SR

Praise for
BEVERLY LEWIS

"No one does Amish-based inspirationals better than Lewis."
—*Booklist*

"Author Beverly Lewis has come up with a new magic formula for producing best-selling romance novels: humility, plainness and no sex. Lewis' G-rated books, set among the Old Order Amish in Lancaster County, Pennsylvania, have sold more than 12 million copies, as bodice rippers make room for 'bonnet books,' chaste romances that chronicle the lives and loves of America's Amish."
—*Time* magazine

"Much of the credit [for the growth of Amish fiction] goes to Beverly Lewis, a Colorado author who gave birth to the genre in 1997 with *The Shunning*, loosely based on her grandmother's experience of leaving her Old Order Mennonite upbringing to marry a Bible college student. The book has sold more than 1 million copies."
—Associated Press

"As in her other novels, Lewis creates a vividly imagined sensory world. . . . And her well-drawn characters speak with authentic voices as they struggle to cope with grief and questions about their traditions and relationship with God."
—*Library Journal*
(about *The Parting*)

"Lewis' readers can't get enough of her tales about Amish life, and this latest installment won't disappoint."
—*Publishers Weekly*
(about *The Forbidden*)

"Lewis provides a satisfying conclusion to the SEASONS OF GRACE series. Touching scenes make it easy for the reader to connect with the characters."

—*Romantic Times* Book Reviews
(about *The Telling*)

"The reigning queen of Amish fiction is back with another tale of secrets, love, and relationships. . . . Lewis has penned another touching novel with well-drawn characters and a compelling plot. It is sure to be in high demand by the author's many fans and anyone who enjoys Amish stories."

—*Library Journal* starred review
(about *The Missing*)

"Once again, Lewis has a hit with the first book in her new ROSE TRILOGY. The charming characters and captivating storyline underscore why Lewis has legions of loyal fans. They will all be anxiously awaiting the next installment."

—*Romantic Times*
(about *The Thorn*)

the JUDGMENT

BEVERLY LEWIS

the JUDGMENT

BETHANYHOUSE

MINNEAPOLIS, MINNESOTA

The Judgment
Copyright © 2011
Beverly M. Lewis

Cover design by Dan Thornberg, Design Source Creative Services
Art direction by Paul Higdon

Scripture quotations are from the King James Version of the Bible.

Published by Bethany House Publishers
11400 Hampshire Avenue South
Bloomington, Minnesota 55438

Bethany House Publishers is a division of
Baker Publishing Group, Grand Rapids, Michigan

Printed in the United States of America

Library of Congress Cataloging-in-Publication Data

Lewis, Beverly.
    The judgment / Beverly Lewis.
       p. cm. — (The rose trilogy ; 2)
      ISBN 978-0-7642-0870-6 (hardcover : alk. paper) — ISBN 978-0-7642-0600-9 (pbk.) — ISBN 978-0-7642-0871-3 (large-print pbk.) 1. Amish—Fiction. 2. Pennsylvania Dutch Country (Pa.)—Fiction. I. Title.
    PS3562.E9383J83   2011
    813'.54—dc22

                                  2010041244

In keeping with biblical principles of creation stewardship, Baker Publishing Group advocates the responsible use of our natural resources. As a member of the Green Press Initiative, our company uses recycled paper when possible. The text paper of this book is comprised of 30% post-consumer waste.

green press
INITIATIVE

*To
Paul and Marge Ferrin,
with blessings and love.
Happy birthday, Marge!*

By Beverly Lewis

THE ROSE TRILOGY
The Thorn • *The Judgment*

SEASONS OF GRACE
The Secret • *The Missing* • *The Telling*

ABRAM'S DAUGHTERS
The Covenant • *The Betrayal* • *The Sacrifice*
The Prodigal • *The Revelation*

THE HERITAGE OF LANCASTER COUNTY
The Shunning • *The Confession* • *The Reckoning*

ANNIE'S PEOPLE
The Preacher's Daughter • *The Englisher* • *The Brethren*

THE COURTSHIP OF NELLIE FISHER
The Parting • *The Forbidden* • *The Longing*

The Postcard • *The Crossroad*

The Redemption of Sarah Cain
October Song • *Sanctuary* (with David Lewis) • *The Sunroom*

The Beverly Lewis Amish Heritage Cookbook

Amish Prayers

www.beverlylewis.com

BEVERLY LEWIS, born in the heart of Pennsylvania Dutch country, is the *New York Times* bestselling author of more than eighty books. Her stories have been published in eleven languages worldwide. A keen interest in her mother's Plain heritage has inspired Beverly to write many Amish-related novels, beginning with *The Shunning*, which has sold more than one million copies. *The Brethren* was honored with a 2007 Christy Award.

Beverly lives with her husband, David, in Colorado.

PROLOGUE

November 1985

Tomorrow holds nary a promise, my dear *Mamm* often says. But thankfully some things are quite certain—we plow, we plant and harvest. We attend canning bees and quilting frolics. Our wedding season always begins on the first Tuesday in November. And this year there are many couples marrying and looking ahead to starting their own families.

My own first cousin Esther Kauffman will wed John Glick, her longtime beau, tomorrow morning. My pretty plum-colored dress and full white apron, which match Esther's own, are hemmed and pressed, ready to slip on right after breakfast.

I should be smiling-happy since I'm one of Esther's wedding attendants. But I must confess to getting a bit tetchy with Esther last evening when she dropped by. She reminded me that her older brother Melvin and I are expected to spend most of the day together, since he's the fellow opposite me in the wedding party. This includes sitting with him at the *Eck,* the corner of the feast table reserved for the bride and groom and the four attendants. So, even though I'll be within flirting distance of Silas Good, I won't get to enjoy the day-long celebration with my betrothed, including the evening meal.

My first thoughts each day are of Silas. His sensible ways and his family's standing amongst the People make me feel so fortunate. Oh, that wonderful-*gut* smile when he looks my way! But no matter how happy I am to be engaged to the most eligible young man in Lancaster County, I must admit there are times when I still think of my friend Nick Franco, the bishop's former foster son. Gone more than a month now.

I must've known a real different Nick than anyone else did. Almost everyone assumes he's a bad seed—most even believe he caused the death of the bishop's only son. But when Nick and I were together, I saw his softer side. That's the part that gnaws at me in the most curious way these days.

Truth is, I ponder where Nick might've run off to . . . and I wonder if he ever misses Amish life. Or me, his best friend.

After all these weeks since his disappearance, I haven't told a soul this—not even my older sister, Hannah, known by most as Hen. But the unusual bond Nick and I shared as youngsters somehow managed to get far deeper into my heart than I realized. I continue to beseech the Lord for poor Nick, praying that God might see fit to forgive him for his years of rebellion.

I pray for my only sister, too. Sadly, Hen's coffee meetings with her estranged worldly husband have turned out to be all but fruitless. And when she's not working at the Amish fabric store, or here at home cooking and whatnot, she has a faraway look in her light hazel eyes, as if caught betwixt and between. I daresay she misses her husband more as the days pass. Misses him . . . even though there are many things that keep them apart.

I am hard-pressed to imagine a solution to their dilemma. So I pray for wisdom from above, knowing I can trust God's timing and way—and His will to be done for them.

As for Nick, it's harder to relinquish him to the heavenly Father, seeing how he always dug in his heels against righteousness. Silas has pointed out to me repeatedly, since Nick's leaving, how difficult he was for his family. His involvement with Christian's accident has certainly tainted him in the eyes of the People. Honestly, it still plagues me what was so urgently on Christian's mind the last time I saw the bishop's biological son, the day before his death. And if it was Nick he wanted to discuss, as I suspect, what could he have revealed about him that I didn't already know?

Despite my struggles with that haunting memory, it is our kindly bishop who must struggle with more bitter memories of his own. He now bears the burden of Nick's part in the untimely death. Just this morning, while I was in the barn, *Dat* said the neighboring bishops, especially Old Ezekiel, are putting pressure on Bishop Aaron. *"If Nick doesn't return and offer a solid explanation by year's end—when the reading of the* Weltende *comes—they'll judge the bishop guilty of failing to get Nick into the church fold,"* Dat said, his eyes moist.

I contemplated the prophetic scriptures in Matthew, where the Last Days are revealed—the teachings on the tribulation and great deception. The ministers always read those sobering chapters at Preaching service near the end of the year. *"Do ya really think the ministers would oust our bishop?"* I asked Dat.

"Oh, they'll try."

"Even though Nick's not the bishop's own kin?"

"There's a debate goin' on," Dat replied. *"That's all I'd better say."*

I paused next to my favorite driving horse, stroking George's thick mane. Secretly I'd ridden this horse bareback many times, all

through the years of Nick's and my late-night riding adventures—
Nick on Pepper and me on George.

Shivering, I knew that if bullheaded Nick was already caught
up in the world—gone to the "edge" and beyond—then he would
never return to the haven of the People.

~

Later in the day, Mamm and I talked quietly in the bright
little room where she found comfort in her midafternoon naps. In
the past few weeks, she'd suffered a bad bout with the respiratory
flu. The illness had weakened her further, compounding her usual
misery of aches and pains.

I could hear *Mammi* Sylvia, my maternal grandmother, preparing the noon meal. "We're havin' one of your favorite dishes
today," I whispered, touching Mamm's frail hand.

Her eyes brightened.

"Smell the delicious veal loaf?"

She nodded, grimacing with pain.

It was hard seeing Mamm in such frail health. Dat doubted she'd
be strong enough to witness Cousin Esther's vows to her beloved
John tomorrow. It was awful selfish on my part, but I felt somewhat
gloomy that Mamm wouldn't be there to see me stand up with
Esther. After all, this was my first time as a bride's attendant.

Yet it is Hen who is most troubled by Mamm's suffering, because
she's been living in town since her marriage to Brandon Orringer.
Now that she's staying here with her daughter, Mattie Sue, in our
smallest *Dawdi Haus*, she's discovering a-plenty what things cause
Mamm pain. Physical and otherwise.

"Did ya hear . . . Deacon Samuel Esh's niece Annie Mast is
soon to have her babies?" my mother said suddenly, though in a
whisper. "Twins, the midwife says."

"Ah, such a wonderful-*gut* blessing for Annie and her
husband."

14

"*Jah.*" Mamm smiled weakly. "They've sent for Rebekah Bontrager to be a mother's helper. Rebekah's father is a second cousin to the deacon, ya know."

"Oh?" I was surprised they'd chosen someone so far away. I hadn't heard a peep from Rebekah for a good nine years. Last I'd seen her, she was twelve. Some of the girls, already intimidated by her blossoming beauty, were sure it was nothing less than Providence she'd upped and moved to Indiana, prior to her courting years. Even Cousin Esther had been quite relieved, considering the way Rebekah had begun to turn the heads of more than one church boy. John Glick included.

"When do ya s'pose Rebekah's coming?" I asked, sitting near the foot of the daybed.

"Tomorrow's what I heard."

Esther's wedding day . . .

"Well, it'll be nice seein' her again," I said, confident she'd be long gone before she could pose a threat to any of my single cousins.

"She's planning to stay *all winter*, Rosie dear." Mamm's eyes held my gaze for an awkward moment, then fluttered shut.

Sighing, I unfolded the afghan at the foot of the bed and lifted it gently to cover her. "No need to worry . . . Silas only has eyes for me," I told myself as I tiptoed out of the room.

Nor is the people's judgment always true:

The most may err as grossly as the few.

—JOHN DRYDEN

Who so loves, believes the impossible.

—ELIZABETH BARRETT BROWNING

CHAPTER 1

*S*unlight was a meager trickle from an ever-darkening sky. The long, rasping shriek of a barn owl echoed in the pastureland to the east, beyond the corncrib. The coming twilight was tinged with the earthy scent of freshly shoveled barn manure that had been hauled out to the dung pit.

Rose Ann Kauffman pulled her black shawl close around her shoulders and hurried across the backyard with Hen Orringer to the small house where Hen and her four-year-old daughter, Mattie Sue, had been residing for the past weeks. The bungalow-like abode was cloaked in ivy on one side of its back porch, making it the more appealing of the two attached dwellings connected to their father's large farmhouse.

Hen reached for the storm door, opened it, and stepped inside the small kitchen. Quickly, she moved to the table and reached for a chair, motioning for Rose to sit, too. "Honestly, Rosie, I never thought things would come to this."

Rose wasn't exactly sure what *this* entailed, but she knew enough to suspect Hen was speaking about her troubled relationship with

Brandon. Settling into the chair, she listened to Hen lament her husband's growing coolness toward her. "The few times we've met for coffee, he always asks about Mattie first. And then he carries on about how he's not getting to see her grow up." Hen sighed. "I can't blame him—Mattie Sue's his daughter, too. But sometimes I just wish he'd act as if he missed *me*."

Rose leaned her elbows on the table. "I'm sure he does, Hen." Her heart broke for her sister, and as Hen continued to talk, Rose noticed again how scattered and *ferhoodled* Hen's feelings were for her husband.

"You've been through a lot," Rose added softly, not saying that it was largely Hen's doing she was in this pickle, impulsive as she was known to be.

Hen continued on, her face dipping with sadness, then momentarily brightening each time she talked of Mattie Sue. Through their growing-up years, Rose had observed this tendency for Hen to open up her heart after suppertime. When Hen had eaten her fill, as she had tonight, she liked to talk. But Mamm would surely say Hen was talking out of turn with her fickle comments. Rose knew their mother would encourage Hen to be consistently loyal to Brandon in both word and deed. Yet that had hardly been the case since Hen had left him to live here.

"You know, Rosie, I really hoped Brandon would miss me enough to ask me to come back." Hen turned to look out the window, her fair hair as neat as a pin, parted down the middle and secured into a tight, low bun. "But he never does. It's like he's only interested in Mattie Sue."

"Aw, ya really think so?"

"Sure seems that way."

"Would you return home if he asked?" Rose said gingerly.

Hen shook her head, tears filling her eyes. "I wish I could. But I've had a taste of this wonderful-good life again . . . and Brandon wants nothing to do with it." She wiped her face with her handkerchief. "He's more interested in his wicked TV than me." Hen went on to explain that Brandon remained firm about watching whatever he pleased—everything from MTV to R-rated movies. "At our coffee visits, he makes a point of telling me what he watches, as if trying to goad me. He doesn't care one iota what I think." She paused for a moment, and then began to spew even more resentment. "And he's never once brought up exposing Mattie Sue to that Madonna business, either. *Ach,* it was just terrible, seeing her mimic that woman. Even worse, he thought it was funny."

Rose cringed. "Have you talked further to the bishop or Dat about it? To seek out their wisdom?"

Hen nodded her head and pulled lightly on her *Kapp* strings. "To tell the truth, Dad's been prompting me to move back with Brandon. He's even asked me to pray with him about it."

Rose wasn't surprised. After all, Hen had made a lifelong marriage vow—for better or for worse. But did the English marriage vow mean turning a blind eye to a husband who seemed bent on introducing a child to the wiles of the devil? She couldn't imagine her brother-in-law wanting to do that intentionally. Brandon hadn't enjoyed the blessing of growing up Plain, or even of belonging to any kind of church fellowship. Nor had he learned anything about Amish life, due to his own indifference, or so Hen had always indicated. Could Rose really blame him for behaving like an *Englischer?*

He doesn't know any better.

"I daresay the Lord will make a way." Rose truly believed that. "If Dat wants to pray with ya, why not do it?"

Hen's eyes welled up again. "On top of all that, Mamm told me recently I should think seriously about the dangers of leaving Brandon alone for much longer."

Rose flinched, guessing why Mamm might be worried.

"Lest another woman catch his eye," Hen said softly. "Dad's

hinted at the same thing, suggesting I go and visit my husband one of these evenings, without Mattie Sue along."

Such talk made Rose's face grow warm and she got up from her chair. "You thirsty?"

Hen nodded. "Sure. I made some mint tea just this morning, before work." She rose quickly and went to the refrigerator.

They bumped into each other as they reached into the cupboard for glasses. Hen set down the pitcher of iced tea, then opened her arms and drew her sister near. "Oh, Rosie, I'm so glad we have each other to talk to again," Hen said, giving her a quick peck on the cheek.

"Jah." Rose stiffened suddenly, not meaning to.

"You're not still angry at me, are you?"

Rose stepped back, frowning. "Why would I be?"

"For what I did—leaving you and turning my back on our close sisterhood . . . when I abandoned the People."

Rose touched Hen's shoulder. She *had* been hurt, and terribly so. Yet now with Hen here again, where she'd grown up, Rose was beginning to feel as if they were making up for the time they'd lost. Even so, she worried that Hen's separation would cause irreparable damage to her marriage—or already had. "Ach, it's hard to know what I think," Rose said quietly, not wanting to continue brooding the loss of her sister for those years.

"I just want you to know . . . I don't blame you for being upset, Rosie."

Rose wished things could resume the way they'd always been. Was it possible to share so fully with Hen once again? She couldn't help wondering how her relationship with her sister might change once she, too, became a married woman. But that was another whole year away.

A knock came at the door and Hen turned to look. "Dad . . . come right in," she called as the door opened. "Rosie and I were just pouring cold drinks—can we get you something, too?"

Dat's gray-flecked brown hair was all matted down after a hard day of toil. A ridge could be seen across his bangs when he removed his hat. His serious eyes signaled to Rose that he wanted to talk privately with Hen.

"Won't ya sit for a spell, Dat?" Rose said, still standing.

He eyed the two of them. "Don't mean to interrupt yous."

"Oh, that's all right." Rose moved toward the door. "I'll come see ya another time, Hen."

Dat reached for a chair and sat down with a sigh, putting his hat on the table in front of him. "No need to leave on my account." He looked Rose's way.

Hen gave her an apprehensive stare as Rose waved good-bye and headed for the back door. *What sort of trouble is brewing now?*

Hen's father shifted his hat on the table and looked up at her. His black suspenders were a bit frayed and his green shirt sleeves were rolled up close to his elbows. His brown eyes were sunken.

"You look tired, Dad," Hen said, going to the kitchen to pour some mint tea for him, even though he hadn't indicated he wanted any.

"That I am."

She carried the drink to him and set it before him on the table. "This might help perk you up."

He thanked her, then hung his head. "Oh, daughter, I hardly know how to tell ya what I came to say."

She froze, her hands gripping the back of the chair.

"Brandon stopped by here today, while you were gone."

Her heart caught in her throat, not just because of what her father had said, but because of the way he frowned so deeply. "He did?"

Dad deliberately folded his hands on the table. "He didn't want you to receive this in the mail." He paused to pull a folded envelope out of his pants pocket. "I haven't read it, but he told me flat-out, he's ready to file for divorce."

She winced like she'd been slapped. *Divorce?*

He held out the letter. "He said everything you need to know is in here."

"Did Brandon say anything else?"

"Just that his lawyer would handle everything." Her father's face looked gray.

Brandon's own brother, no doubt . . .

"Ach, why's he moving so fast?" she whispered.

She opened the letter to see the first line, *Dear Hannah.* Such a shock. He'd used her full name, a name he rarely spoke, as if he were writing to someone else. She made herself slow down and read every life-altering word. *You've abandoned me, Hannah, taking our daughter with you. And for no logical reason. What other choice do I have?*

She read on until she arrived at the final line of the hurtful note: *If you aren't home here with Mattie Sue by a week from this Saturday, I will file for divorce, as well as make a custody complaint.—Brandon*

When Hen finished, she struggled to keep her lip from quivering, not wanting to break down in front of her father. "How will I manage?" she said softly.

"Just as I've always said: with God's help."

Dad lifted his hat and fingered the brim. "I worry if Brandon has his way, he'll try and get sole custody of Mattie Sue." He inhaled deeply.

She dreaded the thought. "He said that?"

"I have a real bad feeling 'bout the whole thing, Hen. 'Specially if yous can't find some way to patch up your differences." He wiped his face with the back of his hand, then told her what had happened to a young couple out in Wisconsin. They'd fought bitterly over the custody of their children, so fiercely that in the end the court had to determine the living arrangements for the little ones.

"Having the court decide—people who don't even know us—is the last thing I want." Hen coughed and struggled to find her voice.

"Of course ya don't."

Mattie Sue doesn't deserve that, she thought.

"Might do the two of you some *gut* if ya went over there to fix him a nice hot dinner real soon." Dad sighed.

"And stay the night?" she blurted, then pursed her lips.

"Well . . . just think back to how things were when you first married. 'Nuff said."

She shrugged his words away. It hurt too much to remember those carefree days, filled with love and reckless abandon. She'd married Brandon fully knowing how very English he was—at the time, it had been part of the attraction. In her heart of hearts, she knew going back to him and making the best of things was the right thing to do. But she was just stubborn enough to want to cling to her hope of returning to a simpler life—for Mattie Sue, and for herself.

"If he pushes you into court, you'll go without a lawyer. No one should represent you but yourself." This wasn't a question but a statement. " 'Tis our way, ya know. No pitting kin against kin."

Oh, Hen knew. Yet without legal representation, she didn't see how things could possibly turn out in her favor. "Jah . . . I know, Dad . . . and I fear that."

Her eyes locked with his, and a helpless gasp escaped her lips.

"Brandon's bound and determined to raise Mattie Sue as a fancy girl, I daresay." He sighed. "Wants nothin' to do with Plain life."

She recalled Brandon's heated account of his run-in with the bishop before they married—how it had left Brandon with no desire to interact with the Amish ever again. It had confirmed in his mind what he'd always thought: that their beliefs made them narrow-minded and backward. The truth was, Bishop Aaron Petersheim had been so indignantly opposed to Hen's plans to marry that he'd attempted to run Brandon off the premises the one and only time he'd agreed to visit her family.

Hen's eyes fell again on Brandon's letter. *Did the bishop foresee then what a mess everything would become?*

CHAPTER 2

What's on Dat's mind? Rose wondered as she made her way down the back steps.

She'd seen the grim look in his eyes and worried it was something concerning Hen's husband. What else could it be? Now that she thought of it, Mamm *had* mentioned a car coming into their lane earlier, while Hen was at work. But Mamm hadn't said who it was or if someone was simply turning around in the drive, lost. That sort of thing happened often on Salem Road, so Rose hadn't thought much of it. Till now.

When she arrived at the main house, Mamm was entertaining Mattie Sue in the kitchen, beneath the golden light of the tall gas lamp. Mamm was smiling as Mattie showed her how to make twin babies using a white handkerchief, as though Mamm hadn't made them herself for Hen and Rose years ago. "I learned it at Preachin' service," Mattie was telling her. "From Becky Zook."

"Well, isn't that something." A soft chuckle escaped Mamm. "Jah . . . and Becky's only three."

"Arie Zook's little girl?" asked Mamm, referring to the daughter of Hen's childhood best friend.

Mattie Sue nodded.

Rose stood there quietly on the summer porch, watching and smiling. It did her heart good to hear Mamm enjoying herself so. And what an expressive child Mattie Sue was. Like Hen had been growing up, Mamm often said.

Mattie raised her sweet face to her grandmother's. "Are Becky and her baby brother going to the wedding tomorrow?"

"Why no, dear one. Weddings are for grown-ups and courting-age young folk." Mamm touched Mattie's blond hair, which was wound in tight braids around her little head.

"What's courting?" Mattie Sue asked innocently.

"Well, now, let's see . . ."

Rose figured her mother might be relieved if she made her presence known just now. She scuffed her feet on the porch and opened the kitchen door. "Hullo, there." She went over to greet Mamm, touching her arm. "How are ya feelin' this evening?"

"Oh, perty *gut* . . . right now, at least."

She glanced at Mattie Sue, who was swinging the hankie. "I'm rocking the baby cradle," her niece announced, grinning at Rose.

"I need to polish my shoes for the wedding tomorrow," Rose said, heading for the stairs.

Mattie Sue jumped up and followed Rose all the way to her bedroom. "Oh, can I help, *Aendi?*"

"Well, sure, honey. You can tell me when they're nice and shiny . . . make sure I do it right." Rose leaned down to get her for-good black leather shoes from beneath the bed. Years ago, she'd seen a bride and her attendants modeling some fancy ones in a magazine. She remembered being surprised at the delicate white satin shoes, with their slender heels. *An English wedding, like Hen's* . . . Sometimes Rose wished she'd never laid eyes on those worldly shoes, because the memory came pretty close to tempting her. After all, her newly sewn dress would look mighty nice with nearly any shoe but these heavy black ones.

"Don't ya need some old newspapers?" Mattie Sue asked. "Mommy always polishes Daddy's shoes like that."

Rose looked over at her new dress and full apron hanging on the wooden peg, then down at the black shoes. "Follow me, Mattie Sue."

"Ach, downstairs again?"

"We'll polish them out on the porch." Rose couldn't help but smile as her niece followed, chattering all the way, some *Deitsch* mixed in here and there.

She's becoming like the rest of us. . . .

~

Hen felt like a wounded child as she sat with her father at her kitchen table. Fear encompassed her, as if she were cornered and had nowhere to run. *Truly, I'm up against a stone wall.* "I should've married inside the Amish church," she admitted.

"None of that matters now, Hen. Brandon's your husband and you must make peace with him. There's no other way."

She pursed her lips, trying to keep from sobbing.

"Let's take this before the Lord in prayer," her father said and bowed his head. "O God and Father in heaven," he began, "we come before you now, in the name of the Lord Jesus Christ. . . ."

Hen soaked in every heartfelt word, grateful for this time with her father, so deeply moved by his concern. As for herself, she quickly wiped her tears away before he said amen.

"Let's trust the Lord for the outcome, whatever it may be," her father said firmly, getting up from his chair, then reaching for his hat. "May God's will be done in all of our lives."

"*Denki* for coming over, Dad. It means a lot to me."

Before leaving, he turned. "You'll put on a cheerful face for Mattie Sue, won't ya?"

"I'll do my best."

"Well, ya simply must." He reached for the back door.

The minute he was out of sight, Hen picked up the letter from Brandon. Hands trembling, she sank into a chair and reread the sharp words he'd penned.

~

Esther's wedding day dawned with an overcast sky. The wind came up abruptly when Rose Ann and the family were about to sit down for breakfast, and dark clouds threatened rain. "If we have a downpour, it'll bring all the remaining leaves down with it," Dat said.

Meanwhile, Mattie Sue was over in the corner with Mamm, who was in her wheelchair. Mattie fussed about her hair being pulled back too tight. "I can't even frown," she complained.

Rose remembered how very taut Mamm had twisted the sides of Rose's own hair when she was little, wetting it down to make it stay "just so" all day long. Sometimes Rose could scarcely blink her eyes while she sat beside her father during Preaching. Mamm thought *rutschich* Rose sat more quietly next to Dat, on the side of the room with the men and little boys—sometimes right near Nick Franco, who made silly faces at her. Rose remembered having to hold her breath so she wouldn't burst out laughing in the middle of Bishop Aaron's long second sermon.

"Just be patient, it'll loosen up," Mamm told Mattie Sue, glancing at Rose.

"How soon?" Mattie put her little hands on her forehead and moved her fingers up and down.

"Pushin' on your forehead won't help none," Rose told her.

"Ach . . . what *will?*" Mattie asked. "I'm getting a headache."

"By the time you're done eatin' breakfast, you'll forget all about your hair," Mamm suggested. It was the exact thing she'd always told Rose.

But Rose remembered all too well that hair pulled back so tight hurt for a good half a day or longer. Rose recalled taking her little hair bob out and then saying it got caught on the rafters in the haymow. Right quick, she'd had the soapiest tongue of any dishonest child living along Salem Road.

Pushing aside the unfortunate memory during the silent table blessing later, Rose changed the subject. "Mattie Sue, can ya tell *Dawdi* what ya helped me do last evening?"

"We shined up Rosie's shoes for Esther's wedding." Mattie Sue dipped her head more rambunctiously than necessary, wrinkling her nose and forehead.

Still hoping to loosen up her hair, thought Rose.

"Did ya, now?" Dat grinned, looking at Mattie between bites of waffles and scrambled eggs.

"She's *Cousin* Esther to you, honey-girl." Mamm wore a frown.

Mattie Sue must not have understood. "You should see 'em, Dawdi. They're just like new."

"Well, almost," whispered Rose from her seat on the wooden bench, thinking again of the worldly shoes in the magazine.

Hen came in through the back door, clutching her shawl tightly about her. "My, the wind sure is kicking up!" she exclaimed.

Mamm stared out the window at the trees swaying hard. Squirrels were racing for shelter, and the windmill spun like a giant whirligig. "Such a dreary day for a wedding," she said.

"Jah, and with the crowd Esther's family is expectin', I

daresay the guests will spill over onto the framed-in porch," Rose added.

"That's why they built the temporary walls—in case of nasty weather like this," Dat said, mentioning he'd gladly take Rose over there in the family buggy and drop her off. "It's no day to walk."

Rose assumed he would return home right away to Mamm. Since Mamm wasn't up to going, Dat wouldn't think of attending the wedding, even though Esther was Mamm's niece. Instead, Dat had plans to load the wheelbarrow full of compost to mulch their flower beds and the now-harvested vegetable garden.

"Sure looks like rain's comin'," Dat said, gawking toward the window, seemingly preoccupied with the weather. "It'll raise the water table, for sure."

"Be sure and take an umbershoot," Hen said, offering a smile.

Mattie's head popped up. "Umbershoot? What's that, Mommy?"

"What's it sound like?" Hen tweaked her daughter's nose.

"Um . . . could it be an Amish umbrella?"

That brought more smiles and laughter. Dat clapped his hands and leaned his head back in a way Rose hadn't seen him do since before Hen married.

"Well, I sure hope the rain clouds blow over," Rose said.

"Jah, no sunshine on the weddin' day . . . no happiness for the marriage. Or so they say," Mamm noted.

"How sad." Rose felt sorry for Cousin Esther. After a quiet moment, she said, "It's just superstition, ain't?"

Mattie Sue's big eyes looked mighty serious.

"*Puh!*" said Mamm, aware of her granddaughter's curious gaze. "Why sure . . . who could possibly know such a thing?"

After the breakfast dishes were all done up, Rose Ann pondered what Mamm had said. She hoped for her cousin's sake that it was a false notion. She'd heard plenty of superstitions growing up, but most didn't prove true. Still, as she took her time dressing, she hoped her own wedding day might be as sunny a day as she knew Dat and Mamm's had been. *Lord willing.*

CHAPTER 3

*R*ose Ann waved to her father as he backed the horse and buggy slowly out of her cousins' lane. The threatened rain hadn't yet come, but she carried along her umbrella for good measure.

Up ahead, Cousin Esther's paternal grandparents were stepping out of their gray carriage. It warmed Rose's heart to see spry, gray-headed Daniel Kauffman smile sweetly at his petite wife before heading off to the horse stable.

"Daniel and Mimi have always been a couple to imitate," Rose recalled Mamm telling Hen just last week. Rose had guessed at the time that Mamm was trying to encourage Hen to be more attentive to her own husband.

Presently, Miriam leaned heavily on her cane, waiting for Daniel to return. Rose hurried to Miriam's side and offered her arm to the darling lady. With a smile, Miriam nodded and they moved forward together. Slowly, cautiously, Rose led her toward the farmhouse, where the wedding was soon to take place.

"Wie geht's?—How are you today, Miriam?" she asked.

"Ever so excited to see Essie and John tie the knot—and on Thanksgiving Day, yet!"

Rose agreed. "They've known each other since they were youngsters."

Miriam's eyes sparkled. "I daresay they've had eyes for each other a *gut* long time. Gracious me, and I did near the same thing— picked out Daniel to be my beau during school recess long ago."

Rose listened with a smile. *How quickly does sixty years of marriage pass?* She wondered how she and Silas would look or act when they were well into their eighties. Would they be as openly affectionate as Mimi and Daniel?

As they approached the house Rose spotted a stand of golden-rod, turned all but silver in the recent wet, chilly weeks, and shivered at the thought of colder weather ahead. How nice if her mother could find solace in Mattie Sue's company.

If Hen stays put longer . . .

She really had no idea what Hen was planning, though it was certain that if Brandon and Hen parted ways for good, the ministerial brethren would want her to stay under Dat's roof and patriarchal covering. Before matters reached that point, however, Hen would probably be advised by the bishop and his wife to do everything in her power to reconcile with her husband.

She reached for the back door and held it open while Miriam lightly thumped her cane on the linoleum as she walked into the summer kitchen, eyes gleaming with anticipation. "*Guder Mariye*— good morning—to everyone," Miriam called, and Esther's married sisters hurried to greet her.

Once dear white-haired Miriam was settled comfortably into a rocking chair, Rose Ann excused herself and headed upstairs to Esther's bedroom. She was eager to see her cousin wearing her plum-colored wedding dress and full white apron. The bride was most likely finished putting all twenty-seven straight pins into her dress and apron . . . and soon to spend her final moments as a single woman with her mother. Rose couldn't help wondering if Esther was having any second thoughts.

Rose found her cousin alone in her room, which was as neat as always. There was a newly crocheted doily on the dresser, and positioned in its center was a pretty oil lamp Rose had never seen before. *A gift from the groom?*

"I'm awful jumpy, Rosie," the bride whispered as they embraced. Her golden-blond hair was parted nice and straight down the middle and smoothed back neatly on the sides, where it twisted perfectly. Despite her nerves, Esther's blue eyes twinkled.

Rose touched her arm. "Maybe when you catch a glimpse of John, the jitters will go away."

A smile brightened Esther's pretty face. "Oh jah, just the thought of my dear beau . . ." She gripped Rose's hands. "Denki . . . ever so much."

"He loves ya, Essie . . . just remember."

Esther's eyes glistened with happy tears, and she reached into her left sleeve to find an embroidered white handkerchief and pulled it out. Dabbing at the corner of her eyes, she nodded her head. "You're right. I have nothin' to worry about."

Rose led her to the window, and together they peered down at the many buggies already parked along the side yard. "See all the folk coming to join in the celebration for you and John? It's wonderful, ain't?"

Esther looked at the sky and grimaced. "Sure hope it doesn't rain and spoil our day." Her breath formed a circular blur on the pane.

The dark clouds did look ready to burst open at any moment. Rose tried to distract her by pointing out the English couple coming toward the house. "You must've invited Donna Becker and her husband." She'd seen them get out of their car, parked along the side of the road.

"Mamma did," Esther said. "She knows Donna through Rachel Glick, who owns the fabric shop. Her cousin, ya know."

"Oh, Donna's as nice as can be. She lives neighbors to Gilbert Browning, the widower I work for Wednesday mornings."

"Why, sure . . . I'd forgotten that." Esther went on to say she'd heard through the grapevine that Gilbert had a special daughter named Beth. "I hear she loves comin' to your place and seeing the foals."

"Does she ever," Rose agreed. "And we love havin' her visit, too." Rose had actually been planning something of a surprise for Beth, but she hadn't yet breathed a word to anyone. Very soon, she planned to talk to Dat about her idea.

Esther made a little squeal of glee. "Well, lookee there!" she said, her forehead close to the window. "My cousins from Wisconsin came for the wedding. Just think, all that way!"

Rose saw a family of seven walking up the lane. "Didn't ya know they were coming?"

"Not for certain, no." Esther straightened and gave Rose a quick hug. "Oh, wait'll ya meet my cousin Peter. He's quite handsome— and fun-loving, too! I wouldn't be surprised if he pulls a prank or two on my groom." Her face flushed pink. "If he wasn't my own relative, oh goodness, would I ever be smitten!"

The wind rose up at that moment, and the eaves creaked. Esther's scrutinizing gaze lingered on her till Rose looked away. She wasn't at all interested in Esther's Wisconsin cousin. But since Esther hadn't been going to Singings here lately, she most likely didn't know of Silas Good's recent interest in Rose. 'Tis best to keep mum on that.

Just then, a knock came at the door, and Esther's mother poked in her white-capped head. "Are ya ready, Essie?"

It was Rose's hint to leave the room. "Happy wedding day," she said with a smile.

"Denki, Rosie." Esther's eyes twinkled. "I'll remember what you said."

"All right, then," said Rose happily as she departed the room for the stairs.

~

Hen sat in her small kitchen sorting through the piecework for her Double Nine Patch bed quilt, trying not to dwell on Brandon's startling threat. Such a dreadful recourse. Had he forgotten *he'd* suggested she take some time to come here?

She wondered—was his change of mind and heart because he was weary of waiting for her return? He must be annoyed she hadn't gotten her fill of all things Plain by now. Her husband must be at a loss, thinking, *What else can I do?*

On top of all that, there was her father's admonition to consider. *Should* Hen stick her neck out and make a private visit to Brandon? Was it possible that might still do some good? *Or might I mess things up even more than I already have?*

In her distress, she looked at the assortment of colorful squares. Soon she'd be ready to lay them out on the floor. She had finished the quilted wall hanging for Mattie's room and was pleased with the outcome. Now she imagined how this completed quilt would look and hoped that, with Mammi Sylvia's expert help, and possibly her mother's, too, it would turn out nicely. *Might very well be my way to sanity.*

She struggled with the thought of returning home even for a few hours, let alone for good. In the weeks she had been living here, Hen had thoroughly embraced the Amish ways, as had Mattie Sue. Still, a hot homemade dinner might be a nice gesture, especially on Thanksgiving evening . . . assuming Brandon was even home. Yet, how much could a single visit accomplish?

I won't know unless I go. . . .

Hen rose from her spot at the kitchen table and went to the

window to look toward the field. The lonely old phone shanty stood a long way from the house. She could almost hear Brandon's response. "He'll wonder if I'm simply reacting to his note if I call," she muttered, frustration rising as she thought about it.

She must get her emotions in check or find herself giving in to anger. Going to sit in the front room, Hen bowed her head. *Lord, our marriage is in pitiful shape.* She sighed, greatly relieved Mattie Sue was over next door with Mamm, reading a picture book.

Hen reached for her Bible and opened to the first psalm. *Blessed is the man that walketh not in the counsel of the ungodly. . . .* She paused, realizing anew that her own father was one of the wisest men she'd ever known. "With a name like Solomon," she whispered, wondering if her father might somehow get through to Brandon. Her husband just didn't seem to understand the comfort she found in her faith and a simpler life, nor her desire to keep Mattie Sue untainted by the world. Or was it that he didn't care? She felt sure he was itching to hurry off to his lawyer brother.

The thought of calling Brandon made everything Hen had set out to do thus far seem for naught. *Yet should I sit idly by and allow my worldly husband to pull all the strings?*

∼

Rose stood across from her cousin Melvin as the wedding party gathered before the bishop. She observed the service with rapt attention, especially the bride and groom, who answered each of the important questions—their vows to each other—with such solemn expressions.

When the bishop placed Esther's small hand in John's, joy shone from the couple's faces. The man of God encircled their clasped hands with his own during the blessing, and Rose couldn't help wondering what Esther was feeling this very minute.

Will Silas and I be so in love on our wedding day?

She held her breath as the bishop offered the final prayer.

"I desire for this couple, O Lord, a good start for their marriage, unswerving middle years . . . and a most blessed end, when one of them breathes his or her last on this earth. This I pray through Jesus Christ our Lord. Amen."

Rose felt a jumble of emotions—more anxious than ever for her own wedding—as she turned to follow Esther and John to be seated again with Melvin and the other two attendants.

Just then, she caught sight of a young woman sitting back near the kitchen with Deacon Esh's wife. Her hair was a rich, deep brown, parted just so, and her brown eyes were bigger than Rose recalled. *Rebekah Bontrager . . .* Rose remembered her clearly despite the passage of years. And regardless of her Amish attire, she was anything but plain. Somewhere along the way, Rebekah had become a beautiful young woman.

From across the room, Rose offered a smile, and Rebekah nodded slightly and smiled back.

At that time, one of the several visiting ministers was asked to give a testimony commenting on the various sermon points; then several more were invited to add their remarks, as well. All of them offered good wishes to the newlyweds and extended the Lord's blessings on their union.

Bishop Aaron motioned for Esther's father to stand and address the People, which he appeared to do gladly. Later, though, when John's father rose to speak, he was overcome with emotion, his voice turning husky as he thanked everyone for coming to witness his son's and now daughter-in-law's vows.

The bishop offered a few more words of admonition before the People turned in their seats and knelt for prayer as he read from the *Christenpflicht*. After the benediction, the gathering came to a close once the final hymn was sung in unison.

The solemnity of the celebration made Rose mindful that this marriage represented that of the Lamb of God—Christ, the

Bridegroom—to His church. And she sensed great awe, even a hush, in the crowded room.

Upstairs, Esther and John gathered all the single wedding guests—both fellows and girls—into the hallway and began randomly pairing them for the feast, an age-old tradition. Until the barn Singing, much later, the assigned couples were to spend the rest of the afternoon and the evening meal together, as would each of the couples in the wedding party.

Rose was suddenly aware of the splashing sound of rain against the windowpanes. It was good the downpour had held off, not disturbing her cousin's wedding vows or the special blessing that followed.

Leaning against the door to Esther's bedroom, she didn't take much interest in the usual matching-up process, knowing she was already obliged to be with Melvin Kauffman. Nice as her cousin was, he certainly wasn't anything like her betrothed.

Esther turned to whisper something to her new husband, John, and the two of them, cute as could be—their heads close together—decided who to further match with whom.

About that time, Silas came running up the stairs, late. *Where's he been?* Rose wondered, hoping to catch his eye. But he wasn't looking her way, and she couldn't for the life of her remember seeing him in the congregation during the sermons given before the wedding vows. Maybe he had been helping the hostlers, who were assigned to feed and water the many driving horses.

Now Esther was in the process of choosing Peter Riehl, her good-looking cousin, for Arie Zook's younger sister Leah Miller. Christian Petersheim had taken a real shining to brown-eyed Leah, and Rose had seen them together at quite a few Singings during the past year or so. For these weeks since his death, Leah had worn a black dress and apron, even though she hadn't actually been engaged to Christian, as far as Rose knew. Rose couldn't help wondering if Leah would still be wearing black today if she weren't at Esther's wedding.

Esther beamed as she eyed the happy couples lined up all the way down the hall. Already, several of the girls were blushing happily at Esther's choice for them. And more than a few of the fellows seemed mighty pleased, too. Some of them were even discreetly reaching for their girl's hand, behind the girls' skirts. But all of that would cease the minute they descended the stairs for the feast. For not having gone to many Singings lately, Esther certainly had a good idea of what was what between some of the courting couples.

Rose smiled to herself. *Has John filled Esther in, just maybe?*

At that moment, Rose realized Silas was without a partner. Instinctively, she stepped forward, then blushed a little, realizing what she'd done as Silas caught her eye. Fortunately, Esther seemed to recognize Silas's dilemma, as well, and glanced around the room in search of an available girl.

Just then Rebekah reached the top of the long stairway. "I have no partner," she said demurely and out of breath.

"Well . . ." Esther started to say, looking around her to see if Rebekah was indeed the only young woman left. Then she motioned for Silas to take his place beside Rebekah. "We're all set, jah?"

With an apologetic look at Rose, Silas moved toward his partner. The predicament was clearly not his doing, and Rose smiled back to let him know she understood. He warmly returned her smile, a silent exchange that did not appear to be lost on Rebekah. Rose's heart was warmed, though her blush returned as Rebekah's questioning eyes came to rest on her.

Slowly, Rose turned and there was Melvin offering his arm. With one more look back at her beau, she followed Esther's brother down the hall and around to the stairs when it came their turn.

Once they were seated downstairs at the Eck, the beautifully decorated corner reserved for the wedding party, Rose glanced at Esther, who was expressing her delight at one of John's surprise wedding gifts to her—a pretty set of floral china, which had belonged to his grandmother. A service for twenty! Simply beaming, Esther made over the lovely plates, matching cups and saucers, and every imaginable service bowl and meat platter while her mother and sisters looked on.

Rose turned to chat politely with Melvin about the freshness the rainy weather had brought to the day, and how very happy the couple looked. The time passed pleasantly enough, and the feast was soon over. Like many couples, Melvin and Rose moseyed outside, and later, when the newlyweds came outdoors to pass around bars of chocolate to the guests, Rose spotted Silas and Rebekah talking over near the old well pump.

Goodness, Rose never would have expected her beau to look so animated. He was motioning back at the house as if he was trying to make a point of something rather important. The more Rose watched, the more uneasy she felt. It was clear that Silas was quite comfortable talking with Rebekah, and obviously whatever he was telling her was greatly appreciated. Even so, Rose checked her concern and reassured herself that there was doubtless plenty for them to catch up on, since they had been childhood friends.

That's all it is.

She turned back to Melvin, who was talking about a horse auction he'd seen advertised in the *Lancaster Farming* periodical that he was planning to attend next week in New Holland, along with Silas. "He's lookin' to buy a new trotter—he and his Dat," Melvin remarked.

Silas had said as much recently. "Jah, they've been looking to purchase a new mare soon," Rose said, thinking Silas might want to get things lined up well in advance of their marriage. He was like that.

"Well, now, how would *you* know 'bout this, Rose?"

She blushed, having forgotten herself for a moment.

Melvin leaned over, peering at her comically. "Any idea?"

"Mind your own *Bisness*," she said, laughing.

"Say, now. Who's *that* girl Silas is with?" Melvin craned his neck to see.

"Rebekah Bontrager . . . visiting from Indiana. I forget the name of the town."

His eyebrows rose. "Well, it's certain no one could forget *her*."

Rose looked right at him. "Seems you did. Rebekah grew up near here, but her family moved away when she was in second grade." *Back when we were both tomboys . . .*

Melvin was still gawking. "I knew I'd seen her somewhere."

"She's your age."

"Twenty-one and still single?" He whistled. "Boy, oh boy . . . how'd she ever manage that?"

He obviously didn't mind making a fool of himself, carrying on so. "If you're that keen on her, why don't ya go over and introduce yourself?"

He turned and grinned, seemingly pleased at her suggestion. "You know, I just might do that." And off he went.

"Perfect," Rose whispered, going inside to warm up. "Maybe we'll just swap partners for the rest of the day." Oh, what she wouldn't give for that!

CHAPTER 4

An afternoon wind swept across the backyard as Hen made her way past the corncrib, toward the lifeless brown meadow where the phone shanty stood, smack-dab in the middle. She shivered, wondering how long before the first snowflakes would fall and cover the countryside with glittering layers of white. She and Brandon had enjoyed several such Thanksgiving Days just playing with little Mattie Sue, keeping warm by the living room fireplace . . . and watching the Macy's Thanksgiving Day Parade.

Hurrying now against the cold, she arrived at the shanty. Promptly, before she lost heart, she dialed Brandon's number. The phone rang once . . . twice . . . then three times. Each ring made Hen second-guess her resolve.

After seven rings, she presumed he was gone from the house. Still, she let the phone ring a few more times. He'd never been interested in traveling to visit his family for the holiday, but she wondered if their recent separation had propelled him out of town to his parents' place.

The phone continued to ring.

He might be watching football. . . .

Eventually, she hung up and stared at the receiver, feeling drained, as if her very future hung in the balance before her. Dad was right. *Isn't he always?* She should not have waited this long to contact her husband again, especially on a holiday.

Heavyhearted, Hen pushed open the wooden door and trudged back over the stubbly field, toward the house. The rain had turned to a mist, and she hadn't bothered to bring her black outer bonnet, or an umbrella. She thought of Mattie's cute remark this morning about the "Amish umbrella." Then, just as quickly, she sighed, sad about her daughter's plight, torn between two parents—and two vastly different lifestyles. *If Brandon follows through with his terrible threat.*

When Hen arrived at the Dawdi Haus, Mattie Sue was carrying around her favorite stuffed animal, a dog she'd named Foofie, with the sweetest brown patch over its eye.

"Can I go over to Mammi Emma's and read to her again before supper, Mommy?" she asked. Mattie Sue liked to pretend to read to her grandmother, which entertained Hen's mother no end.

"Sure, honey," Hen replied vaguely, an idea forming. "Let's see if maybe you can stay and eat there, too." She'd heard that two of her brothers and their families were bringing food for her parents, to go with the roast turkey her grandmother was making—an informal Thanksgiving gathering, since they rarely made much of English holidays.

Mattie Sue seemed happy at the prospect and began gathering up her books. She found her little woolen shawl and pulled it around her slender arms. "I'll ask Dawdi and Mammi if it's all right, jah?"

"Be sure and mind your manners."

"Okay, Mommy." With that, Mattie Sue stood on tiptoes as Hen leaned down for a kiss, and then Mattie Sue scampered out the back door.

Suddenly, all Hen could think of was Brandon and how very foreign her life seemed without him in it. Could she bear to live apart from him the rest of her days? Tears welled up as she went to get her own shawl and wrapped it tightly around her. The notion crossed her mind that she might be better received—once Brandon *did* arrive home—if she wore the English attire he was so fond of. *Something less Plain.* After all, here she was looking completely Amish, something she knew very well he disliked.

But now Hen felt as if she might fall into a panic if she didn't get going. Besides, she'd left nearly all of her fancy English clothing behind.

She hurried next door to see if Mattie Sue could indeed stay with Mom and Dad. Then, heading back out toward the barn, she realized she hadn't driven her car for several weeks. She eyed the family carriage parked in the buggy shed and wished she could be true to her determination to take the horse and buggy whenever she traveled. At least this time, she would spare Brandon the sacred Amish symbol of horse and carriage, too.

My cape dress and prayer cap will be enough to give him fits, she thought with chagrin, hoping it would not be so.

Hen unlocked her car door and got in, feeling hardly any sense of hope that her visit might turn out to be a good thing for their marriage. *What's left of it . . .*

~

When Hen pulled into Brandon's street, she slowed the car to a crawl. She felt terribly out of place dressed as she was, yet driving a car. Oh, the juxtaposition of Plain and fancy!

Seeing the house—*their home*—again gave her an unexpected twinge of pain. Nevertheless, she parked next to the curb, surprised to see a strange car in the driveway. How odd—a Maryland license plate.

Who's here?

Curious, she got out and walked up the sidewalk, past the unfamiliar car, and as she did she noticed through the window a dress hanging in a see-through dry cleaner's bag. *A woman?*

Worry shot through her, though she attempted to dismiss it. More determined than before, Hen hurried to the front door.

Then, glancing down at herself, she knew for certain she'd made an error in judgment by wearing her frumpy-looking brown work dress, with its gripper-snaps to hold on the black apron.

Even though the door was closed, from inside the house, she heard music—the rhythmic thumps of dance music.

What's going on?

Raising her hand to ring the doorbell, Hen trembled.

When no one came, she stood there, confused. She looked at the small porch and recalled scrubbing it with a bristle broom several times each spring and summer. Unsure why she should entertain such an odd memory just now, she considered ringing the doorbell again. But the door opened. Wiggles, the cinnamon-colored cocker spaniel puppy Brandon had bought last month to entice Mattie Sue home, came running, wagging his stubby tail and barking repeatedly.

And there stood Terry Orringer, Brandon's unmarried older sister, her slender hands sticky with dough. Hen expelled her breath with relief.

"Well, I didn't expect to see *you*," Terry said, motioning Hen indoors with a sweep of her auburn hair. She looked Hen over. "Just in time for a late Thanksgiving dinner."

"Thanks, but I really didn't come to eat."

"Oh, you must be here to see what's-his-name," Terry said over her slight shoulder, laughing in her shrill way as they both walked to the kitchen.

"Are you visiting for the weekend?" Hen asked, faltering. She'd never seen Terry's car before. In fact, the only times Hen had engaged in conversation with her sister-in-law were at the few family gatherings she'd been to at Brandon's parents' sweeping estate in upstate New York.

"I didn't think Brandon should be alone for the long weekend" came the flat answer.

Hen was uncomfortably aware of Terry's casual jeans and comfy blue sweater . . . and her repeated glances at Hen's Amish garb. "When do you expect him home?"

"He's working on a project . . . at the office. So, not anytime soon, I'd guess."

Hen remained in the breakfast nook as Terry worked and Wiggles crouched at her feet. "A project? On a holiday?" *What could be so important? Unless* . . . A wave of dismay nearly toppled her as she stood there, her knees locked. The fear was palpable.

"Something important, he said."

Like filling out papers for his attorney. Hen wished Terry wouldn't play games. Why didn't she just come right out and say it?

Terry looked over at her, frowning as if she wondered why Hen was still standing near the breakfast table, several yards away. "I hope you don't mind, but I've got to keep working here. Brandon requested dumplings instead of mashed potatoes and gravy with his turkey," she said.

Wiggles made a little squeal sound and jumped up playfully, trying to catch the end of Terry's apron string in his mouth.

"Oh, you silly pooch." Terry laughed, shooing him away.

Hen remembered how much her husband enjoyed homemade dumplings at Thanksgiving and Christmas. "Brandon must be glad you're here to cook for him."

"Well, I wasn't going to let my baby brother starve . . . not over the holiday."

Hen felt the sting Terry had no doubt intended.

"Mom and Dad—and my brother here—urged me to drive up and spend a few days."

"Oh?"

Terry stopped talking for a time, busying herself at the kitchen counter. Wiggles wandered off toward Mattie Sue's room, down the hall.

"They must think I've abandoned him. . . ." Hen's legs felt weak again as she lowered herself onto Brandon's chair at the table.

"Well, didn't you?" Terry stared at her, putting dirty hands under the faucet.

"Our problems are personal . . . between Brandon and me," Hen said softly. But she knew that wasn't true. What you did affected everyone around you. Dad had said so many times—Dad and everyone else who knew anything about relationships.

"Where's the little cutie tonight?" asked Terry, changing the subject.

"Mattie Sue's with her grandparents."

"Well, in case you have any misconceived notions, Hen—we're going to win this fight. Just so you know."

We?

The word rang through her mind. But Hen fought the dread that threatened to overtake her, clinging to the memory of a verse in the book of Exodus—*The Lord shall fight for you, and ye shall hold your peace.*

Not responding—and wishing Brandon would arrive—she noticed the newspaper with the article about ADD that Brandon had asked her to read, lying on the table. Reaching over, she picked it up, surprised he'd kept it around this long. Her hands shook, and she found it hard to breathe as she absorbed the description and behaviors associated with attention deficit disorder. Had Brandon solicited his family to help him build a false case against her?

Trying her best to push aside worrisome thoughts, she reread the first few paragraphs. Brandon had not only circled but underlined sections, complete with exclamation points.

He must think I'm afflicted with this disorder.

The paragraphs most marked up were about the impulsive

behavior common in affected persons. Did her husband actually believe her present behavior was due to her having ADD?

Goodness, he's just not listening to me!

Looking up, she saw Terry frying the dumplings she'd been rolling out, humming all the while. It shocked her that the woman could seem so cheerful, particularly after what she'd just said. Exactly why *was* Terry in town?

Refolding the paper, Hen took stock of her own perhaps hasty actions weeks ago, in this very house. She sighed and glanced toward the hall and the bedroom where Brandon had once threatened her with a custody battle. It had been a mistake to come here, especially considering the helpless way Hen felt now. Besides, by the looks of things, Brandon was well cared for.

"We're going to win. . . ." Terry's words echoed in her mind.

Apparently, Brandon's entire family was backing him, determined to help him retrieve Mattie Sue. *He has more support than I do.* She thought of her large Amish family, knowing full well her parents—and the bishop and Barbara, his wife—were opposed to a permanent separation.

"Have you changed your mind about staying for supper?" Terry wiped her hands on the apron she wore—Hen's own.

She rose from the chair. "Denki—uh, sorry . . . I mean no thanks."

Terry rustled her cooking apron about, like she was shooing flies. "Okay, so . . . I'll tell Brandon you dropped by," she said, sending an unmistakable message that Hen should not linger.

She nodded meekly and walked out to go to the front door.

Standing there, her hand on the knob, she looked down at her diamond engagement ring and wedding band. She'd felt so peculiar wearing them around the farm while dressing Plain. None of the married Amishwomen wore rings—not even a simple gold wedding band. *Too much like the English . . .*

Suddenly, Hen remembered an item she'd forgotten to pack.

Something she felt she needed, especially considering the worldliness of wearing such a dazzling ring set. *Let alone any rings at all.*

"Uh, excuse me . . . just a moment." She moved toward the hallway.

"Where are you going?" Terry asked.

Hen ignored her, slipping past to the familiar master suite Hen had designed and decorated herself. She was not about to ask permission to go into her own bedroom!

CHAPTER 5

*R*ose stood on the newly painted back porch watching the rain come in torrents. The screened-in area had been turned into a place to store extra chairs and tables for the wedding day, and to lay out the rolls, pies, and cakes leftover from the noontime feast. Curious as to Melvin's whereabouts, she looked across the glistening yard, toward the barn. There, she saw him with Rebekah Bontrager, who'd apparently become a magnet for first Silas and now Melvin. The three of them were trying to keep dry beneath the overhang of the stable.

Glancing over her shoulder toward the kitchen, she spotted Leah Miller, looking dejected all by herself in the corner. Was she still missing Christian, perhaps? But wait—where was Peter, her partner for the day?

Rose scanned the large room for any sign of him. Surely he, too, hadn't gone to cluster around the new arrival from Indiana. Of course, Rebekah wasn't new at all. It was just that she hadn't been in the area for years now. *Guess Annie Mast hasn't had her twins yet*, Rose thought, wishing the babies would come very soon. Any moment, really.

She turned to look toward the barn again, but no longer saw Silas and Melvin . . . or Rebekah. Had they gone inside to escape the rain? She was curious, but not enough to get sopping wet. The umbrella she'd brought from home was upstairs somewhere in the bride's bedroom. Besides, no umbrella was any match for this cascade of moisture from an angry sky.

Sighing, Rose moved back into the kitchen to seek out Leah, who was nibbling on a celery stick. "You want some company?" Rose asked softly as she approached her.

Leah smiled. "I'm glad ya came over. I thought Peter was s'posed to stay with me all afternoon. Yet here I am, stuck alone."

Again. Rose thought fleetingly of Christian. "Oh, he may have gotten lost somewhere in this big house," she said, making an excuse for him. "Or maybe one of his relatives has cornered him, eager for the latest news from Wisconsin."

Leah blushed pink, her long eyelashes fluttering against her peachy cheek.

"Don't feel too bad, all right?" Rose encouraged her. "I seem to have lost my partner, too."

Leah asked, "Do ya think Peter will end up bein' my date for the Singing later?"

"I wouldn't be one bit surprised. I saw how he looked at you."

Leah sighed. "Really?"

"You have nothin' to worry about." Rose smiled. "Peter's not the only fella looking your way."

Leah ignored the latter comment, looking embarrassed again. "Too bad 'bout the rain," she said, changing the subject.

Neither of them brought up the wedding superstition, but it was implied all the same.

"Come, let's go upstairs awhile," Rose suggested, noticing one of her mother's elderly aunts eyeing them.

"All right." Leah followed her around the side of the kitchen and up the back stairway.

When they'd closed the door of the guest room, Rose went to sit on the tan-and-brown-checked loveseat in the corner. She plumped a pillow behind her as Leah sat on the bed. Next thing, Leah was leaning back, stretching out on the pretty quilt as if exhausted.

Rose could hear the sound of voices coming from downstairs, where the older folk must've decided to have an impromptu Singing of their own. She stared outside, looking at the horse stable as the old melodies rose and filled the house.

"You live neighbors to the bishop," Leah murmured, rolling up on her side to look at Rose. "Guess I always envied you . . . so close to Christian and all. Just a meadow away."

"He was fond of you, Leah. I saw it in his eyes."

Leah looked away. "I miss him, every Singing I go to."

Rose didn't know what to say. She'd struggled for years with Christian's disregard for Nick—it was as if he believed foster brothers were meant to be ridiculed. Surely Leah had gotten an earful from Christian along those lines.

After an awkward moment, Leah asked Rose, "How's your sister doin'?"

"Oh, keepin' real busy."

"Does she like working over at Rachel's Fabrics?"

"She seems to."

"My sister Arie said she sees her there sometimes." Leah paused. "It must feel *gut* to come home again, after bein' out in the world."

It wasn't like Leah to prod. Then again, most everyone in the community had inquired about Hen lately—either of Dat or of Rose herself—presumably out of loving concern.

"I wonder what causes someone to set their sights away from the church and the People," Leah said suddenly.

Rose shrugged. "The world tempts us, sad to say."

"Jah. Reminds me of an interesting book my father's reading."

"Oh?"

"He said the book likens a person's heart to a field. If grass seed is sown, it'll never produce wheat or hay. You can cut the grass down real short, but the field will still grow grass."

Rose considered this. "So they'd have to plow it all up and resow if they want something else to grow," she said.

"That makes sense." Leah pursed her lips. "Like the parable of the sower, ya know."

Rose thought of Nick and wondered if he might need the soil of his heart all plowed up, too. Might that happen out in the English world, just maybe?

~

Hen felt unsettled, standing there in the bedroom she'd shared with Brandon for nearly their entire marriage. The same pretty spread, curtains, and rugs adorned the room, but the space felt cold and strange and it was difficult not to give in to sadness. Closing the door behind her, she heard Terry coming down the hall and locked the latch.

She's following me.

Hen went to look in the closet. The sight of her modern clothes—slacks and tops, revealing sweaters and low-cut blouses—opened her eyes anew to her yearning to live and dress to please the Lord. She contemplated the biblical command for women to cover their head when praying. The practice had been deep-rooted in her as a child.

"Why did I so quickly abandon all of that?" she whispered, going from one drawer to the next, making the painful observation that her personal items had been removed from the top drawers of the closet built-ins. She felt a twinge of nausea but could not imagine Brandon doing such a thing. Hopefully, he hadn't discarded everything.

She caught herself. Why should she care? Wasn't she set on never looking back—remaining wholly Plain?

Opening the last drawer, where she'd always kept her jewelry, she spied her rings and the pretty crystal ring holder she'd come looking for. Thankfully Brandon hadn't tossed *that* aside.

A wedding gift from him. She slipped the lovely holder into her pocket and closed the drawer.

Taking a deep breath, Hen left the walk-in closet and went to sit on the bed, staring at her former spot on the left side. Brandon had always preferred the other side of the bed. Her pillow was still there, but the small framed picture of her was no longer sitting on Brandon's lamp table. In fact, there were no pictures on display of either her or of them as a couple anywhere in the room.

She heard Terry outside the door, rustling about. And then her sister-in-law was calling to her. "Can I help you with something, Hen?" Her question was accompanied by sharp barks from Wiggles and subsequent shushing from Terry. For a split second, Hen thought of asking to take the puppy to its rightful owner. Wouldn't Mattie Sue be tickled at that?

"I found what I wanted, thanks." She opened the bedroom door, forcing a smile. "I'll be on my way now."

Hen hurried down the hall, slowing only to glance in at Mattie Sue's room, which looked just as she'd left it. *As if waiting for Mattie's return . . .*

What will happen to us? she thought with a fright. Was the help of her family, and the Lord, enough to get her through this difficult time?

Hen wondered if she might be able to delay Brandon's deadline a week from now.

Can I buy some time until I figure out what on earth to do?

∾

The rain drummed hard against the windows as Rose and Leah settled in downstairs again with another girl from the church district, Mandy Esh, one of the deacon's courting-age granddaughters. The older folk were still singing their slow church songs in the front room. For a moment, Rose wished she'd joined with her many Kauffman relatives, although most were older than her parents.

"How's your mother today?" Mandy asked.

"The same, really. She hasn't completely recovered from having the flu a few weeks back. Dat and Mammi Sylvia stayed with her today," Rose said, unwilling to go into much detail and put a damper on things.

"I thought so," Mandy said. "Is she ever able to get out to quilting bees and whatnot?" She looked concerned.

"Hardly ever lately."

Mandy shook her head. "Sorry to hear it."

They talked of other things, including the barn Singing for the youth tonight, after the scheduled supper. Mandy also mentioned that she and several of her cousins and older sister Linda, as well as Leah and Arie, were making quilts for a homeless shelter in Philly.

"What a nice thing to do."

"We were meeting at Annie Mast's house, but more recently we've had it at my house—just till the babies come and settle in. Then we'll pro'bly return to Annie's. You're welcome to join us, Rosie." At this, Leah nodded cheerfully.

"I'd like that." She asked when they planned to quilt next and was glad when Mandy said next Thursday, a week from today. "That's the day after I work for Gilbert Browning, so I should be able to help. Well, I mean . . . if I can get away for a while."

"You could take Annie's spot at the frame," Mandy added, "since she's not able to come . . . getting so uncomfortable anymore. Due any day."

"There's a nice view of the pond from where Annie sits at the quilting frame," Leah said, smiling.

"Sure . . . I'll take Annie's place." Rose felt invigorated at the thought of working on quilts after many months of sewing only the faceless rag dolls, so popular with tourists, which she sold at market.

"Wonderful. That'll help us keep goin' on the quilt. We have two to finish before we go again to deliver them before Christmas. Prob'ly in a couple of weeks."

Leah rose just then, excusing herself to wet her whistle and went to the sink for a glass of water.

Mandy's eyes turned ever so serious. She glanced around, as if checking for listening ears, then leaned forward. "Mamma and Linda took several quilts to the shelter the middle of October. And, well . . . I really don't know how to tell ya this."

By the somber look on Mandy's face, Rose wondered what on earth she was working up to. "What is it?"

Slowly, almost falteringly, Mandy said, "I remember what a *gut* friend you were to Nick Franco."

At the sound of his name, Rose started. Mandy looked over her shoulder again, and Rose sensed that whatever Mandy was about to reveal might be something she'd rather not hear. Even so, she asked, "What about him?"

"Mamma saw him at the shelter," Mandy said in a near whisper.

A homeless shelter?

"Well, for goodness' sake. Is she sure?"

Mandy nodded her head. "I asked her the same thing."

Sighing now, Rose leaned back in the chair and folded her hands. "I'm real sorry to hear that."

"Mamma's sad about it, too. We all are, despite what he did to Christian."

Rose opened her mouth but thought better of it. She had no

business defending Nick. "Has the bishop or anyone else been told?" she asked.

"I wouldn't be surprised if the bishop hears 'bout it soon."

Rose wanted to burrow her head in the crook of her elbow and pray right then and there. *Poor Nick, homeless. Please, Lord, watch over my friend!*

She excused herself and went to stand on the back porch again, overwhelmed by the news—shaking at best. And Mandy's attitude was like that of many. *I don't blame her.*

Rose was reminded of the night she'd ridden double with Nick on his favorite horse, Pepper, to the high meadow. Truth be known, she cherished that memory even to this day. Yet she knew she must sweep her mind free of all such fond recollections, including the afternoon near the creek in the dark ravine where Nick had revealed his love. And the day he'd carried her, when she'd hurt her knee. She had never forgotten how safe she felt in his arms. Safe and ever so cared for.

She must release those memories before she said her marriage vows to Silas while standing before the bishop and God. *But how?* The thought of Nick's leaving could sometimes bring tears to her eyes.

Staring at the sky, Rose sighed deeply and wondered when the miserable surge of rain would ever let up.

CHAPTER 6

Thoroughly rattled, Hen surprised herself by not reacting openly when Brandon turned into the driveway just as she began to walk down the front sidewalk. Inwardly she held her breath, wondering what he'd say as he opened his car door and unfolded his long legs to get out.

"Well . . . surprise, surprise." He grinned as he walked toward her, then gave her an obligatory peck on the cheek. "Happy Thanksgiving, Hen."

She ignored his patronizing tone and waved toward the house. "I stopped by to see you . . . and while I was here, I picked up my ring holder, too."

"Oh?" He looked down at her left hand. "You're not hocking your diamond, are you?"

She grimaced. "I would never do that."

His shoulders relaxed; he seemed relieved. "You must have received my letter."

"Dad gave it to me . . . said you stopped by."

He gave her a half smile. "How good of him."

She suddenly felt empty.

"What is it, Hen?"

"All of this just seems so sudden."

"We're separated, aren't we? Time to make it legal if you're going to keep living away from home. Why drag this out?"

She looked at him, astonished. "We're talking about our marriage, Brandon . . . our family."

"Touché," he replied. "Exactly what I'm thinking. It's clear you don't take it seriously."

"Well, it's unnecessary to hurry things like this. It really is."

"Then I take it you're coming home with Mattie Sue, right?"

She glanced at the house. Hen wasn't sure, but it looked like Terry had just backed away from the window. Hen heard the puppy yipping loudly. "Why must Mattie Sue be in the middle of things?" she said quietly, feeling strange standing there for the whole neighborhood to see. "She's happy where she is."

"Without her father?" His eyes were fiery now, just as they were whenever he mentioned their daughter. "You haven't brought her to visit like you said. What kind of mother keeps a child away from her daddy?"

She stepped back, surprised. "Brandon . . . please. That's not what I'm saying. You should know that."

"Well, then what?" He glanced down the street, shaking his head. "Drop Mattie off and pick her up in a few hours."

She looked at him—his face, his hair, his mannerisms. Really looked. He seemed different somehow; incredibly so. What had happened during the weeks they'd been apart? Had they forgotten how to relate to each other? "You know how I feel about the worldly things coming into . . . our house."

"Hen, you're never going to make a case against me because I watch TV when Mattie's around." He reached for her arm. "Don't you see? You're the problem. *You*, Hen."

She pulled away. "That's not fair!"

"All right. It's your absurdly high standards!"

There was no reasoning with him. Brandon had never understood her stance against his seeming desire to expose their daughter to the evils of the world, or his refusal to attend church. And since he didn't, Hen felt it best she simply go. "I'm sorry to upset you," she said quietly, moving past him toward her car. *And I'm sorry I stopped by.*

"Yes, why don't you go back to your precious Amish life . . . but remember what I said." Brandon headed toward the house, then turned. "I am not kidding about the deadline, Hen. I already have the papers ready to file."

She had never known him to be so rude or pushy—at least not to her. Dejected, she got into her car and drove away.

Dusk had fallen as the last of the supper dishes were put into a large tub and swished clean by several preappointed women. Rose was secretly glad to be among the wedding attendants, one of the few weddings she'd gone to where she wasn't involved in clearing the tables or helping in the kitchen. Not that Rose ever minded doing so. It was a matter of sharing the work load, and when her own special day rolled around, she would call upon various family members to do the same for her and Silas.

Now that Melvin was back from the barn, she sat in a corner of the front room with him and listened as he freely shared his impressions of Rebekah Bontrager. "She's really nice, not stuck up like you might expect for being so . . . uh—"

"Pretty?"

Melvin shrugged sheepishly. "Jah, and I was a little surprised that she and Silas already knew each other so well."

"Of course they do, from when she and her family lived here."

Melvin took a bite of his pecan pie. "I could be wrong, but I think they may have kept in touch since she left."

"How do you mean?"

"My gut says so."

"Maybe *you'd* like to ask her home after the Singing." Rose forced a smile.

Melvin was quiet while he finished eating his slice of pie. Then, when he'd smacked his lips sufficiently, he leaned closer. "Listen, it's not my imagination, Rose Ann. I think Rebekah's sweet on Silas."

Rose blew out a sigh. She doubted Melvin knew that she and Silas were betrothed.

"And I'd say the two of them are mighty comfortable with each other . . . the way they were talkin' when I went out there."

"Well, Silas gets along with everyone," she said.

Melvin shrugged. "There's no need for me to try and compete with Silas Good for her attention." He pushed aside his empty plate. "I'll see you later." He moved away from the table, leaving Rose alone with her thoughts.

What a foolish imagination he has! She brushed off his comments—Melvin had no idea how much Silas loved her. Nor did her cousin know Silas the way she did.

But sometime later, when Silas and Rebekah came indoors, wet from the rain and both of them wearing smiles, Melvin's observations came back to her. And it wasn't until much later that Silas sought Rose out and asked if she'd be his partner for the barn Singing . . . which helped greatly in dismissing Melvin's jolting remarks.

CHAPTER 7

$\mathscr{S}$alem Road was shrouded in twilight as the headlights of a car shone into Solomon Kauffman's driveway that evening. The vehicle slowed to a stop and a man got out. Solomon had just hung up his carpenter's apron and was closing up his woodworking shop, carrying a lantern. "Hullo there," he called as he stepped outside, a bit uneasy.

"It's Gilbert Browning, your neighbor. Your daughter Rose is my housekeeper and cook."

"How've ya been, Mr. Browning?"

"Oh, we're doin' all right."

Solomon crossed the yard, motioning to him. "Won't ya come inside?"

"I really can't stay." Mr. Browning glanced back at the car. "Beth's with me."

"Well, bring her in, too."

"It's Rose I need to talk to . . . and you."

Solomon said she was off at a wedding. "She might be gone

till late—those Singings sometimes last close to midnight," he explained. "But I can certainly give her a message for ya."

The light came on inside the car, and Solomon could see Beth, Mr. Browning's special daughter, sitting up front in the passenger's seat.

"I know this is on the spur of the moment, so I hesitate to ask for a favor."

"No need to be *scheie*—shy," Solomon said. "We're glad to help if we can."

Mr. Browning continued to hesitate, then forged ahead. "I've been called away to South Carolina to help my ailing father."

"Bless him, will he be all right?"

"He fell and has a bad break in his hip, and there are some complications." The older man sighed. "Would you mind having Beth stay with you a few days—possibly a week?"

"I don't see why not. Rosie will be happy to look after your daughter. We all will." Solomon thought it might actually be good to further occupy Rose these days, what with all of them still mourning Christian's untimely death.

Mr. Browning seemed relieved. "Beth's got everything packed. She even brought her stuffed animals and some of her writing notebooks."

"Well, she'll have plenty of space in Rose's room."

"You sure this isn't an imposition?"

"No . . . no. Don't even think twice about it," said Solomon, going with him to the trunk to get Beth's suitcase and a bag of the stuffed toys. "The soil's resting now with the start of our wedding season. It's our time for visitin'." He paused a moment. "Your daughter will be well cared for, I can assure you."

Beth climbed out of the car, but she stood in the open door and waited for her father to come around and hold on to her arm, just as Sol had seen Rose do the times Beth had visited here. The girl could be unsteady on her feet. "Hullo again, Beth," he greeted her. Then, when her father came to meet her, Solomon lifted his lantern toward the house. "Just follow me."

One of Mattie Sue's barn kitties ran across their path, and Solomon warned the Brownings not to trip. Then, when they rounded the corner and were near the back steps, Solomon called to Sylvia, his mother-in-law. He led the way into the back porch and the kitchen. "We've got us some company," he said as Sylvia rose from her spot near Emma's wheelchair. "Beth Browning's going to stay with us for a while," he added as Emma turned her head and gave a faint smile.

"*Kumme* right in and make yourselves to home." Sylvia reached to take Beth's bag, overflowing with teddy bears and cats.

"She'll stay with Rose in her room," said Solomon, taking his leave to carry the suitcase upstairs.

When he returned to the kitchen, Mr. Browning, whose eyes looked mighty tired, was talking softly to his daughter. "I put your medication in your suitcase, all right?" He handed a piece of paper with instructions on it to Solomon. "You'll see that Rose gets this, won't you?"

"Not a problem at all."

"It's very important." He wiped his brow with the back of his hand. "There's a phone number where I can be reached, as well." Gilbert Browning frowned and suddenly looked concerned. "Don't hesitate to call," he said, glancing at Sol. "For any reason at all."

"Beth'll be just fine here," Sol assured him. He realized Mr. Browning had come a long way toward trusting them in a short time. It was hard to believe this was the same man who'd sequestered Beth away like Rose had described.

Sylvia stood near Emma's wheelchair. "We'll take extra *gut* care of her."

"*Denki* for thinkin' of us, Mr. Browning," Emma said in her feeble voice, looking now at Beth.

"Thank *you*—all of you." Mr. Browning smiled momentarily.

Then he turned to kiss Beth on the cheek. "I love you, honey," he said.

She wrapped her arms around his neck. "I love you, too, Daddy. Tell Grandpa I'm praying for him." She leaned her head against him.

"Don't worry, now, Beth." Tears sprang to Gilbert's eyes, and he gave his daughter's hand a little squeeze before heading for the back door. Solomon followed close behind, picking up the still-lit lantern on the porch so the kindly Englischer could safely make his way back to his car.

∾

"Goodness gracious, we finally have a chance to talk!" said Rebekah, her brown eyes shining as she reached for Rose's hand. They stood in the privacy of the stable area of the two-story bank barn, with several mules near. "With all that was goin' on today at the wedding, I was hoping I'd get to say hullo to everyone present. Well, the folk who might remember me, at least."

"Did ya get to see Esther, too?" asked Rose, smiling back. "The radiant bride?"

"Jah, and now, counting you, all of her cousins." Rebekah beamed. "Ach, I thought I'd never get back here after we moved. Then, when Annie Mast's mother wrote to Mamma, asking if I'd come to help with the new babies, well, I jumped at the chance."

Rose noticed that Rebekah's childhood dimples had deepened. "It's awful nice of you. Annie must be glad you agreed."

Rebekah nodded. "When Mamma got the letter, she only said it was from one of the Masts."

"Oh, and you prob'ly had no idea which ones, ain't?"

"That's exactly right!"

They burst into laughter.

"So are you getting settled in at Annie's place, then?" Rose asked.

"Took no time at all." Rebekah went on to say she'd brought along very little, planning instead to sew some dresses and aprons fairly soon. "But once the babies come, it'll be interesting to see how much sewin' I get done, jah?"

Rose found Rebekah to be just as engaging and fun as she'd always been. She was truly sorry her family had ever moved away. "I'm sure there will be plenty of hours when the twins are sleeping," Rose added. "Newborns tend to do that quite a lot the first few weeks."

"Well, I'll learn as I go. 'Tween you and me, I've only helped with infants a couple times."

Rose found this tidbit interesting. Most all the mother's helpers she knew had frequently assisted with newborns on up to preschool-age children.

"Mostly I've looked after toddlers."

Rose laughed softly. "When they start walking, it's harder to keep up with 'em."

"Ain't that right!" Rebekah told about her older sister's two little ones. "I'm goin' to miss them something awful while I'm here."

"Mamm said you'll be stayin' on till spring."

Rebekah brightened again. "As long as Annie needs me, I will. As for Noah Mast, bless his heart, he's hopin' I'll find myself a nice fella here. Guess they want me to just come back to where I belong."

Rose pondered that, wondering why Rebekah didn't already have a serious beau back home. If she had, surely she wouldn't have come. "Wouldn't you miss your family if ya stayed?"

"Oh sure. But just maybe, if I settle down here, they'll all return to Lancaster County someday."

Rose wondered if the Bontragers really would be willing to move back after living this long in Indiana, where they had land to spare.

Just then, Silas walked into the barn. He immediately looked puzzled when he saw Rose talking to Rebekah. She decided to wait till he came over to talk to her and continued getting caught up on her friend's activities, including Rebekah's stint as a schoolteacher.

"I'd prob'ly still be teaching, but the school board decided to bring on an older woman for the one-room schoolhouse," Rebekah said, still wearing her contagious smile. "A Mennonite teacher."

"Is that so?"

"Interesting, ain't? I'd say the church district we're in out there is . . . different."

"There are plenty of diverse church *Ordnungs* just a little ways north of here, too, ya know."

"Well, where I'm from, we're allowed to have bikes with inflatable tires, for instance."

"Goodness, that'll never happen here."

"Can you just imagine?" Rebekah glanced toward the fellows all clustered together across the barn. Her voice dropped to a near whisper. "Though I heard through the grapevine, some months back, that one of your boys here had taken to card playin'."

"Not Rook, but face cards?"

"I'm talking 'bout the wicked cards with kings and queens and whatnot. I doubt you'd be surprised if I told ya."

Rose listened, curious to know what Rebekah might say.

Rebekah continued. "This same fella supposedly bought himself a pair of Rollerblades. The bishop's wife found 'em in the haymow."

Rose said nothing.

"And I heard he ran off, too," added Rebekah.

Rose wondered how Rebekah knew so much about Nick. "I s'pose you also heard other things."

"Jah, 'tis awful sad." Rebekah touched the back of Rose's hand. "Everything all right?"

Rose wasn't about to say it was, because it just wasn't. And she didn't know when anything related to Nick would ever be.

She looked again for Silas and saw he was still clear across the barn. He had just taken off his black felt hat and was scratching his head. No doubt it was a signal for her to excuse herself and be available for him to wander over and talk with. After all, she'd spent nearly all her time so far with Rebekah.

"They want me to just come back to where I belong." Rebekah's words spun round and round in Rose's mind as she excused herself and headed straight for Silas Good, glad, after most of a day apart, to finally claim her place at his side.

CHAPTER 8

*H*en watched contentedly as Mattie Sue and Beth Browning showed each other their stuffed animals later that evening. Most of Beth's were cats and teddy bears, and she asked if Mattie Sue could count all of them. Mattie was up to eleven when Hen noticed her mother was starting to droop. "Looks like it's almost bedtime for Mammi Emma," she said softly from her spot across the kitchen.

The girls looked up, and then Beth went to stand beside the wheelchair and placed her hand on Hen's mother's slender arm.

Hen didn't know if Rose had ever told Beth about the accident that caused her mother's paralysis from the waist down, so Hen merely said that her mother wasn't well.

"I want to write a healing prayer for her." Beth's eyes were moist. "I'll write it in my notebook."

"That's kind of you, honey." Hen eyed her mother, who was already asleep. "Mattie Sue, go and call Dawdi Sol for me, please."

But her daughter continued to count Beth's stuffed animals near the woodstove, not acknowledging Hen's request.

"Mattie," she said, slightly louder, getting up from her chair. "Did you hear what I asked?"

As if in a daze, Mattie Sue glanced up. "Oh, sorry, Mommy . . . what did ya say?"

Hen repeated herself before noticing Beth was now sitting on the wooden bench facing the wheelchair, a few inches from Mom. Beth's eyes were intent on Mom, and she was whispering under her breath. Hen asked her, "Are you all right, Beth?"

"Your mommy's not breathing so good," Beth said.

"I think she's just tired." But in case she was mistaken, Hen moved close to her mother, watching . . . listening. After a moment, she assured Beth, "Jah, she's resting now . . . please don't worry."

All the same, Beth sat like a statuette, her face turned toward Mom's—her lips pursed shut.

Just then, Hen's father came into the kitchen. Mattie Sue got up and trailed behind as he moved to the wheelchair. "Emma, dear." He leaned down to scoop her up. "Time we head for bed, jah?"

Mom sighed deeply, not opening her eyes. She lay limp in his strong arms, resting her head against him as a sweet smile played across her lips. "*Gut Nacht, alliebber*—good night, everyone," she said, eyes still closed.

"Sleep well, Mom," said Hen, watching with a heavy heart.

"Good night, Mrs. Kauffman," Beth said as she followed them to the doorway of their bedroom.

Mattie Sue clung to Hen's long skirt. "Mommy?"

"Yes, honey?"

"What's a-matter with Beth?"

Hen swallowed the lump in her throat. "Come here, sweetie." She reached down and lifted Mattie Sue into her arms, glancing toward Beth. Carrying her little girl out to the back porch, she began to explain what Rose had told her about Gilbert Browning's daughter. "God made some of us very special," she said. "I mean, some people never really grow up inside. They might look like they're older than you are, but in their mind—and heart—they're still like little children."

"Like me?"

She whispered, "Jah, honey."

Mattie Sue's eyes grew round. "Is that why Beth has so many stuffed animals with her?"

Hen nodded. "That's right."

"I like her, Mommy." Mattie Sue turned, looking back to see Beth. "She's really nice."

"I think so, too."

Beth returned to the kitchen, tears streaming down her cheeks. "I didn't know . . . but can't your mommy walk?" she asked Hen, who put Mattie Sue down quickly.

"She hasn't walked in eleven years—not since her accident." Hen hoped she wasn't saying more than she should to the tender-hearted young woman. "Did Rose Ann tell you about it?"

Beth frowned, her head tilted a little. Then, hesitating, she went to sit near the window and stared out at the darkness. "I miss Rosie," she muttered, sniffing softly. "I really do."

She must miss her father by now, too, Hen thought. She wondered if it might not be a good idea to have Beth head upstairs for bed sooner rather than later, considering her state. She'd get her settled in with Mattie Sue nearby. "Let's read a story together," she said. "What do ya say?"

Mattie Sue was all for it. "In Aunt Rosie's room?" She began pulling out several new library books, offering them to Beth. "Did ya bring your pajamas along?" she asked a little shyly.

Beth brushed away her tears. "Yes, my favorite Strawberry Shortcake ones. I'll show you."

Hen was relieved to see Mattie Sue go to Beth's side, and in a few minutes, when they were all in Rose's room, Beth said she wanted to unpack her things. *Mattie Sue can be a blessing to Beth,* thought Hen as she made some room in one of Rose's dresser drawers, knowing her sister wouldn't mind.

She looked at her wristwatch and realized Rose might not be home for another three hours or more. *If her beau takes her riding,* she thought, so relieved that Nick Franco was out of the picture. *I hope forever. . . .*

~

Rose was happy to walk outside with Silas now that the sky had cleared. They headed around to the back of the barn, where they were less obvious. She'd kept her eye out for Rebekah off and on after the Singing, hoping the so-called new girl might not end up alone for the remainder of the evening.

"You seem quiet tonight." Silas leaned down to smile at her in the white light of the full moon.

"Just concerned about Rebekah, I guess." She sighed.

"She seems happy enough."

"She told ya that?"

"I just think she's glad to be back where she grew up."

Rose nodded and gazed out at the brilliant fields. "Aren't we lucky to live in such a pretty place?"

"Jah, and sometime soon, I'd like to take ya on a tour of a spot I think's the prettiest—my father's dairy farm."

"It would be nice to get better acquainted with your sisters someday, too."

"Oh, they'd welcome that, for sure."

She thought of Rebekah—how odd that she'd been called upon to help with the Mast twins when there were plenty of young single women already here, such as Silas's own unmarried sisters. "Too bad it's so late in November . . . for Rebekah's sake." Typically by autumn of each year, the fellows had already picked their girls to date or court.

"Well, she didn't come here to get a beau, even though she's quite solidly Amish. She's never been one to push the boundaries of propriety."

"I'm just thinkin' about what she told me," Rose said.

"What's that?"

"Something Annie Mast's husband said."

"Oh?"

"Apparently Noah hopes she'll find a husband here." Rose didn't wait for Silas to respond. "I have to say I like her a lot . . . she's grown up so much."

"We all have, jah?" He chuckled, reaching for her hand.

She listened as he began talking about other things, but one comment he'd made niggled at her: *What does he mean, Rebekah's "solidly Amish"?*

She dismissed it as they strolled together out near a small pond, talking softly and enjoying each other's company. It had been a long time since they'd gone walking, and she always cherished their private times. It would've been silly to stick her neck out and repeat what Melvin had mentioned earlier. Truly, the notion of there being something special between Silas and Rebekah seemed altogether flawed now.

Rose breathed in the fresh, crisp night air, smiling as Silas's hand interlaced with hers. *I'm with my darling and nothing else matters!*

～

At first Beth seemed resistant to letting Hen help her to bed, then tuck her in for the night. Hen had taken great care to give Beth her privacy while she changed into her nightclothes, waiting in the hallway till she said she was ready. Meanwhile, Mattie Sue was downstairs at the kitchen table, talking to her own stuffed animals, lining them all up on the kitchen bench.

"I miss Daddy," whimpered Beth now as Hen sat on the edge of Rose's bed. "I want him to come home soon."

"Your grandpa needs his help right now. I'm sure your father will return just as soon as he can."

Beth frowned. "If Grandpa dies, we'll have to move again."

"Why do you think that?" Hen asked gently.

"Daddy says Grandma's too weak—she can't live by herself. I remember how sad he looked when he told me. Almost as sad as when Mommy died."

"Well, let's not worry about that now." Hen pulled up the top quilt and folded it down near Beth's willowy neck. "You'll feel better when you see Rose, jah?"

Beth's face peeked out from the quilts. "She's my *best* friend," Beth said firmly. "I prayed for a friend . . . and God answered my prayer." She closed her eyes for a moment, then opened them.

Hen nodded, trying to understand her childlike faith, as well as the way she seemed to want to be treated. "When you wake up, Rose Ann will be right here, next to you." She pointed to the other side of the bed. "I promise."

"Why's she gone so late?"

Hen smiled, recalling how she had asked her mom the same thing about her older brothers when they had been courting. At the time, Mom had shared her own concerns about the long hours. *"How can it be wise for young folk to stay out most of the night?"* A good many older parents felt the same way once their daughters, especially, turned sixteen and were considered courting age.

"Rose is out with her fella," Hen explained.

"Her boyfriend?" Beth's face beamed in the light of the gas lamp. "Who is he?"

"That's up to Rosie to say." Considering Amish tradition, there was no way Hen would commit Rose to more.

"Will you say a bedtime prayer?" Beth asked, bringing her hands out from beneath the covers and folding them under her chin.

Hen agreed, wondering how much longer Mattie Sue would be content alone downstairs. To comfort Beth, she began to say the nighttime prayer she'd learned verbatim as a little girl. "Holy Father, we ask that we may spend this coming night—which you have ordained for our rest—and all the remainder of our lives under your divine protection and shield. O holy Father, defend us and cover us with the wings of your compassion . . . Beth especially. Amen."

Beth smiled up sweetly at her. "I've never heard that prayer before," she said, eyes glistening. "Is it written down somewhere?"

"Jah, in the German prayer book."

"In English, too?" Beth asked.

"I think so." Hen wondered why she asked.

"First thing tomorrow, I'm going to write my healing prayer for your mommy." Beth's lower lip trembled. "When I look at her, it hurts me."

"It's very hard to see her suffer." Hen got up and went to the door, pausing there in case Beth might say more. But Rose's English friend simply closed her eyes, her hands still folded near her face, and for a moment, Hen had the feeling Beth was silently praying.

Something maternal stirred within her, seeing the innocent young woman with the mind of a child behave in such a trusting manner. A fleeting thought crossed her mind—someday she would love to have another baby. But with Brandon threatening divorce, the chance of another child seemed terribly remote . . . if not impossible.

Hen sighed as she made her way to the stairs. *If only Brandon might come to know the Lord. Then we might see eye to eye. . . .*

～

All the lanterns were still blazing when Rose and Silas arrived back at the barn. Yet the lights were nearly dim in comparison to the dazzling moon, and as Rose entered the upper level, she paused to let her eyes adjust to the contrast.

To her surprise, she noticed Rebekah standing alone near the stacked bales of hay, holding one of the white barn kittens close to her face. Rose hurried to see her and asked without thinking, "Do you need a ride back to Masts'?"

Rebekah's eyes widened as she continued to pet the tiny cat. "Denki, that'd be right nice. But is it okay with Silas?"

Rose suddenly felt awkward about acknowledging Silas as her beau, yet few other conclusions could be drawn.

She looked back toward the open barn door. Silas stood there, watching her curiously. "Just a minute, I'll see if he minds." Rose went to him and asked quietly if they could give Rebekah a ride. "It's too far and cold on foot, ain't?"

He removed his black felt hat and did what he often did when he was ill at ease, pushing one hand through his thick blond hair. "No need for her to walk in the dark . . . no."

"So it's all right, then?"

"If ya want."

She turned.

"Wait . . . Rose." He paused, looking serious. "Next time ask me first, jah?"

She blushed with embarrassment. Never before had Silas spoken like that to her, although she realized now it was certainly warranted. She nodded, wishing she *had* waited to ask Rebekah till she'd seen how Silas felt about it. After all, he'd talked of wanting to ride together for a while—just the two of them—before taking Rose home tonight.

Rebekah smiled prettily when Rose returned. She wasted no time falling into step with Rose, and the two of them followed Silas out of the barn. *I best be minding my manners,* thought Rose as Silas pushed his hat back on his head. *I don't want to displease my betrothed.*

She watched Silas walk toward his horse and the open buggy. But his hat brim cast a shadow over his face, making it impossible to see if he actually was in agreement with her unusual request.

CHAPTER 9

Rose awakened the next day to find Beth sitting up in bed, leaning against her pillow. She had been surprised and delighted to learn from Dat's note last night that dear Beth would be staying with them for the week. Curious, she watched her friend whispering the words she'd evidently written in the blue spiral notebook on her lap. It sounded like a prayer. The more Rose observed her, the more she realized the phrases were well written . . . and that Mamm, surprisingly, was at the heart of what Beth had composed.

Unable to remain silent, Rose stirred to let Beth know she was awake, lest she be guilty of eavesdropping. "Did ya sleep all right, Beth?" she asked quietly, so as not to startle her.

Beth smiled sleepily. "I must've. . . . I feel wide-awake this morning."

Rose sat up and pushed her own pillow against the headboard, then leaned back. "Was that a prayer you were reading?"

Beth nodded. "It's a healing prayer." She paused, fingering the notebook. "From my heart to God's."

Rose didn't know what to say. For as often as she'd prayed in her life, she'd never written down a single one.

Beth closed her notebook. "Remember when we talked at my house about God?"

Rose hadn't forgotten.

"You said He knows everything, even the day we are born . . . and the day we'll die, too." Beth looked at the ceiling for a moment. "Well, the very next day I wrote a letter to God about that." She leaned forward and tilted her head to look outside at the sky from where she sat. "I've been talking that way to Him for a long time, mostly in my notebook pages."

Rose listened, not knowing what to think or say. *Beth's so naïve,* she realized anew.

Beth's eyes were filled with an appealing light. And Rose did not want to discourage her, especially if God *had* put it in her heart to pray for Mamm. "The Lord knows all of our thoughts and the intent of our heart," Rose told Beth.

"Will you read my prayer?" Beth handed the notebook to Rose.

She accepted it but held Beth's gaze, not wanting to intrude unless Beth was absolutely certain. "Are ya sure?"

With eyes shining, Beth nodded. And Rose began to read aloud.

Dear God,

Daddy says you never sleep, so I wonder if you're looking over my shoulder while I write this prayer. There's someone in this house who's suffering. She needs your help. Every time I look at Rosie's mommy, I feel like crying. I wonder: Do you cry for Mrs. Kauffman, too?

In my mommy's Bible, I read once that you healed people when you lived on earth. That's why I'm writing this prayer, because you see everything. When you read this, will you help Rosie's poor mother? If it's in your will, I know I'm supposed to say.

I hope you read this prayer very soon!

Love,
Beth Browning

Brushing back her tears, Rose struggled to see the last few lines. "Oh, Beth . . . this is the sweetest thing."

Beth touched her hand. "I didn't want to make you cry. Are you all right, Rosie?"

Rose blinked and smiled, trying to regain her composure. *Why can't all of us be more like Beth?*

∼

Solomon hitched Upsy-Daisy, one of his driving horses, to the family carriage and headed for Quarryville to the land-development office that morning. Brandon had worked there for at least four years now, but Sol had never so much as stopped by.

He had known today upon waking what he needed to do. Regardless of the result, he must at least *try* to make a connection with his son-in-law. But when he neared the street where Brandon's office suite was located, Sol suddenly wondered how he was going to secure his horse. Standing outside the buggy, he looked around for someplace to tether the mare. Unlike other business establishments, there was not a single hitching post to be seen.

Just then, a sports car crept in next to the horse and carriage. And Sol must've been wearing concern all over his face, because the lady driver hopped out and pointed to her side mirror. "Tie your horse here," she said with a toss of her reddish hair. "I'll be parked here all morning."

"Denki. Mighty kind of ya."

She smiled. "My grandpa's Amish. Maybe you know him."

"Oh?" Sol felt awkward talking to this pretty young woman who looked about Hen's age.

"My Dawdi Dan lives up near Smoketown, though."

He knew more than two handfuls of Dans, but he shook his head. "We rarely get up that way."

Sol wanted to ask why she wasn't Plain, too. "Have a *gut* day, and thanks again."

"Any time," she said, and hurried toward the small building.

Sol turned to his horse now, telling the mare he wouldn't be long. Then he tied her to the sports car's sideview mirror, looking about him to make sure someone didn't think he was as crazy as he surely looked.

∼

Mattie Sue had been pestering her mother since breakfast about making a batch of cookies. Without Mattie's knowing, Rose had happily offered to put both girls to work making the cookie dough for the upcoming common meal this coming Sunday. It was then she realized Beth would be present for church. How would she manage the nearly three and a half hours of the Lord's Day gathering?

Has she ever been to church anywhere? Rose wondered.

She recalled Mattie Sue's recent introduction to Preaching service and hoped Beth might do all right sitting in back, where Hen and Mattie sat, since they were not members.

Rose called the girls to come and measure out the ingredients, and Beth stood up and swayed, seemingly dizzy. Mattie Sue tried childishly to steady her, looking up to see if Beth had regained her balance . . . something Rose had observed twice before this morning.

Mamm let out a moan and Beth frowned deeply, her face sinking as if she was heartbroken. Beth looked first at Mamm, then back at Rose. "I better not help make cookies," she said. "I'm going to sit with your mommy . . . all right, Rose?"

Rose felt sorry for her mother and for Beth, who appeared overly preoccupied with Mamm's condition. "Why don't you sit with her while Mattie Sue finishes measuring, then help Mattie mix all the ingredients?"

But Beth planted herself next to the wheelchair, hovering near like a mother robin. "I want to stay right here."

Rose didn't have the heart to try to persuade her away, not with

Beth's own grandfather in such poor health and the girl clearly missing her father. So she said no more. She was conscious of Beth's remarkably gentle way with Mamm as Beth and her mother—with heads nearly touching—talked softly, about just what Rose did not know.

Being around Mamm must make Beth long for her own mother!

Reflecting on this, Rose was both glad and sad for Beth. To think Mamm, in her great pain, was able to extend this kind of comfort.

Rose suddenly thought of her friend Nick and the recent loss of his mother, whom he'd known for only a short time. Indeed, Nick had come to mind several times since she'd heard from Mandy Esh about his being spotted in Philly. Nick must surely be in trouble if he was living at such a place. If so, shouldn't she try to help him? Maybe someone could go there and try to find Nick—talk sense to him? For the life of her, Rose didn't know if she could stand idly by. *If what Mandy Esh's mother saw was true.* She hoped against hope Laura Esh was quite wrong.

Hen broke the silence and interrupted Rose's musing. "There's a lot of turkey left over from yesterday, if anyone's hungry for a sandwich later." Hen was helping Mattie Sue with the cookie making, glancing now at Rose . . . and then at Beth. Rose could tell that Hen, too, was wondering how to get Beth's mind off Mamm.

"Would ya like that, Beth?" asked Rose. "Some delicious turkey?"

Beth turned. "I'm not hungry."

"Well, later, maybe?"

Beth shook her head slowly, looking back at Mamm.

Hen frowned and Rose sighed. Was it a mistake to have Beth stay here? "I know for sure Mamm's goin' to eat a nice dinner at noon," Rose said, hoping that might set Beth's thoughts on the big meal of the day—and stir up an appetite.

"Can I sit beside her at the table?" asked Beth.

Rose and Hen exchanged glances. "Don't see why not," Rose said.

"We're going to cut out some dress patterns after the dinner dishes are washed and put away," Hen said casually. "How would you like an Amish dress to wear . . . just while you're here?"

Beth's eyes gleamed. "Oh, could I?" She got up and walked over to Hen and Mattie Sue, who were carefully spooning out the dough onto the cookie sheets.

Mattie Sue grinned up at her as Beth stood watching. "We can be sisters together, ain't so?" said Mattie Sue. "With matching dresses."

Beth gave her a winning smile.

"Will it be all right with your father?" Hen asked suddenly.

"I think so," Beth said, then added, "Jah."

Rose smiled at the expression and recalled that Beth had worn Amish attire before, although a boy's britches, suspenders, and straw hat. *A dress and apron will be far better!*

Soon Beth was helping Mattie Sue—both of them counting the dozens of mounds of cookie dough. Rose was so taken with the sudden change in Beth that she was reminded of the unexpected shift in Silas's demeanor last night, though a far less pleasant change than Beth's. To this moment, she felt chagrined by the surprising scolding he'd given her for offering Rebekah a ride home.

Silas had been strangely quiet for a good portion of their ride afterward, once Rebekah had hopped down from the open buggy, waving cheerfully before hurrying up the long lane to the Masts' farmhouse.

What was I thinking? The last thing Rose wanted was to cause a problem between herself and her fiancé. After all, Silas was as good as his family's name.

The peculiar things Cousin Melvin had told Rose crossed her

mind again. But . . . didn't she know better? Besides, Rebekah was much too nice to be a threat to any girl in the church district.

Let alone to a friend like me.

∼

Even though it was the next to last day of November, Sol thought the present cold snap was tolerable. *Not nearly as miserable as some years around this time.*

He smiled inwardly at the way the young woman had offered her car's side mirror for a hitching post. How humorous the situation must look to clients coming in and out of the parking lot west of the building where Brandon worked.

Sunlight filtered in through the glass windows in the lobby of the land-development office as Sol entered. Not having come here before, Sol looked at the wall directory to find the correct suite number. When he'd located it, he moved to the elevator and pressed the button indicating the second floor.

He leaned against the wall, holding his felt hat in front of him. *If Hen knew what I was up to.* He hadn't told anyone his plans, and he didn't know what even dear Emma would think of his desire to sit down with their son-in-law and discuss such important matters. No, it was better that Emma didn't know. She hadn't been sleeping at night here lately. In fact, he was sure she hadn't slept well for weeks, and he worried she might never get the rest her weakened body badly needed. Poor thing, she scarcely had a minute of relief. There were times when he wished with everything in him that he could get Emma to see a specialist somewhere.

The elevator doors opened, and Sol spotted the suite number on the door directly across the hall as he stepped out. He pushed his shoulders back, crossed the wide hall, and opened the door.

CHAPTER 10

*S*olomon's gaze swept Brandon's impressive suite as he entered the lobby area, where several comfortable chairs and end tables were placed along one side of the room. He was met by the cheery-faced receptionist—the same young woman who'd offered her car's side mirror for his horse. "We meet again," she said, her eyes wide as he removed his black felt hat. "How may I help you?"

"Name's Solomon Kauffman," he began. "I'd like to see Brandon Orringer."

She glanced at her computer monitor, then back at him. "Might this be for the purpose of building or land development?"

Brandon's also a builder now? He was surprised; he hadn't heard this from Hen. Then again, she might not have known. "Brandon's my son-in-law," Sol said, still holding his hat.

"No kidding!" she burst out, then quickly softened. "Excuse me, sir . . . I had no idea."

"Quite all right."

"So . . . I don't mean to pry, but is his wife also Amish?"

He didn't know exactly how to respond. "Well, she was raised that way but left . . . to marry Brandon."

The woman's eyes rolled drolly, as if she fully understood. "Marry Amish to stay Amish, jah?"

Sol was startled—that saying was used all the time by the bishops in the area. But Sol was wasting his time making small talk. It was Brandon he wanted to speak to. Plenty of wood needed chopping, among other chores. And Emma . . . goodness, but he could scarcely be gone from home even a short while, things were that bad for her.

The receptionist squinted at the monitor. "I'll see that you get in right after this appointment, Mr. Kauffman. Do you mind waiting?"

He shook his head, turned, and wandered to the water fountain up the hallway. Just as he returned, he heard what must have been Brandon's angry, raised voice, complaining about an upcoming zoning hearing that was dragging on too long.

Sol cringed. *Has Hen ever borne the brunt of his temper at home?*

He scanned the narrow coffee table, making note of several magazines and newspapers there. Headlines regarding trends in real-estate development and land-use policies, zoning laws . . . and land-development ordinances. Restless, Sol went and took another long drink from the water fountain, trying to block out Hen's husband's continual spewing. The man sounded incensed over cost overruns for a cluster of townhouses he was in the process of building, as well.

Sol heard a door closing and Brandon's voice disappeared into a soft muffle. The receptionist was standing near her desk, offering a rueful smile. "I do apologize for Mr. Orringer. It's already been a rough day around here. Actually, a rough week. Mr. Orringer even worked yesterday—on Thanksgiving."

Sol went to sit near the receptionist's window and placed his hat on a nearby chair. "How long has Brandon been a builder?" he asked the woman.

"Not long." Her curious gaze met his, as if to question him: *Didn't you know?*

He wasn't willing to own up to not knowing much at all about his own son-in-law.

"He acquired a partner just recently. A Bruce Kramer."

"I see."

"I'm sure he'll be happy to fill you in." She looked Solomon over. "Brandon's been walking around here like his shirt buttons might pop right off," she added.

Sol wouldn't have expected Brandon to be a man of humility. He was English, after all.

Sol took his time choosing a magazine to read, wishing his father-in-law were here to talk to. As it was, Jeremiah might be wondering what was keeping him and start splitting logs without him. With winter coming on, they'd need plenty of wood for the cookstove. Sol could only hope the bishop might've wandered over from next door to help . . . or one of Sol's sons, maybe. Jeremiah was hard to keep down. He'd recovered nicely from his stroke last spring, but now he liked to think of himself as a new man. Which, of course, he was anything but.

"Mr. Kauffman," the pleasant receptionist said a short time later. "Mr. Orringer can briefly see you now."

Sol picked up his hat and moved quickly past the man who was leaving Brandon's office. "Hullo," he said kindly. The man blew out a breath and said nothing, but Sol sensed the irritation seeping through his dark suit.

Brandon looked perplexed as Solomon entered the office. "Well, Mr. Kauffman," he said cordially. "I didn't expect to see you here."

"Thought I'd drop by."

Brandon didn't rise as Sol might have expected him to. Instead, he motioned for Sol to take a chair on the opposite side of the well-polished desk. "Any chance you've got some farmland to sell?"

"Pardon me?"

"Just joking," Brandon said. "I assume you came to see me about something?"

Solomon cleared his throat. "I'd like to invite you to dinner. Something I should've done years ago."

Brandon leaned forward, elbows on the desk, his hands folded beneath his chin. "What would that accomplish?"

"We might get to know each other."

Brandon regarded Sol carefully, his eyes penetrating. "So . . . I take it Hen isn't coming home."

"On the contrary. I fully expect she *will* return to you." He paused. "When she's ready."

"Well, I can't wait forever. At some point I have to protect my interests."

"Your interests?"

"My daughter, Mr. Kauffman. I can't have her growing up Amish, now, can I?"

Sol rubbed his beard, ignoring the slight. "But you *did* tell Hen to get the Old Ways out of her system, didn't you? I assume you meant her Amish upbringing."

Brandon glanced downward, where his fingers tapped against the desk. "She told you that?"

"Is it true?"

"In so many words, but—"

"Then she's going to need time. Are you a man of your word or not?"

Their eyes met, and Brandon's lips tensed into a firm line. A moment passed as the two men regarded each other. "I'd like her to return home tomorrow," he said. "But as I've stated in the letter, she has until one week from tomorrow. If she's not back by then, I'm filing for divorce."

Sol placed his hands on his knees and shifted forward. "Can ya give your wife a bit more leeway . . . show her some extra patience?"

"I've given her nearly two months already."

"Well, then, what's a little more time?" Sol truly wished for a better resolution to all this. "But in the meantime, you're always welcome for dinner. You might find we're not as backward as you've been led to believe."

"I work late, Mr. Kauffman. No time for pointless dinners," Brandon replied tersely. "Thanks for the invitation, though."

"So, another month, then?"

Brandon shook his head no. "For what reason?"

"Well, to get some wise counsel instead of rushin' into a divorce . . . just maybe?"

"Do you have a counselor in mind?" asked Brandon, eyeing him.

"Our bishop's a wise man—chosen by God, in fact."

Brandon blew air out of his mouth. "I'm acquainted with that man, and let me tell you, I'll never set foot in an Amish bishop's house. And I'm sure Hen would never consider going with me to a marriage counselor of my choosing."

"No . . . prob'ly not." Sol sighed. What was the answer to this terrible dilemma? "But . . . will ya give it more time, at least for Mattie Sue's sake?" he asked.

"What . . . so you can indoctrinate my daughter further?" Brandon practically sneered.

"More time, Brandon. Is that too much to ask?"

Breathing loudly, Brandon stared at his desk. Then, quite reluctantly, he said, looking at Sol, "Two weeks, and not a minute longer."

"All right, then." Sol got up and put on his hat. "I'll let Hen know," he said as he headed for the door.

～

Rose looked across the front room at her mother, whose gaze was focused out the window, at the sky. Seeing Mamm grow weaker as each day passed, Rose's heart was filled anew with compassion.

Hen had suggested they set up a long folding table nearby, so they could work together in the same room. Already, they'd begun to lay out yards of Amish-green fabric and different-sized dress patterns cut from brown grocery bags. Some scraps were large enough for Rose's market dolls.

Meanwhile, Mattie Sue and Beth played in the corner with their toy animals. Rose could hear Mattie Sue trying her best to rename some of Beth's cats and teddy bears, much to Rose's surprise. It seemed that Hen's little girl was bent on taking the leading role. Rose felt sure it was due to Beth's developmental delays, and at times she cringed when Mattie Sue talked up so sassy to Beth, more than four times her age.

Mamm stirred in the wheelchair and called to her. "Rosie, dear . . . I need something to help me with this pain." There were tears in her eyes, and her hands were clasped in trembling fists. "I need it . . . right quick."

"What do ya want? Is there something ya should take, Mamm?" Rose asked, surprised at this request from a mother who never took pain medication.

"The new painkiller the Quarryville pharmacist suggested. I haven't tried that yet."

Rose could scarcely believe her ears. "Are ya sure? You know how awful sick you got last time on a mere aspirin." *Frighteningly so.*

"But this isn't the same . . . and I feel like I'm losin' my mind," Mamm said.

What should I do? Rose wondered. "It could make your stomach wrench, Mamm."

"The pharmacist said it was safe to try. Oh, Rosie, I can't stand it any longer." Mamm began to cry.

Rose's heart broke. "All right . . . I'll give it to you with a nice warm cookie. How's that?"

"Milk might help, too," Mamm added quietly.

"Jah, milk." Rose hurried to the kitchen, hoping she was doing the right thing for her dear mother.

Opening the gas-run refrigerator, she recalled the days when Mamm was healthy and full of life. All the happy, energetic hours of hoeing the family vegetable garden together or of gathering wildflowers while Mamm's gentle hand brushed against the tallest stems. Together with Hen, they'd sold hundreds of pretty embroidered items and other handiwork at market, and attended numerous canning bees and comforter knottings. Always, always, Mamm had been the fastest and hardest worker. To see her like she was now, day in, day out, struck Rose to the core. *She taught me the importance of hard work*, thought Rose, pushing down the lump in her throat. *Mamm taught me to cook and bake, and how to sew my faceless rag dolls, too.*

But those happy years had been stolen away by an upturned carriage on Bridle Path Lane, and no one knew just what had taken place. Not even the smallest clue had been left as to the cause of the dreadful accident that had left Mamm confined to a wheelchair.

Rose located the medicine bottle in the corner cabinet. *Is this the wrong thing to do?* she fretted. Mamm was so desperate. Maybe, just maybe the pill would take the edge off her pain without causing the horrendous stomach upheaval she'd experienced with other pain relievers.

She poured a small glass of fresh cow's milk, direct from the bishop's milk house that morning. Then she returned to her mother with the medicine and a cookie. "Here you are," she said, holding the glass for Mamm. "I hope you'll be all right." *This time.*

"Go an' get your father," Mamm said in a husky whisper, the pill in her hand. "I want him near . . . in case I get queasy."

She's expecting the worst, thought Rose, the muscles in her neck tightening. "All right, Mamm . . . I'll go to fetch him now."

Rose rushed to get her shawl from its spot on the wooden peg near the back porch and stepped out the door. She did not find her father in his woodworking shop, where he typically was. Thinking he might be out doing some late-season plowing with the bishop or one of her older brothers, she ran around to the back of the barn, scanning the fields in all directions.

Not willing to give up—wanting to give her mother the comfort of Dat, as she'd requested—Rose headed across the meadow to the bishop's farm. "Surely Dat's around somewhere."

As she hurried past the neighboring barnyard, she scanned the area, not seeing her father. She rounded the bend and peeked into the stable, wishing she had time to go and curry Pepper, Nick's favorite horse.

Another time, she thought, deciding to see if Dat and his good friend Bishop Aaron might be inside having a quick cup of coffee. Sure enough, they were there, enjoying Barbara's famous sticky buns at the table. Evidently the bishop had helped her grandfather with the woodcutting, so the men were relaxing a bit. Dat was saying as much and thanking his friend.

"Sorry to interrupt," Rose said, going into the kitchen and catching her breath. "Mamm's in an awful bad way, Dat. She wants you to come be with her." Rose kept her voice low. "She's trying the new pain medication . . . thought you should know."

"Ach, no!" Dat fairly leaped off the bench. His forehead twisted with worry as he reached for his old work coat and flung it on, motioning for Rose to follow him outside.

"Let us know if we can help," Barbara called after them, and Rose waved her thanks.

"Rosie, you remember how terrible sick she gets, don't ya?" Dat shot at her over his shoulder as they dashed across the field toward the house. "What on earth were you thinkin'?"

She explained she'd tried to discourage Mamm, but to no avail. "She was just so frantic—on edge. And it's something she's never tried, ya know. Oh, I do hope she'll be all right," Rose worried aloud.

"Well, hopin' isn't *gut* enough. A moment's relief just ain't worth a possible reaction. And with her so weak right now, there's too much risk."

Dat was clearly irritated—so much so that Rose wondered if something else was bothering him as he huffed and puffed his way back to the house. *Ach, but what?*

CHAPTER 11

Within the hour, Mamm was experiencing horrible nausea. Sympathetically, Dat carried her into the bathroom, dread masking his bearded face as he closed the door.

Successive retching sounds tore at Rose's heart, and she felt responsible for Mamm's physical torment. If only she'd refused her mother! She was concerned, too, how exhausted Mamm—and Dat, too—would be by morning. In the past, her father had sat up all night, making sure Mamm was all right. *He'll do the same again.*

Meanwhile, Beth Browning moped pitifully about, pacing the length of the front room. She looked to be worrying herself sick. Rose ushered the girl outside to the back porch and pushed her short hair back from her face while Beth knelt over a large bowl, shaking and vomiting like she had a bad case of the flu. It was astonishing to witness Beth's strange kinship to Mamm.

In the midst of the wave of illness in the house, Barbara Petersheim stood at the back door with a hot dish of Busy Day casserole, nearly enough to feed the whole church district. Or so Rose thought as she eyed the size of it and let her in.

Checking to see if Beth would be all right alone, Rose said she wouldn't be long and left her on the porch to accompany Barbara into the kitchen. "Mamm's terribly ill," Rose said quietly, glancing back at Beth and explaining that her mother was having another alarming response to a pain reliever. "Oddly enough, Beth seems to be imitating Mamm's illness."

"Oh dear. Could it be some kind of sympathy sickness?"

Rose had heard of this sort of thing but never known anyone to experience it. "Hard to say, really." She gave a small smile and changed the subject. "Awful nice of you to bring food," she said, glancing toward the bathroom door. "Though, more than likely, two of us won't be eatin' supper."

"Oh, just whoever's hungry, then."

Quickly, Rose remembered her manners. "But it's so *gut* of you to help out, Barbara. Truly 'tis." She showed her where to set down the casserole dish on the cookstove, saying she would stoke the fire beneath to keep the meal warm for a bit.

"I'm awful sorry your mother's struggling like this on top of her ongoing pain," Barbara said.

"Dat's with her now." Rose ushered her toward the front room, hoping to move out of earshot for Barbara's sake. "I just feel so bad 'bout giving her the new medication. I really do."

"She must've been desperate, jah?"

Rose bowed her head. "Still, I'm awful sorry. . . ."

"I know, honey-girl." Barbara's sweet smile touched Rose deeply. "You meant well."

Rose's lip trembled and Barbara gently reached for her and let her cry in her ample arms. "I never should've given it to her, after the other times. Dat said as much."

"Now, now . . . ya can't blame yourself, Rosie. It's all right to cry. Soothes the soul, when need be."

After a moment, Rose removed a handkerchief from her dress sleeve and dried her tears. "Poor Mamm . . . and now Beth, too."

"I daresay Beth'll be fine. It's your mother I'm worried about." Barbara's eyes were moist now, too. "A body can't live day in and day out with such constant pain."

Rose had sometimes thought the same thing. No question about it, Mamm was deteriorating, unable to bounce back from something like the respiratory flu as quickly as she once did. "Dat allows Mamm to do things her way, 'least when it comes to gritting her teeth and enduring pain," Rose explained, knowing the bishop and Barbara were well aware of her mother's long-standing wish not to make any further efforts to see a specialist.

Suddenly, Rose heard weeping coming from the bathroom, and she covered her face with her hands. "Oh, Barbara, what'll we do?" she whispered. "Poor, dear Mamm!"

"Let's pray."

Barbara led Rose to the small sofa and knelt there with her, both of them offering silent prayers for Mamm while the sound of pain-wracked sobbing filled the house.

~

Solomon cradled Emma in his arms and gently placed her frail body on their bed. He covered her with a red and violet afghan. All the while he beseeched God to help his wife make it through this, vowing that he would find a way to convince her to see a specialist, lest she weaken further and die.

He wondered if he should have Rose Ann run to the phone shanty and call for Old Eli, the Amish folk doctor in Quarryville. Years ago, Sol had taken Emma there in the family carriage. Eli had insisted Sol not pay for the visit, citing the many instances where Sol had been quick to extend his generosity to others. But as it turned out, Eli's hot and cold applications gave Emma only temporary relief, and by the time they had arrived home, the shooting pain in his wife's back had returned with a vengeance.

Now, sitting on the bed, he wondered what to do next. There

was no health insurance to cover Emma's medical costs, though he knew the church's benevolence fund would assist if necessary. Emma had always been adamant about accepting her lot in life, as she believed this to be. Yet Sol could no longer hold his tongue on the matter. *Oh, Lord, grant me your wisdom. . . .*

"Thy will be done . . . in heaven and on earth," Emma whispered, opening her golden-brown eyes.

Sol pushed several stray hairs away from her damp forehead. "Amen and amen." He leaned down to press his cheek next to hers, checking for a fever. She was surprisingly cool, even clammy. He didn't have the heart to ask if she was without pain, though she did seem to be calmer than earlier today. "I'll stay here with you, even into the night if necessary."

"Sol, you need your rest."

He kissed her forehead, then lightly placed his hand over her eyes, hoping Emma might relax. "Not as much as you do, dear."

A slight knock came at the door, and Sol rose slowly. When he opened the door a crack, he saw Beth's big, worried eyes peering in. "Jah?" he whispered.

Beth stood there silently, her forehead wrinkled in a deep frown.

"You mustn't worry over Emma," he said, seeing the girl's distress. "I'll take care of her."

Slowly, Beth nodded and closed her eyes for a moment. Then she leaned her head on the doorjamb and sighed, her shoulders rising and falling with her breath.

"Is Rose in the kitchen? Maybe you can help set the table for dinner."

Beth lifted her head and tilted it inquisitively, like a little bird. She looked into the room, past him, to Emma. "Oh . . . dear lady," she said softly. "Poor, dear lady."

Solomon felt so awkward, never before having encountered a young woman like Beth—slow in her mind and unpredictable, too. Abe Esh, the deacon's twelve-year-old grandson, was like her in many ways, but he was a boy, after all. It was far easier for Sol to relate to him. Standing there with Beth so near, he wished Rose might call for her.

Instead, it was Emma who called Beth's name just then. How strange that she must've sensed her there, standing all forlorn in the doorway. And, with Emma's lips shaping Beth's name, the young woman tiptoed to the bedside, knelt quietly, and put her head down on the brightly colored afghan.

For pity's sake! Solomon inched to the foot of the bed as Beth began to say a childlike prayer, pleading with the heavenly Father to "look down with compassion and mercy on Rosie's mommy."

Such an unexpected yet beautiful thing to behold. Solomon found himself wiping away silent tears.

～

Hen felt bad for not sharing with her sister about Brandon's ultimatum, but she desired to keep the dreadful news between just her and Dad until she knew what to do. Or at least until she found the right moment to talk with Rose. As it was, she half feared Rose might plead with her to return straightaway to the house in town. Yet how could she, with her husband so opposed to the Plain values and traditions that were once again a part of her?

Hen picked up the newspaper she'd purchased yesterday evening at a gas station on the way home from seeing Brandon. She found herself quickly absorbed in reading about the after-Thanksgiving sales, recalling the few years she'd crawled out of bed before dawn to go and stand in nearly endless lines at various stores. "No more," she muttered to herself, spotting the types of secular toys her daughter had always pleaded for and usually received "from Santa," thanks to Brandon and his parents.

Presently, Mattie Sue wandered downstairs and into the small living room, looking rather glum. Earlier she'd asked Hen to wrap her head with braids, unlike most young Amish girls. Yet, seeing how determined Mattie Sue was, Hen had wound her daughter's hair the way she'd asked. Mattie came over and plopped down on the sofa, sniffling. Then, leaning her head against Hen's arm, she asked in a sad tone, "When can I see Daddy again?"

Hen had thought of taking her tomorrow, on a quiet Saturday morning, to see how Brandon might actually respond to Hen's staying and doing needlework while Mattie Sue visited. She recalled how adamant he'd been about wanting Mattie dropped off, and with a sigh, she realized she had no idea if he would even be home tomorrow. What if she found only Terry there again? Hen certainly wasn't looking forward to a similar awkward encounter.

"I miss my puppy dog, too." Mattie Sue wiped her eyes. "Don't you?"

"Yes, and I know you miss Daddy even more than Wiggles." Hen leaned down and kissed the top of her head. "Maybe next week I'll take you."

"But I don't want to wait."

"Well, it might not suit Daddy right now if we just popped in."

"Why not, Mommy?" Mattie asked, beginning to carry on like she had when they'd lived with Brandon not so many weeks ago.

At that moment, Hen heard a car creeping into the driveway, and when she got up to look, she noticed a familiar blue Dodge Caravan. *Well, what do you know,* she thought. "Mattie Sue . . . go look outside. Someone you know is coming to visit."

Mattie Sue ran to the back door window. "It's Diane Perlis . . . and Karen!"

"*Mrs. Perlis,* remember, honey."

Mattie Sue was much too surprised by the visit to correct herself. And before Hen could say otherwise, she darted out the back door without a coat and ran across the yard to her little friend. Mattie Sue hugged Karen as if they hadn't seen each other in years. A lump came into Hen's throat as she stood in the open door witnessing the affectionate greeting, suddenly realizing she was depriving her daughter of not only her father but of her dearest friend.

"Hen . . . hi!" called Diane, looking at her now with eyebrows raised at Hen's full Amish attire. She was a slip of a woman with a thick fringe of bangs and stick-straight brown hair that hung past her shoulders.

"Good to see you, Diane." Hen wandered down the steps, shivering in the cool air.

Sporting pale pink sweats and a pink and white jersey, Diane gave her a quick, casual hug. "I've been calling and calling your house for weeks. Then, finally, Brandon picked up the phone this afternoon." Diane looked over her shoulder at the girls and lowered her voice. "He said you're hiding out in Amishville."

Sounds like him. Hen grimaced.

"He's joking, right?" Diane's gaze swept Hen from the top of her Kapp to her black leather shoes. She went on to say how concerned she'd been not hearing from Hen. "Last I knew, you were all fired up about taking a job at an Amish fabric shop, but I never dreamed in a hundred years you'd—"

"Diane, *please*," Hen whispered. "The girls . . ."

Frowning, Diane moved closer. "Hen, have you left Brandon?"

Hen felt dejected. "You're jumping to conclusions." She wondered what Brandon had told her. "Come inside, out of the cold," she called to the girls.

"Do we have to, Mommy?" complained Mattie Sue, putting her hand on her hip.

"You're not dressed warmly enough. Please come inside."

Karen, who was Mattie's age, tugged on Mattie's arm and led her into the house. Once Karen removed her own jacket and left it on the floor, the girls ran upstairs, jabbering all the while.

"Karen really misses playing with Mattie," said Diane, settling onto the settee and stretching out her long, thin legs.

Hen didn't know what to say. Sure, Mattie had missed seeing

Karen, but English friends were no longer in Hen's plan for her daughter—not since coming home to Salem Road.

"And you have to know I've missed seeing *you*," Diane said, turning to look at Hen, who was pushing pieces of wood into the belly of the black cookstove and then filling the teakettle with water.

"I've missed you, too."

Diane stared at her. "So what're you doing living out here in the boonies?"

"Amishville, you mean?" Her ire was rising. "This is my home, Diane . . . my life."

"But you married Brandon."

"Yes, I did." Hen had no obligation to bare her heart to Diane Perlis.

"Why go backward, Hen? I don't get it."

Hen returned and sat down in a wing-back chair across from Diane. "My husband and I are working this out."

"Right." Diane curled her lips into a peculiar smile. "I see that."

Looking away, Hen wished Diane would stop pumping her with pointed questions. *Questions with no answers.*

After a time, the teakettle whistled sharply. Hen was relieved and rose to pour hot water into a china cup. "I assume you want some tea?" She raised one of the saucers to Diane as she balanced the filled cup.

"Why not? Maybe some Amish tea's just what the doctor ordered."

Hen nodded and poured hot water into a second cup.

"Listen, Hen, we're both adults. I'm going to give it to you straight. There are plenty of women who'd give their eyeteeth for a good-looking, successful guy like Brandon." Diane's eyes widened and she shook her head. "If he was my husband, I wouldn't risk leaving him for a minute."

"Well, I'm not stupid," Hen blurted, wishing she'd kept her mouth shut.

"Then you'd better go home to him."

"You don't understand, Diane."

"You're right . . . I don't." Unfolding her legs, Diane rose and wandered to the table and sat down. She spooned a token bit of sugar into the hot water and chose a tea bag. "I mean, really, you two were just the best together, Hen. Why would you want to give up your life with Brandon for . . . well, any of this?"

Hen considered Diane's remarks as she added a heaping amount of sugar to her own tea. She stirred it slowly, deliberately, without looking up.

∼

Hen had already put Mattie Sue to bed for the night and was thinking of curling up with a good book when Rose let herself in.

Once she was downstairs, Hen immediately saw the anxiety on Rose's face. "What is it, sister?"

"Mamm's awful sick," she said, then asked her to follow her back to the main house.

"Oh, poor thing." Hen pulled on her woolen shawl and hurried along.

They walked outside together as Rose told of the painful stomach upset that had plagued Mamm today after taking a new pain reliever. "She's had similar symptoms in the past with other medications, but never anything so severe."

Fear gripped Hen as she mounted the back steps of their father's house. "Shouldn't I drive her to the emergency room?" she asked.

"No, Mamm's opposed to it."

"I wish she weren't so stubborn." Hen sighed. "Is she resigned to . . ."

"Only to the will of God," Rose replied.

Hen prayed silently, pushing away thoughts of losing their mother. A dart of pain shot through her heart. *Not just yet—not this night!*

Stepping softly into her parents' bedroom, Hen was struck by the sight of her father's bowed head, his hands folded in prayer. "Oh, Mom . . ." She could not speak further and took the chair next to Rose, pulling it up close to the bed, where their dear mother lay still as death.

CHAPTER 12

*O*t took a long time for Rose to get to sleep that night. She worried she might wake up and discover that Mamm had slipped away from them, into Gloryland. Even though such a thing would be wondrous for Mamm, it was quite devastating for Rose to consider.

I'd miss her terribly! Rose thought when she awoke in the middle of the night, realizing she must've fallen asleep after all. She shivered and sat up to reach for the additional folded quilt at the foot of the bed. She did so quietly, not wanting to awaken Beth, who lay next to her, still as the round moon shining a brilliant beacon beneath the half-open window shade.

Rose trembled at the deathly quiet. The house seemed to sigh as she lay there, her eyes closed in hope of falling back to sleep. But her eyes flew open again at the slightest sound coming from the room directly below. Was Dat still up, pleading for mercy from the Almighty?

Concerned about Beth's excessive attention to Mamm's health, Rose made herself lie still. She continued to strain her ears to listen as she tried to picture what might be happening downstairs. Was the Lord answering their prayers and allowing Mamm to recover from the day's terrifying ordeal? Would God give Mamm the strength to live?

She was certain Dat was pacing the floor, praying. . . . Or had he fallen asleep sitting in the chair next to the bed?

If so, what was that sound just now? Surely not Hen . . . or Mammi Sylvia looking in on Mamm. Perhaps she'd imagined it, just as Gilbert Browning had suggested when Rose had first heard in the Browning kitchen the small stirrings made by Beth overhead. But, as she'd later discovered, she had not been imagining anything of the kind.

Glancing now at Beth, who'd asked earlier to sleep with two of her teddy bears, Rose sighed with frustration. She would never get back to sleep until she looked in on Mamm. So she slipped out of bed and reached for her bathrobe, lapped over the footboard. She pulled it on and made her way, quiet as a cat, down the hallway to the stairs.

When she reached her parents' open bedroom door, she peered inside. Dat was stretched out on top of the quilts, lying near Mamm. They were holding hands as they slumbered, and Rose's breath caught at the sight of it. She squinted to see if her mother's chest was rising and falling, and for the longest time she waited, holding her breath and watching fearfully.

Then, at last, a great breath escaped her mother's lips. The sweet murmur reassured Rose, and she leaned her head against the doorframe. *Thank the dear Lord . . . the worst must be past.*

Rose willed her heart to slow its beating as she returned to her own room. The day had given her a fright. Oh, she never wanted to find out what it might be like to lose dear, dear Mamm!

Once upstairs, she tiptoed to her side of the bed, wondering if the bishop and his wife experienced such heartbreak each morning, upon first awakening. That first jolting pain—remembering anew that Christian, the only son of their union, was dead. No longer would he sit at his designated spot at the dinner table, or haul hay with his father. *No longer will he live the Plain life of his calling.*

Few talked about the loss, far as Rose knew. Yet, she assumed the bishop and Barbara and Christian's three sisters and their families must surely dwell on it. *Surely!*

She imagined Barbara weeping in silence in the wee hours, or while riding alone in the family carriage running errands or going to quilting frolics and canning bees. But did she and the bishop ever openly discuss their loss the way Dat and Mamm seemed to talk about everything?

Rose honestly didn't know, and yawning, she rolled over to face the dresser, her back to Beth, who must be missing her father terribly. Just like poor little Mattie Sue . . .

Everybody misses someone in this old world. Staring across the room at her top dresser drawer, Rose thought of Nick. There, she kept the two notes he'd written her when they were youngsters. The third and most recent note—the one he'd left her on the day of his disappearance—had never made it to the small drawer. She'd seen to that. The too-telling note had been reduced to ashes out behind the barn.

But there were times, like this hushed and longing-filled moment, when Rose wished she hadn't been so hasty. She felt so awful torn now, in the predawn hours when things seemed murky and ever so difficult to resolve.

I don't know what to think anymore. Rose sighed.

⁓

Following breakfast the next day, Barbara Petersheim came again to see Mamm, who'd stayed in bed at Dat's urging. Dat had told Rose earlier, before heading out to his woodworking shop, that Mamm was feeling less nauseous and had even slept a few hours—all wonderful-good news.

Rose had taken a small dish of chipped ice in to her mother before breakfast and offered some chamomile tea to help settle her stomach, too. *"Later, Rose,"* Mamm had whispered, which gave Rose further hope.

Presently Rose regarded Barbara, whose thick brown hair must've been washed just today, because it still looked damp. She wore a black dress and apron, the garb of a mother in mourning. And with the dark shawl wrapped around her, she reminded Rose of Nick's fondness for dark shirts—the grays and blacks he always wore.

Morbid, really.

"How's Emma this mornin'?" Barbara asked Rose.

"No worse, thank the Good Lord." She explained that her mother was resting.

"Mind if I wait till she's up, then?" The two women were, after all, close neighbors and had been friends for decades—even before Rose's oldest brother, thirty-one-year-old Joshua, was born.

"Sure, that's fine," Rose said. "Have some tea with me."

A few minutes later, Mattie Sue and Beth came over from the Dawdi Haus, Hen following close behind. The girls each had a stuffed animal toy in their arms. "Mommy's going to the fabric shop," Mattie Sue told Rose, "so can we play over here?" Mattie eyed the bedroom but ten feet away, where her grandmother lay sound asleep.

Hen came in the back door. "All right with you, Rose?"

Rose said she didn't mind. "I'll put them to work helping me bake a cake."

Mattie Sue's eyes brightened. "That'll be fun. Ain't so, Beth?"

But Beth had turned and was focused on the door ajar, where Mamm was beginning to stir, calling for Rose.

Beth needs a distraction, Rose decided, hoping the little surprise she had planned would get her mind off Mamm. "Excuse me just a minute, Beth," she said.

Barbara followed close behind Rose. After their short visit with Mamm, Barbara whispered, "I believe your mother's goin' to pull out of it."

When Rose and Barbara returned to the kitchen, Mattie Sue was eager to say the cat's name and all about where she'd "found" her, calling to Beth to come show off *her* cat, too.

Barbara made over both girls' toys, then set the animals together side by side on her lap. "Did ya hear the news, Rose? Annie Mast gave birth to identical twin girls last night."

"Oh, first we've heard."

Mattie Sue frowned. "What's identical?"

"Well, the babies look almost exactly alike," explained the bishop's wife.

"Like mirrors of each other," Beth said softly.

"Jah, that's right." Barbara's face beamed.

"What're their names?" Rose asked.

"Don't know yet."

Mattie Sue seemed taken by the news. "Can we go an' see the matching babies, Mommy? Can we, pretty please?"

Rose looked at Hen. "Are ya heading that way . . . just maybe?" She motioned discreetly at the girls.

"Why, sure. I just need to pick up some facing. Won't take long at all." Hen's smile gave it away: She, too, wanted to go and see the look-alike Mast babies.

"I'd better stay here with Mamm, though," Rose said.

"No, *I* will," Beth said, and by the tone of her voice, she meant it.

Rose was stumped. What could she say? It wasn't wise for Beth to be the only one looking after Mamm, even for a short time. And Rose certainly didn't want to offend Beth by saying she would run next door to ask Mammi Sylvia to come instead.

Barbara, bless her heart, seemed to sense her quandary and suggested *she* would be glad to stay with Mamm. Beth's lower lip protruded into a sulk, but within a few seconds, she was smiling again as Mattie Sue reached for her hand and led her out to Hen's car, their kitty-cats tucked under their arms.

"We're going to see babies that look just the same!" Mattie Sue sang as they went.

Rose quickly prepared a basket of homemade breads and jams and other food items for the newly expanded family, then slipped through the back porch and closed the door. Outside, she caught up with Mattie Sue and Beth, who were holding hands and jabbering to beat the band while waiting to get into the car.

∾

During the morning drive to the fabric store, then to the Masts', Hen apologized to Rose. "I don't know what I was thinking. I should've hitched up the horse and carriage and taken it instead of the car."

"Not to worry," Rose replied, but Hen seemed preoccupied with it, as if driving the car again so soon after visiting Brandon the other day was a grave error. "Ain't like you're drivin' it all the time," Rose told her.

"It's such a temptation, though. I'd be better off never driving at all."

This worried Rose. Surely her sister didn't mean she was abandoning all hope of reconciling with Brandon! She did not know what to think about this, or what to say, so she merely watched as the trees and fence posts whizzed past them.

"You don't know this, Rose . . . but I've been given a time limit to return home," Hen said softly, doubtless so the girls wouldn't hear in the back. She beckoned for Rose to lean closer so she could whisper. "Brandon's threatening me with divorce."

No! Tears sprang to Rose's eyes and she pursed her lips, not uttering a sound. The thing she had feared most for her sister was coming to pass.

Hen reached for Rose's hand and gave it a squeeze. "I'm sorry, Rosie. I wish I hadn't said anything."

When Rose had composed herself, she turned to glance at Mattie Sue, sitting behind Hen and looking out the window, quietly pointing out different Amish neighbors to Beth. Did poor Mattie Sue have any inkling of what might lie in store?

When they pulled up to the Masts', Rose saw Silas's courting buggy and sleek black horse up ahead. Surprised, she looked down into the hollow and saw him standing near the springhouse with Rebekah Bontrager. Then, lo and behold, if he didn't hand her something white. It looked like an envelope!

"I think they may have kept in touch," Cousin Melvin had stated to Rose at Esther's wedding. Yet Rose had doubted him. As she continued to watch in amazement, Rose noticed again how very comfortable the two of them looked together. Silas was so engrossed in whatever he was saying, he still hadn't noticed Hen's car parked just up the way.

Bowing her head now, Rose struggled to steer her thoughts away from the things Melvin had said on his sister's wedding day.

Hen set the brake and opened the door on the driver's side, and Rose reached for the door handle and stepped out, unable to pull her gaze from the sight of Silas and Rebekah still talking in the private, sheltered area.

Not wanting to let on to Hen how she felt, Rose straightened her long black apron and followed her sister to the back door of the old farmhouse, their skirts rustling. Mattie Sue and Beth trailed behind Rose, still talking excitedly.

Rose wasn't about to peek over her shoulder again, because each look stirred up more unsettled curiosity—curiosity that could lead to jealousy, come to think of it. She wasn't even sure she should bring it up to Silas when she saw him next. Even so, no one could argue the fact that it was highly unfitting for him to come to see Rebekah.

Is there a secret between them? Rose wondered as they entered the back porch.

CHAPTER 13

*H*en hadn't realized Annie Mast's newborn twins would be impossible to tell apart. Except for a single pink strand of yarn tied loosely around one of the baby's wrists, they looked exactly alike. Baby One and Baby Two were the names Annie had assigned to them "for now." Annie and her husband were still deciding whether to give them names that sounded similar—names like Annie and Mandie, or Arie and Mary—or names that were unique.

The wee babes stirred up such a yearning in Hen. Sitting there in Annie's front room, Hen could hardly wait to hold one of them. And once Baby Two was in her arms—the one without the pink wrist yarn—she found herself blinking back tears and looking away, in case Rose, or even Annie, saw her struggling so.

Mattie Sue sat with her on the sofa, leaning her head against Hen's arm. Gently rocking the baby, Hen couldn't keep her eyes off the tiny round face. All the while, the infant slept soundly in her arms, her little pink lips pursed and occasionally making sucking movements.

"How will you tell which twin is which, without the yarn?" asked Beth out of the blue. She had been standing near the woodstove, shifting her weight back and forth, as she often did.

Annie smiled tenderly, her eyes tired. She wore a thick yellow bathrobe. "A mother just knows."

By the nod of her head and the look on her pretty face, that seemed to satisfy Beth.

"The yarn is for my husband's benefit."

They all chuckled at that.

"How long before you give them real names?" Beth asked.

Hen felt sorry for Beth—the question was more like that of a child than a young adult. *Such an innocent young woman.*

Annie responded kindly. "Oh, we'll decide pretty soon, I think. Prob'ly tomorrow."

Hen leaned her head to touch Mattie Sue's. "Honey, you were this little once," she whispered.

"I was?" Mattie Sue's eyes widened.

"Teeny tiny."

"Did I smell this good, too?" Mattie Sue sniffed the baby's fuzzy head.

"You certainly did."

Just then, the back door opened, and in came a beautiful brunette, who quickly removed her woolen shawl and outer bonnet and hung them on a hook near the door. Annie introduced her to everyone. "This is Rebekah Bontrager, who used to live near Salem Road with her family some years ago." She explained that Rebekah was here to help with the newborn twins. Hen vaguely remembered a girl Rose's age with the same name attending the one-room schoolhouse.

Rebekah said hello to all of them, glancing at Rose, who offered a little nod in return. Rebekah slipped an envelope into her pocket, then made a beeline for Baby One, asking Annie if she minded.

Meanwhile, Rose seemed rather transfixed, her eyes on Rebekah, who caressed and cooed to the tiny infant in her arms.

Annie talked in cryptic tones about the home birth and the fact that the midwife, over the years, had helped to deliver "forty sets of twins, as of now." She looked up tenderly at the wee babe in Rebekah's arms from her spot in the willow rocker.

"It's going to be a challenge to keep these two bundled up and warm this winter," Rebekah said.

"Seems the cold's already settled in to stay," Annie added.

Some time later, Rebekah handed Baby One to Rose, then excused herself to her room, just a few feet away.

"Rebekah didn't sleep much last night," Annie explained, folding her hands. She chuckled. "None of us did, really."

Hen couldn't imagine having twins of any age. But with two newborn babes, the next six to eight weeks would be very demanding, mother's helper or not. "Rebekah's young, so let her take care of the babies as much as possible," Hen suggested.

"Well, we certainly don't want to tire you out further," said Rose, handing Baby One back to Annie, who smiled down into the wee face and kissed the baby's forehead.

"Do we have to go already?" Mattie Sue whined to Hen.

"You heard Aunt Rosie—we just dropped by for a short visit."

"But, Mommy . . ." Mattie Sue whimpered.

"Honey, please," Hen whispered. "We'll visit Annie and her babies another time."

Mattie began to sob as if her heart might break. This baffled Hen, but Rose hurried over and consoled her niece, leaning down to kiss her cheek and take her hand before leading her out to the back porch.

"I'm real sorry," Hen told Annie. "She's just not herself here lately." That was all she felt she should say. She couldn't help but wonder if Mattie's sorrowful response to their leaving was a way of acting out because of their separation from Brandon. Did her daughter feel so terribly displaced?

Hen felt a pang of guilt as her heart ached for Mattie Sue. Adjusting the receiving blanket, she placed Baby Two in the wooden cradle with the soft pink bedding. The other matching cradle, lined in white eyelet, was set right next to it, a small white and yellow afghan folded neatly at the bottom.

"You and your husband are doubly blessed, Annie," she said, gazing at the look-alike baby in Annie's arms.

"Denki for stopping by . . . and for the nice goodies, too."

"We'll be seeing you again." Hen suddenly realized Beth must have gone out to catch up with Rose and Mattie Sue. "Good-bye!"

"God be with ya, Hen."

Quite unexpectedly, tears sprang to Hen's eyes, and she made her way toward the wide porch. She felt the warm drops against her cheek as she opened the back door. Standing there on the dormant lawn, she wept for Mattie Sue . . . and for herself. She wept, too, for the babies she would never bear. If Brandon pushed through with his divorce, she would follow the way of the People and remain single the rest of her life, never to love again or to marry . . . or to bear more children.

To think I could lose my only child to a court ruling!

All the way home, Rose thought how peculiar it was of Silas to drop by Masts' and visit Rebekah. What more did they have to talk about, following Cousin Esther's wedding? It was both strange and annoying, but Rose refused to jump to conclusions.

When she opened the kitchen door back at the house, Rose heard Mamm moaning and held her breath, worried her mother was suffering the lingering effects of yesterday's scare.

Barbara peeked out of the first-floor bedroom. "Rosie, *kumme schnell*—come quick!"

"What is it?" Rose's heart was in her throat. "Has Mamm taken another bad turn?"

Barbara waited till Rose was near, then lowered her voice. "I fear Emma's sinking into despair. She says the bones in her spine feel like they're grinding against each other. Her back is worse than ever," Barbara explained.

"Does Dat know?"

"He's been checking on her every hour." Barbara wiped her own eyes. "Such a *gut* man . . . your father."

" 'Tis true," Rose agreed. "Ach, I never should've gone to see the twins."

"No . . . no, I fear you're shackled by your mother's infirmities, Rose Ann." Barbara's eyes were soft with sympathy. "Your grandmother Sylvia was here and is returning in a few minutes, she said."

"Oh?"

"Jah. She's bringing over cold packs from her icebox."

Rose heard Mammi Sylvia coming in the back door just then and she touched Barbara's arm gently, thanking her. "You needn't stay any longer. It was so nice of you to help out."

"How are Annie's babies?"

"Adorable," Rose said. "And Annie looked awful tired, as you'd expect. But, oh, such perty babies she has! You'll have to go over and see them soon."

"I surely will." Barbara leaned out from the doorway, as if looking to see where Rose's grandmother was keeping herself. "Would ya have a minute to walk back to the house with me?"

"Why, sure. Just let me look in on my mother first." Rose sensed Barbara had something important to share. Swiftly, she turned and went to Mamm's bedside. Her mother's eyes opened partway, and Rose whispered, "I'm awful sorry I ever gave you that pill."

"Rosie . . . no, no . . . ain't your fault. I was in rough shape even before that, dear."

"I pray you'll recover soon."

Mamm nodded slightly, then seemed to drift back to sleep.

"Rest now," Rose said as Mammi Sylvia entered, looking tired herself and carrying the cold packs. Rose told her she was going to walk with Barbara next door. "But I'll return right quick."

"Ach, you take your time," Mammi Sylvia said.

She feels sorry for me. Such pity was simply not warranted and Rose felt embarrassed.

She headed outside with the bishop's wife, aware of the bright sky. A brittle crispness hung in the air, like a prelude to the first snow of the season. Thoughts of Silas and Rebekah threatened to intrude, but she pushed them out of her mind.

"Won't be long till Christmas," Rose said. Then, catching herself, she said she was sorry, this being the first without Christian. "I just wasn't thinkin'."

"Oh, but you were . . . about celebrating the Lord's birthday." Barbara looked at her, smiling pleasantly. "Don't ever think you can't enjoy Christmas because of what happened to our son."

Doesn't she think of Nick as theirs, too? Rose felt so heavyhearted for the bishop and his wife. "It'll be very difficult, I'm sure."

"Jah, 'specially for Verna, who was always so fond of her brother," replied Barbara.

Rose waited for a mention of Nick, but no such remark came just then. She wondered if her father had heard anything more about the brethren's determination to question Nick. Or to locate him.

Barbara picked up her pace, and they walked through the pastureland between Rose's father's land and the bishop's. This stretch had always been a fun place to explore, especially when Rose and Nick were children. She and Hen had romped here, too, dodging cow pies and the brambles near the wooded area, north of the grazing land.

"After Christian died, I couldn't bring myself to go through his clothing and personal things. Same with Nick."

"What did Nick leave behind?"

"Mainly his Amish clothes, I 'spect, since they're still hanging on their pegs. But I really don't know." Barbara placed her hand on her bosom. "You see, I closed off both their rooms . . . just left things be." She stopped walking and reached for Rose's hand. "I know how fond you were of Nick and thought, just maybe, you should be the one to take a look at what's left in there."

Surprised at this, Rose suddenly felt unsure. Just how much did Barbara know of Nick and Rose's devoted companionship? Rose felt the need to guard the years with Nick, out of loyalty to her friend. "It was kind of you to think of me," she replied, her heart in her throat. "I'm willing to help however I can."

"Well, come along, then. I'll show you his room."

Rose followed obediently, quite curious.

CHAPTER 14

*S*olomon knew from past experience that once an Amish-person owned a car—a temptation for many youth during *Rumschpringe*—it was mighty hard to abandon the lure of speed and return to horse and buggy.

As he split wood that midmorning, he couldn't help thinking Hen's car parked on his property might soon become a bur in his flesh. Especially when she still occasionally drove it, like earlier today, taking along Rose Ann and Mattie Sue and Beth, too. The bishop was likely to ask her to sell the car and give the money to the church's charity fund here before too long. That is, if she continued to dig in her heels and stayed put. Her stubbornness on this latter point weighed heavily on all of their minds . . . especially Solomon's. The extra time Brandon had given Hen to get herself back to him would pass all too quickly, he knew.

The whole thing was complicated. His wayward daughter had come home and he'd scarcely had a chance to kill the fatted calf. Secretly Sol wanted to revel in the fact that his prodigal had returned.

If only she hadn't succumbed to worldly drift as a youth. He picked up his ax to split more wood. And as he worked, he considered his visit to Brandon yesterday. *My son-in-law, of all people.* It was still hard, even after seeing him several times since Hen's coming home, to feel much of anything but pity for Hen's husband. The man was rattled and on edge. His lips poured forth evidence of his impatience and irritation. Solomon almost wished he hadn't made the trip to Quarryville.

Such futility . . .

He wouldn't think of voicing these things, though. Truth was, Brandon needed someone to come alongside him, put a big, burly arm around his suited shoulders, and guide him along on his life journey.

But who?

It was hard to watch such a bright young man choose to go his own way . . . making the gathering of riches an imperative. Not caring whom he stepped on or hollered at as he worked so hard to get where he was bent on going.

Pausing to pull out his old pocket watch, Solomon saw that it was time to check on Emma again. With her growing weakness and her pain taking its terrible toll, he wondered if she would even make it to Christmas.

Shivering with dread, he quickened his pace toward the house. *Will I greet the New Year as a widower?*

$\sim$

Rose and Barbara stood just on the threshold of Nick's bedroom. *Is she nervous about what might be found?* Rose wondered, feeling awkward about stepping foot into her dear friend's private space.

They looked around. The bed was still made and the dresser cleared of everything but a man's hairbrush and a homespun doily Barbara had no doubt crocheted.

"I'll go and get some boxes for any giveaways," Barbara said, leaving the room just that quick.

Rose went to stand at the window. She looked west toward her father's house and realized Nick had had a clear view of her own distant windows from this vantage point. She was glad she'd never told anyone how close they'd been through the years. Not even Hen knew about the sunny afternoon they'd spent in the ravine by the creek. Try as she might, she could not erase Nick's startling words from her mind: *"I know you better than anyone. . . . I loved ya first. . . ."*

Turning, she stared at the wooden pegs mounted to the wall, where Nick's dark work shirts still hung, and his black Sunday trousers, vest, and frock coat. "You had it so *gut* here, growin' up under the bishop's roof," she whispered. "Did ya ever stop to think that, Nick?"

And now you might be homeless, she thought sadly.

Sighing, she remembered the first week Nick had lived here. Mammi Sylvia had declared right off that he was but *"a scamp of a lad."* Christian had muttered a derogatory remark about his smelling like the devil, even saying he wondered why his father had picked such a runt to help with farm chores. Rose had caught Christian mocking Nick to his sister Verna in the barnyard as Rose came through the meadow on her way to the milk house to get some fresh cream. But she'd always heard from Dat and Mamm that the bishop had chosen Nick precisely *because* he was the most needy of all the available foster children.

Even then, Christian thought little of Nick. . . .

Staring at the large braided rug near the bed, she heard Barbara's footsteps and turned to face the door.

"Here we are." Barbara was carrying two large boxes. "This should do it."

They began with the drawers filled with his pajamas. Barbara emptied the drawer of underwear and socks. At one point, Barbara sniffled loudly, tears welling up. Rose knew it was best not to comment about it, lest the bishop's wife struggle even more.

How would Nick feel if he knew I was doing this?

After only a few minutes, they were nearly finished. Rose turned to look at Nick's Sunday clothes on the wooden pegs. She was about to ask if Barbara had someone in mind for those when Levi, the Petersheims' oldest son-in-law, called up the stairs to Barbara. He was saying something about a neighboring bishop having just stopped by.

Promptly, Barbara excused herself. "I'll be right back, dear," she said.

Barbara's footsteps were hurried on the stairs, and there was the sound of several more male voices in the kitchen below. Rose began to work on the bed, removing the quilts, blanket, and sheets from the mattress. Taking off the cotton mattress pad, she raised the box spring and spotted something drop to the floor beneath.

Rose got down on her hands and knees and stretched to reach for what looked to be a snapshot. She held it up to the light—it was indeed a photograph, torn down the middle, the ragged line falling between a young man and woman. Discoloration indicated the rip had been taped back up some time ago.

Rose suddenly felt shy, as if trespassing on Nick's personal belongings. Yet she peered into the faces of a dark-headed teenage boy holding hands with a blond girl. Glory be, the boy's resemblance to Nick at age sixteen or seventeen was downright uncanny. She held the picture closer to make sure it wasn't him.

Then, turning the picture over, she searched the back for an indication of who this couple might be—but found nothing.

Flipping back to the front, she studied the attractive girl, whose eyes were very much like Nick's. *Could it be his mother . . . and father, before they married?*

The room seemed to close in on her in that moment. She was so taken by the old picture that her hand trembled as she crept into the hallway and listened for Barbara and Levi and the others, but she heard only silence and assumed they'd gone outdoors.

Why would Nick leave this behind?

Surely, Rose assumed, he'd forgotten to take it along. *In his haste.*

⁓

The minute Rose returned from Petersheims', Hen planned to take Mattie Sue to see Brandon, despite her protestations yesterday. She should've done it before now, but knowing how busy her husband was, she'd put it off. Plus, she had hoped to have him visit them here, just as she'd suggested the day of her packing and leaving. But now she felt bad about keeping Mattie from her daddy. For as long as she could remember, from their first date until now, Hen had felt guilty for some reason when it came to Brandon. Only the reasons had changed.

Before Hen left, though, she wanted to finish cleaning the little Dawdi Haus, as well as prepare food for the Lord's Day tomorrow. Since her grandmother and mother adhered to the Old Ways of not cooking on Sunday, Hen did the same while living here. *No boisterous play, sewing, cooking, or cleaning . . .*

She finished redding up Mattie Sue's bedroom, then dusted her own room. While rearranging several things on the dresser, her eyes caught the pretty ring holder. How glad she was to have it here, where it could be useful, instead of stuck in a drawer at the house. Since returning to Amish country, she'd stopped wearing her birthstone ring, a brilliant red garnet. Brandon had surprised her with the gift the second year of their marriage, on her twenty-third birthday. Touching the red ring and ring holder now, Hen sighed, then turned to gather up the colorful handmade rag rugs, taking them downstairs to beat on the white porch banister outside.

She noticed several gray buggies parked diagonally at the bishop's and wondered if his sons-in-law had dropped by. But then she saw a circle of men all in black—unquestionably the ministerial brethren.

What's happening?

She hoped no one had been hurt, or worse still. Christian's death had shaken her in many ways, but she hadn't grasped until recently just how angry she was at Nick Franco—such a troublemaker. To think he'd caused his own brother's death!

Hen returned indoors. It was wrong to harbor such resentment, yet she had never understood why she'd had such difficulty with Nick. Was it because he reminded her of her own rebellion, late in her teen years? Or was it that she viewed Rose Ann as the flip side of herself—pure and innocent—and had always worried Nick's friendship with her sister might somehow taint Rose?

Inside, Hen ran the wet mop over the wooden plank floor both up and downstairs, wanting to do a quick yet thorough job. The small space she and Mattie Sue lived in now was but half the size of Brandon's and her home. *Will I ever live there again?* The thought crept up on her.

But it wasn't the loss of that home she feared most. Hen worried that their love had faded, more rapidly than she'd thought possible. Brandon had not pursued her the way she'd expected, although at least in part because of his strong aversion to the Plain community.

And here I've grown reattached to it. . . .

She rinsed out the mop and hung it up to dry, then went to the main house to see if Rose had returned yet from Barbara's, where Mammi Sylvia had indicated she'd gone for a short visit. The men in their black wide-brimmed hats, trousers, and coats lingered near the barn, and now it was obvious Bishop Aaron was the focus of their attention.

As Hen stepped into her mother's kitchen, Dad closed the door to his and Mom's bedroom behind him, his face pasty white. "Dad . . . is she—?"

"Not well at all." He shuffled into the kitchen and sat forlornly at the head of the table. "Yet she refuses to see Old Eli . . . or any doctor." He covered his face with his big, callused hands. "Even if one of them would agree to come to the house, well, she just won't hear of it. I don't know what to do. It's like she's giving up, and I'm not ready to let her."

Hen moved closer and sat at her mother's own spot at the table, absorbing his concern. They sat without speaking for a time. At last she said, "Dad, you're right—we can't let her waste away. It's not right."

He sighed like a wounded child. "Mamm believes her days are numbered. There's nothing I can say to make her think otherwise."

She's always known her own mind.

The back door opened just then, and Beth and Mattie Sue wandered into the kitchen. Looking sheepish, Mattie Sue asked, "Can we have a cookie . . . or two?"

Hen said they could.

"This is so hard on your mother," Dad said softly, returning to the subject at hand.

"Well, it's hard on *you*, too, Dad." She looked at him tenderly, wishing there was a way to lift the anxiety so evident on his countenance.

Beth neared the table, still wearing her jacket and hat. "When can I go in and see your mother again?" she asked Hen. Her eyes shone with expectation.

Hen looked to Dad for his decision.

"'Tis best to leave her be now," he said.

Beth just stood there. "She needs me," she whispered.

Hen shook her head and encouraged Beth to go back to play with Mattie Sue. She didn't want any more stress on her distraught father. Beth's presence in the house was becoming a complication, although Hen hadn't voiced this to Rose. "Run along now, honey,"

Hen told her. It was strange talking to a young woman as if she were Mattie's age.

Beth instantly looked sad, but she obediently stepped away from the table to join Mattie Sue, who'd removed her coat and hat and was setting up a game of checkers in the corner of the kitchen floor.

Dad turned to glance at them as the girls mumbled together, then back at Hen. "Were we too harsh with her?"

Hen didn't think so. Sometimes it was necessary to be firm with an individual like Beth, who didn't seem to comprehend what was being asked of her. "Not to worry, Dad. She'll be fine." Hen wished she could say the same about Mom, if only to cheer up her father. But she sadly feared it was the farthest thing from the truth.

~

Rose stood at the Petersheims' back door and noticed several men walking with Levi, who waved to his mother-in-law. It appeared as if the ministers had had a meeting with Bishop Aaron over near the stable. But now they were all getting into their carriages, including Levi, who climbed into his market wagon parked farther down the lane.

Eventually Barbara returned to the house and removed her shawl, looking peaked. Rose held out the mended photograph to show it to her. "Look what I found," she said almost reverently.

"Well, for goodness' sake!" Barbara motioned for Rose to sit with her at the table. She peered down her nose, inching the picture farther away as she looked at it. "I daresay I need my reading glasses . . . why, this fella looks exactly like Nick, ain't?"

"I thought so, too."

Barbara's eyes glistened. "We just never knew what we were goin' to uncover next with Nick."

Rose didn't know what to say.

"I wonder if my Aaron was ever aware of this photo." Slowly, almost reluctantly, Barbara squinted at it again, her chin jutting up. "He lived a double life, Nick did."

"Are those his parents, do ya think?"

"Who else could it be?"

Rose agreed. "Jah, not only does the young fella look a lot like Nick . . . the girl's eyes are exactly, well—"

Barbara put the picture facedown on the table. "This must be the long-lost father who left his wife . . . and young Nick."

"Did you ever learn anything more about him?"

"*Nee*—no." Barbara shook her head. "Only what the social worker told us."

Nick himself had told Rose that his father had run off. "Sad, isn't it, that his dad wasn't there to see him grow up?"

"Well, if ya think about it, God gave Nick a wonderful-*gut* father." Barbara straightened the cape portion of her dress and sat taller. "But the lad wasn't interested in bein' the bishop's son, that's for certain."

Rose felt a flutter of sadness. "I'm sorry 'bout the unhappy years . . . when he was livin' here."

"I wouldn't say *all* of them were." Barbara paused a moment. "When Nick was little—when he first came here—he seemed 'specially fond of me. I've never told anyone this, but when I would carry the dirty clothes down to the cellar on washday, if he was around, he'd often tell me to be careful on the stairs, or even try to carry the clothes himself, small as he was. And he called me his "Amish Mamma" . . . 'twas the sweetest thing."

Rose listened, taking this all in.

"And you prob'ly don't remember, but the autumn Nick came, we had a wonderful fourth cutting of hay—and a bumper crop of corn, too." She sighed, a faraway look in her eye. "Seemed like a kind of blessing then, Nick's comin'."

"When did all that change?" Rose ventured.

Barbara shook her head. "He missed his mother just terribly.

I'd find him in a pool of tears some mornings, and he'd just sit and sit at the kitchen table long after Christian and the bishop left for the barn. Sometimes he'd stare out the window, like he was a lost soul."

Rose wasn't surprised. She, too, had known Nick to be moody and sad. Brooding about just what, no one had seemed to know.

"Would ya like to keep the picture, Rose?" offered Barbara.

She hesitated, surprised. "Are ya sure?"

"This picture would hurt Aaron no end. Seems Nick's still causin' him trouble . . . from afar."

Does she know Laura Esh saw Nick in Philly?

"Bishop loved Nick, ya know . . . like a son," Barbara added.

The man of God had always been so kindly toward Nick— just as he was to all of his children and grandchildren. " 'Tis *gut*, jah? A child needs to soak up that sort of love . . . like the love our heavenly Father offers." Rose paused, a catch in her throat. " 'Specially a child nobody wants."

Barbara's eyes were bright with tears. "Ach, you're right, Rose." And with that, she lifted herself off the bench with a groan that sounded as if she might begin to weep. "You're ever so right," she murmured and made her way to the sink.

CHAPTER 15

*H*en paused on the steps with Mattie Sue as they approached Brandon's front door that afternoon. The sound of his sister's singing seeped through the door.

Why is she so happy? Hen wondered.

Wiggles jumped up on the back of a chair and was barking through the window. The adorable cocker spaniel seemed to smile out at them.

"Mommy, look—Wiggles remembers us." Mattie Sue hopped near the window, making faces at the puppy.

"Wiggles remembers *you*, sweetie."

The house key was still linked to Hen's key chain, but she wouldn't think of using it after being away all these weeks. She pressed the doorbell, stepping back so Brandon—or Terry—would see Mattie Sue first when the door opened.

The dog continued barking while Mattie egged him on from where she stood. Then the door flew open, and there stood Brandon. In seconds, Wiggles was yipping at his feet and coming to jump up on Hen.

"Daddy—surprise!" Mattie Sue leaped straight into her father's arms.

Hen leaned down to pet the puppy, glad her husband was occupied with Mattie Sue's affection. They did not make eye contact as he carried their daughter into the house. Hen said not a word as he made over Mattie, who'd insisted on wearing her Amish clothes and both bonnets—her white Kapp tucked beneath the black outer bonnet.

Brandon set her down to untie the loop of Mattie's woolen shawl and removed it. Without speaking, he also took off her black bonnet to reveal the prayer covering and little bob at the nape of Mattie's neck. He set the shawl and the bonnet on the back of the sectional and turned to open his arms to hug Mattie Sue a second time, still ignoring Hen, who'd gone to stand in the living room.

"You've grown at least an inch since I saw you last." Brandon kissed Mattie's cheek and lifted her up once more, spinning around until she began to squeal.

He should not be deprived of seeing her, Hen thought, moved by the tender scene.

Soon Brandon put their daughter down and took her hand, walking with her to Mattie's former bedroom. "It's a nice surprise to have my little girl stop by," he told her, and Mattie Sue chattered right back about having missed him. Almost as quickly, she stated, "There isn't anything left to play with in my old room," as she peered inside.

"Well, you can play with Wiggles whenever you visit . . . and also when you come home to live here again."

Mattie paused, looking worried. "Can Mommy come, too?"

Hen felt her knees go weak and looked for a place to sit, choosing the far end of the sectional. Her neck prickled; she wondered what Brandon might say.

"Don't worry about that, honey," he said. "Things will be fine . . . in the end."

"But I really want to live on the farm with Grandpa and Grandma Kauffman . . . and George and Alfalfa, too!" Mattie Sue recited the names of her grandpa's driving horses, the old whine returning. Hen had hoped their former power struggles had ceased with all the instruction she'd taken care to give her daughter since leaving the modern world behind. *"Obedience training,"* as Brandon had tauntingly dubbed it the one time he'd visited them there.

"You'll be very happy living here again," Brandon said firmly. "You've forgotten what it's like, that's all."

"No, I don't want to, not without Mommy."

"Listen, honey, let's go to your closet and pick out something pretty to wear," Brandon said, more sharply now. "I'll wait for you to change your clothes."

"Ach, but my Amish dress and apron *are* perty!"

"You heard me. Take off those clothes for make-believe—and talk English, please."

"Daddy . . ." Mattie Sue began crying.

"Do what I said—change into one of your normal outfits."

What on earth? Brandon had always been the more lenient parent, but now he had a definite edge to his voice. Astonished, Hen rose to defend her little girl.

Just as she did, Terry came in carrying a tea tray containing cookies and bite-size cakes. "Would you care for something?" her sister-in-law asked almost too politely. "For your sweet tooth?"

"That's very nice, thanks." Hen watched as she set the tray down on the coffee table and left the room.

Hen stood there, aware that Mattie Sue's bedroom door had closed and Brandon was walking this way. She suddenly felt wilted. What would he say now?

His eyes were fiery darts. "Can't you dress her in regular clothes *sometimes?*" he asked.

"She likes to match Mommy, she says."

He looked toward the kitchen and rubbed his chin. He paused, eyes passing between the kitchen and Hen. Then at last he said, "Uh, there's something else. . . ."

What more? Her shoulders tensed immediately.

"Did you put your father up to coming to see me at the office?"

She shook her head. "I don't know what you're talking about."

"He dropped in to invite me to dinner." Brandon gave her a sideways look. "You didn't know?"

"First I've heard it."

He seemed uncommonly disgruntled by this. "I told him to save his breath."

"Is an invitation to have a meal with my family really so troubling?"

He shrugged off her comment and stared at her—no, looked right through her.

"Dad's just being hospitable, wants to get to know his son-in-law, perhaps."

"I disagree. He had an agenda."

He reached for a small lemon cake on the tray and popped it into his mouth without saying more. She didn't know how it could be, but Brandon looked taller. Or had he lost weight? He stood so straight, even defiant in his stance, appearing to be more confident than ever . . . but also less familiar.

For reassurance, she picked up the steaming teapot and poured some tea into her cup—one Diane Perlis had given to her for her collection. Diane's uncalled-for remarks about Brandon yesterday flitted through Hen's mind as she reached for her cup and saucer. With the way he was acting, Hen could hardly think of mustering up any romantic feelings. Brandon's behavior—his carrying on about Mattie Sue's clothing—made Hen anxious to leave. How could she possibly return home to him anytime soon? *If ever.*

Glancing over his shoulder toward the hallway, Brandon shook his head. Mattie Sue was taking a long time to change her clothes. *Too long for his schedule,* thought Hen miserably.

"Your dad pressed me for more time," he finally said.

"Excuse me?"

"I'm giving you two weeks to get your tail feathers home."

"Brandon, please."

So Dad did have an agenda. She wondered what else they'd discussed.

"No, Hen, you listen to me for a change!" He came around the sectional and sat down, leaning forward as if he might pitch right off the cushion. "I'm tired of you calling the shots. Mattie Sue is my daughter as much as yours. Get that through your head." His voice rose with each phrase. It had been years since she'd seen him this irate. The memory of his fury over Bishop Aaron's strong words so long ago came to mind.

She didn't dare tell him to shush, but she worried Mattie would hear. "We aren't going to fight this way, Brandon."

"No, not here—but in court, if you're so stubborn."

"Well, I care about protecting Mattie from the evils of the world."

"Oh, you think you're the better parent . . . is that it?"

"I'm concerned about how she's raised."

"And I'm not?"

Truth was, he'd had plenty of chances to prove what sort of parent he was—a permissive one who didn't give a thought to exposing his daughter to things even another secular parent might find inappropriate.

"Is that it, Hen? You think I'm a lousy father."

It would not be a good idea to respond to his baiting. Hen lowered her eyes as she'd often done as a child.

Huffing loudly, he got up and headed into the kitchen.

I'll just sit here and stay out of the way. After all, she had done his bidding, hadn't she—bringing Mattie Sue to visit? On the other hand, she'd disregarded his request to drop off their daughter unaccompanied. This, she assumed, was the main reason for his anger now and his frustration earlier with Mattie Sue. How could he take it out on their daughter?

Hen had brought along a small sewing basket and reached in to find scissors, a pincushion and needle, and the unfinished pillowcase she was embroidering, to occupy her time. Unlike when she had lived here, Hen felt surprisingly calm as she kept her fingers busy. Soon Mattie Sue inched down the hall, wearing a pair of jeans and a soft purple turtleneck sweater that looked almost too tight. Her pouting face was tear streaked, and she had her pointer finger in her mouth.

"Honey, come sit here." Hen patted the sofa cushion.

"I don't like these clothes." Mattie buried her face in Hen's embrace. "I want to dress like you, Mommy."

"I know, sweetie." She sighed. "You were obedient, honey . . . I'm proud of you for that."

"I love Daddy, that's why . . . just like when we obey God, jah?" Mattie looked up at her with big, innocent eyes.

Hen kissed her cheek. "Bless your heart. What a dear girl you are."

Mattie Sue reached for a cookie on the tray, looking back over her shoulder to see if it was all right with Hen. Hen nodded, then looked toward the kitchen doorway. She could only wonder what Brandon and Terry were doing.

They sat in the living room for a good five minutes while Wiggles played with Mattie Sue and barked teasingly. A few more minutes passed and there was no further sign of Brandon. Mattie had slipped to the floor and was rolling an old, empty spool back and forth to the puppy, seemingly enjoying herself.

"Daddy doesn't like my clothes," Mattie told the dog.

Wiggles wagged his tail.

"He doesn't like anything Amish," Mattie said sadly. She went to retrieve her little black bonnet and put it on Wiggles' head, but he merely shook it off, yipping at her. Then Mattie put the bonnet on the floor and hid the spool inside. Wiggles nuzzled at it with his tiny nose, curled up, and sat down on the bonnet.

As more time passed and Brandon stonewalled, Hen began to feel trapped in the well-furnished living room. The framed floral prints on the walls had been mostly her idea, as had the colorful throw cushions and ottoman. She and Brandon had made the decisions regarding the style and fabric for the large sectional together, however. The same for the window treatments.

Not really so long ago . . .

She wondered if her husband might've gotten caught up in his work where he preferred to sit, in the breakfast nook. How tactless to ignore them. *Terribly rude . . . if not punishing.*

Hen was utterly bewildered at his and Terry's silence. And the longer she sat there, the more resentful she became.

It would be so easy to walk right out the front door.

Not wanting to give way to anger, as in the past, Hen carefully folded the finished pillowcase and put it back in the basket. "Why don't you go and see what Daddy's doing?" she suggested gently.

Mattie Sue nodded and went to the kitchen, Wiggles scampering behind. Meanwhile, Hen drank her unsweetened tea. Even though nearly everything on the tea tray, as well as the tray itself, belonged to her, she felt she was partaking of hospitality from a stranger.

The stranger who used to be me.

Soon she could no longer drink the tea without sugar, so she spooned up a bit from the salmon-pink Carnival glass bowl. She studied the delicate bowl, remembering the day she'd found the old piece at an estate sale not far from Salem Road.

Three years ago . . .

The day had started out with a chilling drizzle and wind, and Hen had bundled little Mattie Sue up very well to drive the back roads near her father's house. She'd seen in the paper that the Hank

Smucker family—Amish she'd known growing up—were clearing out a farmhouse: *Everything goes!* the ad had declared, and she hoped to look for a matching sugar bowl and creamer to replace the cheap set broken in the move to their new house.

While she drove, the clouds pushed back to reveal sunshine, warming the day at last. At the sale, Hen put Mattie Sue in her umbrella stroller, freeing up Hen to browse among the many knick-knacks. She'd noticed several sets of cut-glass salt and pepper shakers, as well as old sugar bowls and creamers, and had experienced a few pangs of homesickness for the farm—and for her family.

Two full years had passed since she'd seen both sets of grand-parents, or her married brothers and their wives and children.

Hen had held the lovely Carnival glass sugar bowl and remembered filling a similar bowl for her mother, hearing Mamm comment with a chuckle on all the sugar they must consume in a single day. *"Dawdi Jeremiah says sweets make the world go round,"* her mother had often remarked, a twinkle in her eye.

Round is right, Hen had thought with a smile.

She liked the etched designs and the color of the set, so she'd purchased it and watched with interest as gracious, plump Mrs. Smucker carefully wrapped the pieces. All during the drive home, while Mattie Sue slept in her car seat, Hen reflected on all the wonderful things she'd already begun to miss.

The early rumblings of my yearnings, Hen thought now as she set down the dainty sugar spoon. She held the cup and saucer to her lips and took a small swallow. Her eyes scanned the room for other treasures she might not want to leave behind should Brandon have his way and divorce her.

But no . . . she didn't really care much about material possessions. Let him have the things they'd cherished as a couple. Even though *she* had been the one desirous of collecting teacups and saucers. Looking again at the beautifully arranged tea tray, Hen changed her mind just that quick and couldn't help wishing she might keep at least some of her nicer things. *Items with family stories behind them* . . .

Brandon was talking to Mattie Sue in the kitchen. It sounded as if they were playing a game. Leaning back on the sectional, Hen closed her eyes and wondered what might've happened if she hadn't attended the Amish household sale that day. *Would I be where I am now? Or did simply having a child trigger my latent longings?*

~

An hour passed, and Hen heard Brandon cajoling Mattie to wear her modern clothes to her Amish grandfather's farm. "That way you'll have something to wear next time you visit me here."

Hen wondered how Mattie Sue might reply.

"But I like my dress and apron."

Hen heard Brandon moan. "No more talk about this. Keep the clothes."

She half expected Mattie to complain as before but was surprised when she said nothing. Hen gathered up her things, waiting for Mattie Sue to reappear in the room.

What nerve of him to pressure their daughter about her clothing! He reminded her of a spoiled child. No wonder Mattie behaved the way she sometimes did. Hen could not imagine being in Mattie's place, being treated so poorly as a youngster. No, if anything, her own childhood had been remarkably happy.

I want that for Mattie Sue, too. But am I willing to risk losing her altogether?

Later, Hen secured Mattie Sue in her booster seat and they drove the old byways leading to Salem Road. The thought of acquiring a family lawyer of her own crossed her mind, if only fleetingly. Such a move would terribly offend her father. But what sort of mother did not protect her child from the reprimands and demands of the likes of Brandon Orringer? Had he changed so radically during their separation, or had he always been this heartless and scheming?

CHAPTER 16

*L*ate Saturday afternoon Rose found her father in his woodworking shop sawing a board in two. She waited till he noticed her standing there quietly before asking permission to take Beth for a ride in the pony cart, "as a surprise."

He flicked sawdust from his beard. "Would she enjoy that, ya think?"

"Oh, I know she would." Rose reminded him of Beth's fondness for the new foals, and the horses, as well. "She can hardly wait to help me water them every morning."

"Well, take things nice and slow, ya hear?" He turned back to his work, then looked over at her. "You'll be in charge of the reins, jah?"

Rose guessed what Dat meant and nodded.

"All right, then," he agreed.

She noticed how tired he looked. Worry could wear on a person, she knew, thinking how concerned they all were for Mamm. *Especially Dat.*

Later, when she went looking for Beth, she found her in Mamm's room, sitting with the chair pulled up next to the side of the bed, reading a prayer she'd written from her blue notebook.

"Denki ever so much," Mamm said, reaching for Beth's hand. "Your sweet prayers most surely touch the heart of God."

Rose stood at the door, observing the endearing sight. When Beth looked up, Rose beckoned for her to come to the doorway. Gently letting go of Mamm's hand, and taking time to tuck it back under the quilts, Beth came over to Rose. "I have a little surprise for you," Rose whispered.

Beth glanced back at Mamm, who'd already closed her eyes. "Your grandma says she thinks your mother's pain is less when she's lying down," said Beth.

Mammi Sylvia wasn't the only one who thought this; Rose did, too. "Hen will look in on Mamm now . . . so you and I can go out to the horse stable. All right?"

"What for, Rosie?"

"It's a secret. Get your coat and scarf and follow me."

With a limited amount of daylight hours, there was precious little time for Beth's first-ever pony cart ride. Even so, Rose led her to the horse stable. Beth's face shone with glee as she steadied the large pony while Rose hitched it up to the cart. "Oh, Rosie, I'm so excited!"

"Me too. It's something I've been thinking 'bout for a while . . . and now that you're staying with us for a few days, it's the perfect time."

When the hitch was secure, Rose threw a woolen blanket inside the wooden cart her father had made years ago. "We'll ride around the barnyard," Rose said, helping Beth inside, then raised her skirt and climbed in beside her. "It's a bit tight in here . . . but we'll manage."

Beth gripped the side and her melodious laughter lifted to the air. "This is wonderful-*gut*." She mimicked Mattie Sue's choice of words, giggling with each step of the pony.

"Are you all right?" asked Rose. "Do ya want to go a little faster?"

Nodding, Beth asked, "Can he trot?"

"He sure can."

"Then let's go!" Beth shouted.

Rose hadn't felt this happy in some weeks. She clicked her tongue and off they flew, laughing all the way.

Around the barnyard they went, though one time was not enough for Beth, who kept asking for "once more."

As they went, Rose recited the only rhyming prayer she'd ever memorized. "A Horse's Prayer" had been penned by an unknown author, and the bishop's wife had comically recited it through the years. Nick, too, had sometimes said it in an entertaining singsongy fashion that Rose had never forgotten: "Uphill wear me, downhill spare me. On the level let me trot. In the stable forget me not."

Beth giggled at the poem and asked Rose to repeat it, which she did.

Around they went, and they might have made three complete circles past the barn and surrounding buildings, but as they came back toward the driveway the second time, Rose noticed a car pull up slowly to the house. *Who's this?* She'd seen Hen's car behind the grove of trees, so this was someone else stopping by.

A woman got out and Rose recognized Donna Becker.

"Is she coming to visit me?" Beth wondered aloud.

Rose had an odd feeling seeing Donna there, but dismissed it as she and Beth climbed out of the pony cart. Quickly, they walked over to greet Donna. "How've ya been, neighbor?" asked Rose.

"Oh, I'm just fine," Donna said, glancing at Beth. "But I'm afraid I have bad news."

Beth stiffened where she stood near Rose. "Is my grandpa getting worse?"

"Yes, Beth. Your father called and said he is struggling . . . he's very low."

"I dreamed he died last week," Beth said sadly. "I don't like those kinds of dreams . . . especially when they come true. Sometimes they do."

Rose startled at this; she had read about people who had such premonitions in dreams, much like Joseph in the Bible. Was Beth one of those?

Rose slipped her arm around Beth's shoulders, stepping near. "We'll take care of Beth as long as need be."

Donna smiled in the fading light. "That was the main reason Gilbert called—to ask if you'd mind keeping her at least another week."

Rose looked toward Dat's woodshop. "I'm sure it's all right, but I'll let my father know."

"My grandpa's going to die." Beth's voice was flat and low. "I just know it."

"Your father asked for your prayers," Donna said. "He said the time may be near. . . ."

Beth did not cry as Rose expected. Instead, Beth raised her face to the sky and whispered something Rose couldn't make out.

"Well, I should get back to my husband." Donna patted Beth's arm and held Rose's gaze for a moment. "I'll be in touch again when there's further word."

"Denki," Rose said, her arm still around Beth. Then, after Donna had backed out, Rose asked, "Are you all right?"

"This has happened before," Beth said. "Why do I have dreams about people dying?"

"Your grandfather might get better," Rose said, feeling sorry for her. Beth sounded so heartsick. "When did you last see your grandpa?"

"Daddy and I haven't seen him and Grandma for a long time. They used to visit us in Arthur—ya know, in Illinois, where we moved from. But that was when Mommy was still alive."

Rose recalled Beth saying she and her father would have to live with her grandmother if her grandpa passed away. But seeing how stressed Beth was, Rose did not think it wise to mention that.

Suddenly, she realized how much she would miss seeing Beth if the Brownings moved. *Too many losses lately.* Rose thought sadly of both Christian and Nick as she helped Beth back to the pony cart, where they realized they were in no mood for more riding. So Rose unhitched the energetic young horse with a little help from Beth. When they'd finished, she and Beth walked arm in arm back to the stable, leading the pony.

∼

On the morning ride to Preaching service the next day, Beth was filled with questions about the Amish church, asking Rose one thing after another. Wearing the blue for-good dress Hen had sewn for her, Beth looked authentically Plain, sitting with Mattie Sue in the small space at the back of the buggy. She and Mattie Sue bobbed their heads up and down, mimicking the horse, which struck Rose as humorous.

Later, after the three-and-a-half-hour service, Rose commented to Hen how surprised she was at Beth's quiet demeanor during the hymns, prayers, and the two sermons. "She seemed to soak it up, like she comprehended the order of service—and even some of the German, too," Rose remarked.

"Beth does seem to be in harmony with folk," Hen replied. "In one accord, like the bishop says."

During the third seating of the common meal, when the younger children were served, Beth and Mattie Sue sat next to each other at the table. Several of Silas Good's younger school-age nieces were perched on the long bench near them, smiling and enjoying the light meal of bread and *Schmierkees*, dill and sweet pickles, and red beets. There was snitz pie for dessert, which brought smiles to everyone's face.

Rose had been very surprised, earlier, to see Annie Mast's fair-haired mother sitting with Silas's mother during the table seating for the adults and ordained brethren. Never before had Rose seen the Masts and Goods this chummy, talking with their heads together, laughing and smiling. She couldn't help recalling Silas's strange visit to Rebekah at the Masts' the other day.

Much later, after she helped clear away the cups and saucers and table knives, Rose lost track of Mattie Sue and Beth amidst the many young people. She had a hankering for some fresh air, though it was almost too cold to venture outside. Nevertheless, she and her sister-in-law Suzy—Enos's wife—took off walking across the back lawn, toward the barren fields.

"You look like you lost your best friend," Suzy said, her light blond hair neatly parted down the middle.

"I do?"

"You looked glum all during Preaching. Somethin' wrong?"

You weren't paying attention to the sermon, Rose thought, but she dismissed it and said, "I'm worried 'bout Mamm. So is Dat."

Suzy indicated that Enos had said as much. "Evidently, Sol went around and told the boys how poorly she's been doing."

"All of them?"

Suzy nodded.

"Dat can scarcely bring himself to leave Mamm's side anymore." She shared with Suzy how Dat was constantly checking on Mamm. "It's takin' a toll on him—on all of us."

"He's here today, jah?"

Rose nodded. "Mammi Sylvia stayed home with Mamm."

Suzy sighed and looked sad. "Are ya sure nothin' can be done for her?"

"It's been years since she's seen a doctor." Rose paused and glanced at the sky. She shivered. "Only the dear Lord knows what'll happen. Our lives are in His hands."

"That's right." Suzy looked her way, offering a faint smile. "Still, 'tis awful hard seein' her suffer."

Rose agreed as they walked all the way up to the windmill, then headed back toward the house, the air damp and mighty nippy for wearing only shawls. Her mind wandered to the torn picture of what was probably Nick's parents, nestled where she'd placed it with his childhood notes to her. Such thoughts seemed to crop up so unexpectedly, and at the oddest times.

"I hear ya have Beth Browning as company," Suzy said, bringing her out of her musing.

"Anymore, she's nearly like family."

Suzy nodded. "I just hope it's not too taxing for Emma, having a stranger underfoot."

"Actually, Mamm seems to find some comfort in Beth. And it's uncanny how drawn Beth is to her, too."

"I feel for ya, Rosie." Suzy stopped walking and faced her, touching her arm. "You and Mamm are so close after the many years you've looked after her."

Rose nodded. "But I sure won't be the only one missing Mamm when it's her time." She sighed. "Sometimes I honestly think she's anxious to go Home to Jesus."

They rounded the barn at the southeast corner. From there, Rose could see Silas with a group of other young men his age, including Annie Mast's younger brother Benuel. Fleetingly Rose wondered if Silas might be asking Benuel about Rebekah, who was not in attendance today. Without a doubt, Rebekah was at home with Annie and the twins and would be for a number of weeks yet.

Will she get time off to go to Singings while she's here? Rose wondered, hoping now that Rebekah wouldn't show up.

Silas glanced her way and nodded his head, eyes smiling. Her heart swelled and Rose could hardly wait to see him at Singing tonight.

Dare I ask him about Rebekah? The last thing Rose wanted was to stir up trouble. Nevertheless, her curiosity nagged her.

She spotted Annie Mast's mother and Silas's mother walking toward the corncrib, talking earnestly. And near the woodshed, Rose's father and Reuben Good were chewing the fat, while the bishop stood alone over near the stable.

What's going on?

CHAPTER 17

The afternoon had grown increasingly colder, and all but a few families had headed home to milk cows. The bishop and Solomon were folding up the last table and bench for the family who had hosted the service. They would soon resume their normal life once again—at least until the barn gathering for the young folk later this evening.

"Well, the ministers next district over want me to go to Philly and talk to Nick . . . and bring him home," Bishop Aaron told Solomon. "Like the Good Shepherd searching for a lost sheep, I s'pose."

"Oh? I'd guessed it was only hearsay that Nick's hidin' out there. So he *did* go to Philly, then?"

"Won't know for certain unless I go. But who's got time to hunt down a needle in a haystack?"

Sol held his tongue, sensing his friend's need to talk.

"Knowin' Nick, I doubt he'd fess up to anything significant regarding Christian's death, anyway . . . assuming there's anything to say." The bishop rubbed his long beard. "Waste of time, the way I see it."

"But if it helped save your ministry, wouldn't it be worth it?"

Aaron wiped his brow with the back of his hand. "There'd be no forcin' Nick to come clean about what he did . . . or didn't do. The men demanding this really have no idea who or what they're dealing with. Nick's as rebellious as the winter is long." He sighed. "But that's what they seem to want. That, and for him to repent fully and join church."

"Same as what you always wanted for Nick, ain't?"

Aaron sighed loudly. "What I want now doesn't seem to matter." He paused, a faraway look in his eyes. "Between you and me"—and here the bishop glanced over his shoulder—"I think some of them are a-hankerin' for a squabble."

"Why's that?"

The bishop folded his arms across his burly chest. "Got themselves a long memory, I daresay." Fed up as he no doubt was with the demands of the other brethren, he seemed strangely resigned. "It's all bound up in the past."

"Meaning?"

"You prob'ly don't even know it, but the ministerial brethren were mighty outspoken about my decision to take in Nick—not only the neediest boy I'd found, but the most unruly. When 'specially Bishop Ezekiel got wind of it, he said only time would tell if my actions were wise or not. And, considering how Nick's turned out, I'm looking downright guilty of poor judgment."

Sol was stunned. "First I heard of this." Yet he knew as well as anyone that Old Ezekiel had not a progressive bone in his body.

Aaron straightened. "My disobedience to Bishop Ezekiel has come back to haunt me, I daresay." He motioned for Sol to move closer. "Ezekiel's even gone so far as to suggest that Christian's death might very well be God's judgment on me . . . because I unwisely picked Nick Franco to be our foster son."

Shocked, Sol shook his head. "That just can't be. The old bishop believes such a harsh thing?"

"Seems so. He suggested that no good would come of this back when Nick first arrived and was already hard as anything to manage. He simply would not submit to my authority." Aaron pulled out his kerchief and wiped his face.

Sol was unable to speak as he considered all this. Moments later, when several of the womenfolk came into the room to redd up the floor, he said, "You never breathed a word of this to me, Aaron."

"No, I wanted the whole mess brushed into a corner somewhere." Aaron moved toward the front door and stepped into the frigid air. He looked remorsefully at Sol. "You had enough to think about then, what with Emma struggling so. I felt for ya, I truly did." Aaron shook his head. "Still do. Your wife's in constant pain . . . and your daughter's left her husband."

"Emma endures both mental and physical suffering."

"One is due to Hen," Aaron said.

They stood there silently for a moment. The sky seemed to lower as smoke from someone's pipe on the other side of the house wafted over the big roof, its sweet aroma filling their nostrils.

"So now that she's left Brandon . . . what're ya thinking?"

Aaron bore a pained expression. "Guess if I was truly God's man for the church, I would've succeeded somehow in keeping your dear Hannah in the fold. The Lord knows I certainly tried." Aaron remarked how he'd practically run Brandon off Sol's premises the only evening Hen had brought him over for supper, back when.

"We were all mighty upset," Sol admitted, pulling hard on his uneven beard.

"Jah, the Lord himself knows just how desperate a time it was."

Sol nodded in agreement. Still, it could not compare to what his friend was now experiencing. He wondered if Aaron might be waiting for him to offer to go along to look for Nick. But with

Emma so awful weak, Sol wouldn't think of leaving her. And he had numerous orders to fill this week, as well. It wasn't right to deprive his family of that income to seek out the likes of Nick Franco in Philly. Still, it would be ideal if the bishop's foster son agreed to return and make recompense. But, as Aaron had said, the likelihood of that was mighty dim, if not hopeless. "So you truly think the brethren are holdin' a grudge against ya . . . 'bout Nick?"

Aaron's eyes were fixed on a flock of geese gleaning in the cornfield across the road. He never once moved his head to acknowledge one way or the other. Sol placed his hand on Aaron's back. "I'm awful sorry about the disunity. 'Least it hasn't caused a ruckus amongst the People," he offered.

"Not just yet." Aaron turned toward him. "Thing is, I'm standing my ground, refusing to *make* Nick come home, even if I *could* locate him. How absurd, when ya think of it. I'm of the mind to think it should be *his* doin'."

Words like these were exactly why Sol looked up to the man chosen by divine lot to oversee the local church. "I'm with ya on that."

Aaron continued. "I don't expect Nick to ever set foot in my house again, but at the same time, I won't quit praying for him to do just that."

Solomon said he'd continue to pray, as well, still reeling with the disquieting information that the most revered bishop in the county was putting such pressure on Aaron.

∽

The Sunday evening barn Singing was well populated with nearly all the courting-age youth from the local district, as well as a dozen or more from a neighboring one. Rose couldn't help overhearing one of the ministers' sons from the other church talking about his father and others wanting to get to the bottom of what had happened to Christian Petersheim that fateful day.

The idea greatly disturbed her, mostly out of concern for Nick. And also because Christian's passing had taken its toll on the whole community, especially the bishop and dear Barbara.

In her heart of hearts, she did not believe Nick was capable of causing someone's death—no matter what his cryptic words had implied.

In the note I burned . . .

≈

Much later, when the cold air had stilled, Rose and Silas rode alone in his courting buggy. She brought up the new youth who'd come to the Singing. "They aren't from our district, which seems a bit odd to me."

Silas chuckled. "It appears word got out that a new batch of girls recently turned sixteen over here."

She smiled; she'd guessed there was more to it than the other boys just showing up because their songs were faster than the neighboring church's, or whatnot. But this made plenty good sense.

Funny how fast word spreads about eligible girls!

They visited pleasantly for a while, until Rose began to shiver. Silas reached back and brought out another lap robe and placed it over her. Then, just as quickly, he slipped under it, too, trusting the horse to keep going as he got resituated next to Rose. Silas, for his part, seemed relaxed and happy, even talking about the possibility of her coming to see his father's dairy farm—"the milking operation is mighty impressive." He held the reins lightly with a single hand. "Ya needn't be shy about comin' during the daytime. My family already suspects you're my girl."

She blushed at that. It was awfully hard to keep such things secret from families, especially when two of Silas's sisters were regulars at youth gatherings. "I could prob'ly visit this Wednesday, since I won't be working for Mr. Browning that day." She explained that Beth Browning was staying with them. "For the week, anyways."

"Wednesday morning's fine with me." He smiled at her. "I'll come pick you up."

"Denki . . . sounds *gut*." Rose couldn't wait for him to hold her hand tonight. So far he hadn't, and she wondered if it had anything to do with what she'd witnessed between Silas and Rebekah at the Masts'.

Not knowing in the slightest how to bring up that uncomfortable topic, Rose gazed at the night sky. Tiny specks of snow drifted onto her face and she felt momentarily at peace. "Seems like December's been here for a long time already."

"Hog butcherin' weather, for sure."

She again contemplated what she wanted to say about Rebekah. Did she dare reveal her concern? She glanced his way, but he was focused on the road again. Just as well, maybe.

The road stretched out before them like a narrow gray strand, dotted on either side by golden lights in the farmhouse windows. She'd noticed the clouds looking denser, grayer that afternoon—like goose down. Dat and Mose, the third oldest of her five brothers, had spread fresh manure around the rosebushes days ago, then sowed rye in the vegetable gardens as green fertilzer and to prevent erosion. There was no turning back; winter was here to stay.

Rose drew a slow, deep breath after thinking it over. "I can't help wonderin' how Rebekah Bontrager must feel, being away from her family with Christmas coming up."

Silas mumbled a single syllable, though Rose couldn't make it out.

She continued. "I saw her yesterday, standing outside at Annie Mast's—near the springhouse." She paused and waited to see if he might respond. "My sister and I, and her little girl, went with Beth Browning to see the new twins."

Silas said nothing, and Rose felt she must press forward. "You were there, too."

Silas shifted in his seat, bringing his free hand up to hold the reins. "I stopped off to make a quick delivery, is all."

A *delivery?*

"Something for Rebekah," he volunteered.

"Rebekah?" Her mouth felt like cornmeal mush.

"It was a letter I should've written sooner . . . before she ever arrived here."

Rose was all ears, though apprehensive about what was to come.

"You see, she and I exchanged a few letters a while back— months ago, actually. It was during the time you were stayin' home with your mother, after your Dawdi Jeremiah had his stroke."

She remembered her months of loneliness all too well. Except for Nick, Rose really hadn't had anyone to talk to, because, even when she'd been awake, Mamm had not often been up for much conversation back then. *Even less so now . . .*

"Just five or six letters."

Rose was somewhat shaken to learn that Silas's romantic interests had strayed during the months she hadn't gone to Singings and such. Goodness, did that mean Silas and Rebekah's present communication might be less innocent than Rose had hoped? She cleared her throat. "What did ya write to her yesterday?"

"That I was engaged to you. I wanted her to understand why I'm not pursuing her while she's here."

That's good, she thought, relieved he'd let Rebekah know he was spoken for. But she wondered why Silas hadn't written to say he was engaged prior to Rebekah's coming. "So then, she knows for certain we're a couple?" Rose asked, still feeling somewhat cheerless.

"I made it clear—you are my betrothed." Silas looked at her quickly, then away. "I should've told you before now about writing her. For that, I apologize."

She recalled Silas stating that Rebekah was *"solidly Amish,"* as if comparing her to other girls—possibly even herself, although she couldn't imagine why he'd find her own commitment to the Plain tradition wanting. After all, Rose had been the one to join church at just fifteen, a younger age than most girls. Much earlier than the young men in the church district typically did, too. *No, surely he wasn't comparing her to me.*

When Silas reached for her hand later, Rose felt heartened and welcomed the old thrill. She decided she had been right to bring up the niggling topic after all, and was glad Silas had been so forthcoming. *A right gut trait in a husband.*

Yet as they drove on into the night, her mind traveled in circles. It haunted her, recalling how fond Rebekah had been of Silas as a preteen. What had seemed so nearly perfect between Rose and Silas in the past months had come about in spite of Rebekah Bontrager.

CHAPTER 18

The next two days brought sleet and even colder temperatures. Woodsmoke puffed out from chimneys along Salem Road, more than Rose had noticed thus far in the season. With the last of the leaves gone from the trees, the landscape looked bleak, even tattered, and the sky was the eerie shade of steel wool.

"'Tis downright dismal," Mammi Sylvia remarked to Dawdi Jeremiah as they sat with Rose in the kitchen of the main house.

"Well, you can't have summer in December, now, can ya?" Dawdi jokingly replied.

Rose kept busy stoking the cookstove for warmth in the kitchen and the sitting room, filling it from the woodbox just outside the back door. She checked on the oil space heater in the front room, wanting to keep things nice and cozy for Mamm. For her part, Mamm didn't want to move from her comfortable nest, no longer interested in even being at the table for meals. Mammi, Hen, and Rose took turns with Mamm and, more often than not, Beth Browning was either sitting near or pacing just outside the room. As much as Beth had previously enjoyed playing with Mattie Sue, she spent less time doing so now, focusing most of her attention on Mamm. It was as if Beth had adopted Mamm as her own.

∼

As Wednesday morning dawned—before Rose left to meet Silas—she sat in bed reading one of her favorite novels, *A Girl of the Limberlost*, wishing she could someday see the beautiful area where the long-ago story had been set. *Might it be close to Rebekah's parents' home?* she wondered.

Later, when she'd washed and dressed, Rose asked of both Hen and Mammi Sylvia if her being gone for a little while would cause a hardship for either of them. Hen reminded Rose she was scheduled to work that afternoon. "Till four-thirty—only a few hours today."

Mammi fairly shoved Rose out of the house, eager to tend to Mamm, Rose thought. So Rose took off walking down the driveway, expecting Silas to be prompt as always. She eyed the spot near the road where Nick had clasped her arms the pitch-black night he'd taken her down Bridle Path Lane—a supposed shortcut. Not wanting to dwell on that, she quickened her pace and turned west toward the designated location to meet Silas.

Her fiancé was as punctual as she'd assumed. He smiled and waved as she walked toward his father's gray family carriage. "It looked like it could sleet or snow, so I brought the family buggy," he explained quickly. The enclosed buggy would also shield them from prying eyes—a good idea, since they had another year before they would announce their wedding.

She smiled at him, appreciating the warmth and shelter of the carriage as she carefully raised her skirt to climb inside.

In due time, they arrived at Reuben Good's great spread of land, just four miles south of Dat's farm. Silas's younger sisters, Sarah and Anna Mae, ran out to greet them as Rose stepped out of the carriage. The girls walked with her and Silas toward the barn, and

Rose noticed her betrothed's face light up like a lantern when he began talking of the large herd of dairy cattle he would oversee— "forty milking cows, with additional heifers for replacements."

They strolled through the stable, past the box stalls for birthing, and out through the barnyard, with Sarah and Anna Mae happily tagging along. Even compared to her father's expansive acreage, the place was enormous. Silas mentioned the many workers the daily production required, obviously excited to have been chosen to take over the sizable operation.

Rose wondered if she would be expected to help with the milking. Oh, she'd do so, if need be, but it was not her favorite thing. She surveyed the grand main house, where she and Silas would eventually reside. Its white clapboard exterior gleamed in the sunlight and was the center of activity, with several smaller houses connected to it. She was eager to set up housekeeping here and make a home for Silas and their future children.

Rose continued to follow Silas demurely as he showed her the outbuildings and narrow mule lanes rimming the vast fields.

Sarah and Anna Mae urged her to come again soon before they headed back to the house to finish cleaning and baking. "Your sisters are real sweet," Rose told him later.

"Jah, well, they can sometimes be mischievous, too."

Rose liked the sound of that.

" 'Course, maybe I get special treatment, since I'm their brother," he added with a twinkle in his eye.

Rose chuckled at that. "They seem like good girls. Close as your Mamm seems to Annie, I wonder why one of them wasn't chosen to help with her twins."

Silas shrugged. "Guess I hadn't given it a thought."

Yet Rose was unable to dismiss how odd it was seeing Annie Mast's mother seeking out Silas's mother at the common meal. After all, it had been Annie's mother who'd first contacted Rebekah's mother about the twins.

"What's on your mind?" Silas smiled down at her.

She paused a moment, then forged ahead. "Why do *you* think Rebekah was asked to come and help with Annie's babies?"

He shook his head, obviously puzzled. "I've no idea."

"Well, does it seem peculiar that Annie's mother wrote to Rebekah's mom about it?"

"Really?" Silas frowned. "Is *that* how it happened?"

Rose felt ridiculous. "Rebekah said so herself." Evidently that wasn't something Silas and Rebekah had discussed. Rose wished now she hadn't brought up the tetchy subject; Silas's response had explained nothing. Worse yet, she didn't want her intended to wonder if she could think of nothing else—especially on what was supposed to be a special morning for both of them.

~

"Your dad pressed me for more time." Brandon's words rang in Hen's memory as she sat at the kitchen table with pen and paper following breakfast. She had been agonizing over what to write to him, wanting to state the conditions for her return home. *To live under his roof . . .*

Deciding to simply be straightforward about her thoughts, she began to write.

Dear Brandon,

I've been pondering your ultimatum. I hate to think of our marriage ending, and I dread the idea of having strangers decide Mattie Sue's living arrangements. Can't we meet each other halfway?

I will be happy to return home if you'd permit Mattie Sue and me to dress in Plain clothing. It would also be wonderful if we could continue to attend our Amish church and have ongoing fellowship with my family and friends. In addition to this, how would you feel about visiting my parents and siblings on the Lord's Day as a family?

I realize how difficult this has all been for you, Brandon, but I truly think you'd find my family quite pleasant, even fun.

One more thing: If you don't mind, would it be possible for you to watch TV only when Mattie Sue is not in the room?

Surely these things are not too much to ask in the hopes of keeping the peace in our marriage—and in an attempt to retain Mattie Sue's precious innocence. Oh, Brandon, I would love to have the chance to rebuild what we have lost!

I really hope you'll hear my heart in this.

With love,
Hen

She'd thought of asking that Brandon attend Preaching services with her and Mattie Sue, but realized it was unrealistic to expect Brandon would agree. *I may be asking for more than he can handle as it is.*

Hen folded the letter and tucked it away in her stationery drawer in the nearby cupboard. She would read it again tomorrow before mailing. If she had second thoughts, she'd rewrite it completely . . . or discard the idea altogether.

She remembered something her grandfather Jeremiah often said when she was little: *"If you marry in haste, you'll repent in leisure."*

Hen made her way to the wooden hooks near the back door, where she kept her black shawl and outer bonnet. Donning them, she then headed next door to help her grandmother with Mom, hoping by some miracle things might've taken a turn for the better. Apart from that, she didn't see how her mother could continue living.

∾

Her sister strongly encouraged Rose to attend the quilting bee on Thursday morning, even though Rose protested mildly, determined to take her turn looking after Mamm, who, despite her continuing pain, seemed slightly better today. But despite her repeated objections, both Hen and Mammi Sylvia assured her they were planning to be on hand to assist.

"Only if you're sure," Rose replied.

"Go on, now," Mammi Sylvia said, flapping a dish towel at her. *I'm sure getting out of the house more often*, she thought with a pang of guilt.

When Rose arrived at the Esh farmhouse, she was happy to see Mandy and an older sister, Linda. Soon Rose was seated at the north end of the large quilting frame—where she was told Annie Mast typically sat. Not long after, here came Arie Zook, Hen's friend, with her six-month-old baby, Levi, sound asleep in her arms. Mandy offered the downstairs bedroom for a quiet spot for the wee one, and right away Arie was back, looking tired but saying how eager she was to have some "woman-talk." Rose assumed it had been a busy and, perhaps, trying week for Arie as a young mother of two. She didn't ask where Arie's three-year-old, Becky, was spending the day, but guessed either Arie's mother or mother-in-law was babysitting.

One by one, all twelve spots at the frame were filled with expert quilters, including Mandy and Linda's mother, Laura, and a number of Esh girl cousins. Together they worked, talking and laughing, even having a contest to see who could get the most stitches on a single needle. Laura was the consistent winner with eight, although she was humble about it, ducking her head and blushing pink.

There was plenty of gossip, more than usual, what with the wedding season in full swing. Several more couples had been published at the last Preaching service, which meant some of the womenfolk present would have to choose between two, or even three, wedding invitations in a single day.

Hours later, after a pause for the noontime dinner of mashed potatoes, two kinds of meat, and many desserts made by the hostess, they resumed their work. When the quilting was finished, all that was left to do was the edge, which several women would hem once the patchwork quilt was removed from the frame. The group seemed pleased that yet another quilt was nearly ready to be included in the Christmas batch going to Philadelphia next Thursday morning. Mandy said there would be any number of tied comforters, too, which took less time to complete than the intricately stitched quilts.

During a lull in the conversation, Mandy asked who'd like to go along to help deliver the quilts. When Mandy and Linda both turned and openly stared at her, Rose felt her cheeks flush. Not wanting to appear anxious to volunteer, she nodded slowly, agreeing to go with Mandy and her mother, who planned to hire a Mennonite van driver.

The women said their good-byes, and Rose hitched up her horse and buggy and headed home, still aware of Mandy's and Linda's gawking at her. *Why? What do they think they know?*

Yet all during the buggy ride home, Rose had the strangest, nearly giddy feeling about the upcoming trip. *It's not like I'll see Nick there,* she kept telling herself . . . but a part of her surely hoped otherwise.

CHAPTER 19

Seeing Brandon's car pull into the driveway on Saturday and inch toward Hen's Dawdi Haus, Solomon picked up his pace through the pasture. He kept walking, finding it curious that Brandon merely sat there in his car, not getting out. *Cold feet?* Sol wondered. He held his breath and hoped this wretched separation might come to a quick end.

Sol was fast approaching the barnyard now. He figured Brandon might just end up staying put in his fancy car if Sol didn't go over and make some small talk. Maybe he could help his son-in-law work up the nerve to go and knock on his bride's door.

"Hullo, Brandon. Can I help ya?" Sol said through the car window.

Brandon rolled down the glass. "I can't believe I came all the way out to the sticks to talk to my wife." He looked over at the little house. "Would you mind giving her a message for me?"

"Be glad to."

"Tell Hen I received her letter . . . and, in a word, the conditions she laid out are preposterous." Brandon muttered something under his breath, as if talking to himself.

Sol was taken by surprise. "All right." Wishing he could do something to fix this, he glanced at the main house. "Say, we're havin' some mighty tasty roast beef for supper. Can ya stay and eat?"

"No, thanks."

"Suit yourself."

Brandon turned the key in the ignition. "Will you tell Hen one more thing? I'll be contacting my lawyer first thing Monday. Time's up!"

Sol felt his stomach tighten into a knot. "What happened to giving her more time?"

"I've changed my mind. Unless she's getting independent counsel, she'll need to come to his office, since she refuses to do the sensible thing and return home."

Sol's mouth dropped open. Brandon was clearly fed up. "I'll let her know."

He didn't wait for Brandon to back up and leave. Sol waved disgustedly and headed for the barn.

～

Hen flinched and her body sagged when her father repeated the words Brandon had so curtly spoken to him. *We're coming undone*, she thought, closing the door behind her father as he left for the main house.

She headed upstairs to look in on Mattie Sue, who was playing in her room with some of Rose's faceless dolls. Oodles of them were in rows along the braided rug where she sat. "Hi, sweetie."

"Mommy?" Mattie Sue said as she looked up from her cozy spot. "Do I have to wear English clothes to visit Daddy next time?"

If there is a next time, Hen thought crossly.

"We'll see, honey." She didn't want to trouble Mattie Sue with the latest news from Brandon. But she had to do *something*, even if it meant getting her own lawyer. And just what would the bishop say about that?

Oh, she just didn't know how to make any of her plans work anymore. But as Hen sat down on Mattie Sue's bed, she knew one thing for sure: She absolutely refused to take her daughter back to an English life. They were not going back to Egypt, so to speak. And she was not handing precious Mattie Sue over to the world without a fight of her own.

~

Rose was surprised when Hen announced she wouldn't be coming for supper but asked if Mattie Sue might eat with them again. Her sister's face looked nearly beet red, like she was ill with a fever. "You all right, Hen?"

"No, I'm not . . . and please don't ask anything more." She turned to leave by way of the back door.

"Mommy's upset—*bees*," Mattie Sue told Beth where she sat in the corner of the kitchen writing in her blue notebook. "That's Pennsylvania Dutch, ya know."

"What's wrong with her?" Beth looked up as Mattie Sue sat down near her at the table.

"I don't know." Mattie began to cry. She put her little head down on her arms and leaned on the table, sobbing.

Well, what the world? Rose rushed to her side at the bench and put her arm around her niece. "Honey . . . honey," she said, patting Mattie's back.

Meanwhile, Mammi Sylvia stepped into the kitchen, coming from Mamm's bedroom nearby. "Beth, will you go and read some of your poetry to Emma? She's askin' for you."

"Prayers that rhyme," Beth said when Rose caught her eye. Beth closed her notebook and got up quickly to go in and see Mamm.

Mammi Sylvia's eyes grew serious. "Your mother also wants to see you, Rose Ann . . . and Hen, if she's around."

Rose's heart fell. "Is she . . . ?"

Mammi shook her head. "She's not *gut* at all. Her spirits are as low as I've ever seen them." She looked tenderly at Mattie Sue. "I'd be happy to take over for ya here."

Rose kissed Mattie's cheek and went to wait at the door for Beth to exit Mamm's bedroom. She could hear Beth reading the sweetest poem-like prayer. Tears welled up, and Rose wished Hen was here now and not off wherever she'd gone. *Most likely to see Brandon,* she thought with concern.

Truth was, her sister hadn't looked so good. And she'd been curt, too, much like the way she'd been back when she and Brandon were secretly dating.

Comfort and guide my sister, dear Lord. And be ever near to Mamm, too.

Rose wiped away her tears and put on a smile for her ailing mother, hoping to cheer her with her presence, just as Beth surely was now.

～

Hen didn't bother to wait for the front door to open after she rang the doorbell. This was her house, too, so she turned the doorknob and walked right in. Terry had obviously taken leave of the place. The kitchen looked like someone had left all the windows open during a windstorm, and food was standing out on the counters. The dishwasher gaped wide and the table was speckled with crumbs and dribbles of coffee.

She hated the thought of looking downstairs in the family room, where Brandon liked to sit in front of the tube and eat snacks. *Now that I'm gone, he's probably camping out there.*

Glad Terry was most likely gone, Hen wished Brandon would appear. Surely he hadn't left the front door unlocked. It wasn't like living with the Amish, where doors were never locked.

Amishville, she thought, chagrined. "If that's what he thinks . . ."

she muttered as she made her way through the house, heading for the bedroom.

She heard the shower running and thought it best to wait to spring her surprise on him once he was out and dressed. Going to Mattie's former bedroom, she sat on the twin bed and rehearsed what she planned to tell her husband. *No backing down!*

Lying on the bed, she closed her eyes and pictured going to the lawyer's office—*her* lawyer. She would get the best attorney in all of Lancaster, too. It was her best hope for getting custody of Mattie Sue. There was no fooling around with a man like Brandon.

Hen's emotional exhaustion overtook her and she dozed off momentarily in Mattie Sue's cozy bed. She dreamed she was waiting on pins and needles for word from Brandon's hotshot lawyer, hoping the powers that be wouldn't take Mattie Sue away from her. The dream became murky as she heard the sound of footsteps, which she soon realized, as she awakened in a haze, were not in her dream at all.

When she opened her eyes, there was Brandon standing over her, towel drying his hair. "Wha—? I guess I fell asleep."

"Well, hello to you, too," he said. "Do you ever call ahead? Oh, that's right—you don't have a house phone over in farmers' town."

"Brandon," Hen said, sitting up. "I came by to tell you I'm getting representation."

"Oh really?" He eyed her. "Guess you'll have to use my phone to make the call, right? Of course, you'll be lucky to find a law office that's open on a Saturday."

She shrugged off his comment. "Dad said you basically laughed at my requirements . . . for my return home."

"You bet I did!" He turned to leave, then stopped in the doorway. Facing her, he added, "I'm putting the house on the market, too. Mattie and I will make do with something smaller."

Mattie and I . . .

"Maybe we'll move closer to my parents in New York."

The blood drained from her face and she felt faint. Breathing slowly, purposefully, Hen shook her head. "How can you be so sure you'll get custody?"

"Because, my dear wife, you are out of touch with reality. You live in Amishland . . . remember? You prefer horses and buggies to modern transportation, and you dress like a . . ." He paused to eyeball her outfit. "Like something out of the Salem Witch trials."

She felt like crying as Brandon marched out of the room.

Angry enough to raise her voice at him, Hen bit her tongue and headed to the kitchen to look for an attorney's office to call. *Might as well use his phone book,* she thought, shaking with fury. *I can't afford to lose any more time.*

CHAPTER 20

$\mathcal{R}$ose saw Hen drive into the lane and park behind the barn that evening after an early supper. Hen's face looked puffy and red as she walked toward the house. Rose rushed out to meet her. "You all right, sister?"

Hen leaned her head on Rose's shoulder as they embraced. "I doubt I'll ever be right again," she whispered. "I honestly don't see how . . ."

Rose felt hesitant to tell Hen how very anxious Mamm was now. The recent scare with the new pain medication had left her more desperate for her future than usual. *Hen has so much to think about, let alone adding Mamm, too.*

But Rose couldn't just hope Mamm would pull out of her murky depression—she had to let Hen know their mother's situation. So she forged ahead, holding Hen's hand as they walked slowly toward the house. "Mamm's askin' to see you, Hen," she said softly. "She needs the comfort of her oldest daughter . . . and your prayers, too."

$\sim$

It was nearly eight o'clock when Hen left her mother's sickbed. She felt sad that she'd been away when Mamm had initially called for her—sad, too, that in her present state there was little she could do to encourage her mother. She walked back to her Dawdi Haus, where she encouraged Mattie Sue to get ready for bed, all the while praying silently for her mom. *If she can have occasional good days . . . is it possible for her to feel better more often than not, dear Lord?*

Sometime later, while reading her Bible, Hen heard footsteps on the porch and looked up to see Brandon standing at the back door. "Goodness, what's *he* doing here?" she whispered, startled.

Without giving it a second thought, she hurried to let him in. "Brandon?"

He frowned when she opened the door. "I'm taking Mattie Sue home."

Hen trembled. "But . . . she's already in her nightclothes."

"Nightclothes, Hen? C'mon . . . that's so archaic."

Hen ignored his ridicule. "She's going to sleep now."

"I don't care. Get her up!" He stood with his arms folded. "Pack her *normal* clothes—and make it quick."

"Brandon . . . *please*." Hen felt the air being sucked out of her. "Don't do this."

"I'm entitled to equal time with my daughter." He turned, disregarding her plea. Going toward the stairs, he called up. "Mattie Sue, come down here, please."

A staccato of small footsteps followed, then Mattie Sue's happy voice. "Daddy . . . you surprised me!"

Brandon glanced at Hen with a scowl. "What are you waiting for?"

"But—"

"You heard me. Get her things ready."

Mattie jumped into his arms. "Did ya bring Wiggles to visit me, too?"

"No, honey," he stated matter-of-factly. "Wiggles is waiting for you at our house."

Mattie's eyes locked with Hen's and she blinked several times in a row. "I don't want to wear my nightgown outside, Daddy."

"That's all right," he said, putting her down. "Just put your coat on over the top."

Hen assumed Mattie was simply going to run back upstairs and hide, but she darted out the back door instead, running out into the cold, damp night barefooted and wearing only her white cotton nightgown.

Brandon rushed to the door and looked out, huffing air. Hen hoped he wouldn't take off running after Mattie Sue. He turned and glared at Hen. "Do you have any idea what you're doing to our daughter keeping her locked up like this?"

"You are welcome to spend time with Mattie here whenever you wish," Hen replied, struggling to keep her tone even. "Mattie Sue loves everything about the farm. She helps my dad and Rose feed the animals, goes exploring in the meadows, and even makes goat cheese. She's learning to sew and quilt and bake . . . and she enjoys playing with the bishop's grandchildren."

At the mention of the bishop, Brandon winced. "Don't get me started!" He glanced out into the night again. "Call Mattie back into the house, Hen. Now!"

Jolted by his harshness, she moved to the door and waited for him to move away. But just as she opened it, her father was standing there, as if a godsend.

Brandon ran his hands through his hair as though in sheer desperation. He went to the window near the sink and looked out. "Mattie's going to freeze out there," he muttered.

"What's goin' on?" Dad asked.

"I came for my daughter," Brandon answered, turning away from the window. "But she seems to have run away."

"Well, what's that tell ya, son?"

Hen was so relieved her father had come, she went to sit at the table, entrusting the seeming nightmare to him. And to God.

Dad motioned for Brandon to sit at the table and pulled out a chair for himself to join Hen there. "Seems to me there's something wrong with taking a little girl from her Mamma." He looked at Hen.

Though obviously seething, Brandon was suddenly silent.

Dad studied them both. "So, now that I've got ya both in the same room, what can be done to put a stop to this talk of divorce? Ain't at all pleasin' to the Lord God, no way and no how."

Brandon sighed heavily, leaning back with his hands linked behind his head. He stared at Hen, then turned to Sol. "Do *you* have any influence over your daughter?"

"I'm her father."

"And I'm her husband, but you can see where that's gotten me."

"Did ya ever think there might be something each of you can surrender? I mean to save your marriage. Something Hen wants that you're not willing to give her quite yet. And vice versa."

Brandon's expression turned incredulous. "You should've been a marriage counselor, Mr. Kauffman." He paused and glanced at his watch. "Why not practice on Hen instead of me?"

She'd never heard a man speak so rudely to her father. And she was growing increasingly worried that Mattie Sue would catch her death of cold outside. Maybe her daughter had made her way over to the main house. Hen hoped and prayed that was so.

"My wife knows exactly what she has to do to patch things up," Brandon spouted.

"I see."

Brandon shrugged. "For starters, tell her to practice her Amish upbringing."

"So you *do* want her to act more Amish, then?"

Brandon sputtered, apparently caught off guard. He glanced at Hen. "Well, she could listen to her husband, for one thing."

"If you were a God-fearing man, I'd have to agree with that." Dad stared at Brandon, and Hen felt terribly uncomfortable. "Meanwhile, till that happens, I suggest you take yourself on home and leave my granddaughter be to say her bedtime prayers."

Standing up, Brandon looked anything but whipped. He shot a look of defiance at Hen. "Better get that lawyer lined up. I'll see you in court." With that, he paused, staring at her clothes. "And if I never have to see you wearing such a dowdy dress again, Hen . . . well, it'll be too soon."

Hen waited till Brandon left the house, then fell into her father's arms, thanking him again and again. "The Lord must've sent you over here, Dad."

"Jah, the Lord and Rosie," he replied. "Your sister spotted the car and was concerned for you. Now, let's find out where that clever daughter of yours ran off to."

"Oh, poor Mattie Sue . . ." Hen walked with her father to the back door.

"What's this 'bout getting yourself a lawyer?" he asked solemnly.

She wasn't surprised he'd bring that up. "I don't want to lose my daughter. I've decided to fight for her in court."

Her father eyed her, visibly concerned. "Well, now, are ya trusting in yourself, or in our sovereign Lord?"

Immediately, Hen felt convicted. There was nothing she could say that would change Dad's mind. Yet wasn't she responsible under God to do everything in her power to keep her child far from the world? *Just as Dad tried to keep me in the community of the People . . . before I eloped.*

CHAPTER 21

$\mathcal{S}$unday morning, after the breakfast dishes were rinsed and stacked to be washed, Rose heard a knock at the back door. She moved quickly to see who was there, since English neighbors were the only ones who typically ever knocked.

Sure enough, it was Donna Becker—a bright picture to behold in her long red coat and matching gloves. But Rose's heart sank, because Donna looked quite solemn for such a sunny day. "Excuse my loud colors," Donna whispered. "It's my warmest coat."

"'Tis all right." Rose held her breath; she guessed why Donna had come. "Perhaps we should talk out here . . . on the porch." Beth and Mattie Sue were somewhere inside the house, playing together.

"Beth's grandfather passed away in the night," said Donna. "Gilbert called just a while ago."

"How very sad for Mr. Browning . . . and Beth." Rose touched the top of Donna's gloved hand.

"It might be good if you're the one to tell her," Donna suggested with a faint smile. "You know Beth better than I do."

"Jah, *gut* idea." Rose glanced toward the kitchen, wondering if Mammi Sylvia was still sitting with Mamm. "Will Mr. Browning return for Beth . . . to take her to the funeral?"

"I asked the same thing, and evidently Beth does not do well in large gatherings. Besides, it's a long ways for Gilbert to come for her."

"Understandable," Rose whispered.

"So he'll stay on for at least another few days, if not a week. He said he'd call again after the funeral and let us know when he plans to return."

Rose nodded. "When he does, please let him know Beth's doin' fine here. Tell him to take his time." She just couldn't imagine the man's grief . . . losing first his wife and now his father, too.

"I got the feeling his mother will need a bit of looking after. His father had been doing so for some time, as I understand it."

Rose had heard the same. "How sad the dear woman is ailing so and is now a widow, too." She thought suddenly of Mamm. "Would ya like to come in and have some hot tea or cocoa?"

"No, no . . . just wanted to drop by and let you know the latest news." Donna sighed and gave a small smile. "Bless you for taking care of Beth."

"No trouble at all."

"I'm happy to help out, if necessary."

"Denki." Rose smiled and nodded her head. "And, Donna, rest assured I'll break this to Beth very gently."

Donna blinked back tears, patting her face with her red glove. "Beth is such a fragile flower, poor thing. I hope she doesn't take this too hard."

Rose watched Donna turn and make her way out to her car parked near the walkway. Opening the door to the screen porch, Rose stood on the steps, shivering with the cold . . . and sorrow. Oh, she wished she didn't have such heartbreaking news to tell dear, dear Beth!

⌣

Hen had encouraged Mattie Sue to play quietly this Lord's Day morning. So, after breakfast, when Mattie asked to go over to Mammi Emma's to see Beth, Hen was happy to oblige, thankful for some time alone.

From the moment she had awakened, Hen felt ready to return to bed, unable to sleep as she had been for hours last night. Her head throbbed with the pressure of Brandon's harsh words, which still plagued her. His comment about her Plain dress stung her heart. How could she forgive him?

Now she sat on the small sofa in the front room of her little house, her legs curled up beneath her long green dress and black apron. Brandon had stated that he'd see her in court, and after the events of last night, Hen was afraid he would indeed push things that far. Brandon wasn't one to make idle threats—she knew that much from his business dealings.

This same man had wooed her away from her family and the Plain life so easily. She had yearned for the forbidden fruit of the English life as a teen and gotten what she *thought* she wanted in Brandon. Bitter anguish poured from her soul as Hen wept. And remembering the heartache she'd caused her parents, she cried all the harder.

The memory of little Mattie Sue running next door to find shelter last night, when Brandon had come to take her, shook Hen to the core. Rose, too, had reported being terribly upset to find Mattie Sue wearing only a nightgown in such cold weather. Fortunately, Rose warmed her up by the fire, then put her to bed with Beth and kept her there till Dat and Hen came over later.

After Brandon left . . .

Hen gave in to sobs, crying away her woes. Finally, she dried her eyes and straightened her dress in case Mattie Sue returned and found her in a miserable heap. She looked around, aware of God's provision for her and Mattie Sue, here in this restful house.

She prayed for wisdom in acquiring a lawyer and for peace to know she was making a choice that was pleasing to God. Yet she knew in her heart that what would please Him most would be to salvage her marriage, even now. *Impossible as things seem . . .*

Reaching for her Bible, Hen opened to Psalm forty-two. As she read, the last verse caught her eye and pulled tenderly on her heart. *Hope thou in God. . . .* With a catch in her breath, she embraced the loving instruction from her heavenly Father.

Leaving the Bible open on the sofa to the beautiful verse, Hen rose to put on her shawl, ready to go next door to see her dear, discouraged mother.

≈

Rose Ann watched Donna Becker back slowly out of the lane and contemplated the sad news she must tell Beth. With a silent prayer for guidance, Rose returned to the house. She followed the sounds of Mattie Sue's expressive voice, such a contrast to Beth's low monotone, and found them upstairs in Rose's own room. The two of them were perched on the bed playing school.

"C'mon, Mattie Sue," Beth was saying. "You've never been to school before. Not even to preschool. Have you?"

"But I still want to be the teacher," Mattie Sue insisted, her arms crossed. "Can't you be the teacher next time?"

Evidently not to be outdone, Beth turned away and looked out the window.

"Beth?"

Still staring, Beth didn't move.

"Aren't you listening?"

Beth whirled around. "I'm not your plaything to boss around!"

Mattie Sue began to pout. "But I really want to be the teacher."

Beth frowned as Mattie Sue continued her sulk, looking as

though she might even squeeze out a tear. Rose found the girls' interaction fascinating, so she held back, not interrupting.

Four stuffed animals sat on the bed, propped against the footboard, while Rose's library books were open before them. The girls seemed to have already planned out the items they would need for their school.

"Here's what we can do," Beth said finally. "I'll help you teach, since I know a lot about school."

Immediately, Mattie Sue brightened. "You'll help me?"

Beth handed her two books. "First, you need to give the students an assignment from these books."

"What about circle time? My friend Karen says it's real fun. They sit in a circle and talk about the weather and other things."

"Never heard of that," Beth replied.

"Sometimes Karen gets to be the weather helper and put up pictures of suns and rain on a special calendar. Let's start with circle time today."

Beth shrugged, disinterested. "Doesn't sound like the kind of school I went to."

Rose could see this exchange was headed for yet another conflict. She knocked on the door and stepped into the room. "Sorry to interrupt your class, girls, but I need to talk to Beth alone . . . just for a little while."

Her niece frowned, eyes blinking. "It's circle time right now, Aendi Rosie."

"I see that," said Rose, hoping Mattie Sue would quickly comply. "But I need to talk to Beth now, honey."

"Can we play some more . . . afterward?"

Beth looked at Rose; her face was serene, but her eyes had a knowing look. "Is my grandpa worse?" Her lower lip quivered.

"Mattie Sue," said Rose a bit more firmly, taking her niece by the hand and leading her into the hallway. She leaned down and kissed her face. "Go on down and sit with Mammi Emma for a minute, won't ya?" Just then, she heard the back door open and Hen calling. "Your mommy's downstairs," Rose said.

Mattie Sue looked up and hurried off.

Perfect timing!

Rose could hear Beth already crying softly, and she went to her side and slipped her arm around her shoulder. Together, they moved toward the window and stood there looking out at the brilliantly blue sky. "I will not leave you comfortless, the Lord promises us," Rose said, paraphrasing the Scripture verse. She turned to look at Beth, whose pitiful, tear-streaked face made Rose feel like crying, too. "Your grandpa's pain is past now, Beth. He won't ever have to struggle again with the cares of this life." Her voice broke.

Beth covered her face with her hands and cried. Rose drew her into her embrace, holding her as she might her own sister.

"He's with the Lord now, Beth," she whispered.

"But Grandma's all alone" came the fretful remark, through more tears.

Rose stroked her short hair. "God will take care of her, just as we're takin' care of you."

"But we'll move far away, Rosie. I just know it."

She released Beth, still holding her thin hands, and she looked into her childlike face. "Can you trust the Lord for that? He does all things well," she said. "That's another promise from the Bible . . . ya know?"

"I just don't want to leave you, Rosie . . . my best friend."

This tugged at Rose's heartstrings. "Come here, sweet girl." She opened her arms once again and held Beth near.

∾

Solomon helped Bishop Aaron stack hay in his loft all day Monday. All the lifting and heaving of bales was taking its toll on his back muscles. He'd stayed longer than usual, offering to shovel feed to the heifers, too.

But Aaron was ready to call it a day. "Tired as I am, I think I'll go to the cemetery after a bit," Aaron told him as they walked through the barnyard, toward the house. "Just feel the need tonight."

"I'd go with ya, but I ought to be getting back to Emma." Sol looked over at his house; the downstairs windows were flickering squares of gold. "Honestly, I'm afraid she'll pass over Jordan, and I won't be nearby to say good-bye."

"No, it's only *farewell*, Sol. You'll see her again, when God calls ya home." The bishop smiled briefly, then shuffled toward the back porch. They stood there solemnly in the deepening twilight, and Sol offered his handshake to his friend. "You must miss Christian something awful."

Aaron clasped his hand. "Every day." He sighed loudly. "Even worse is goin' into the house and seeing Barbara crying alone, her Bible open in front of her on the table."

Sol's heart went out to both of them. He grabbed Aaron's arm and pulled him into a strong clench, like a father might a wounded boy. " 'The Lord is nigh unto them that are of a broken heart,' " Sol quoted the verse quietly.

"Jah . . . jah." The bishop nodded in agreement. "He surely is that."

"God be with ya, Aaron."

"And with you, Sol."

Just that quickly, they parted ways. Aaron moseyed up the back stoop of his house, and Sol headed toward the path his booted feet had created through the years. It was a single narrow strip of dirt, somewhat akin to a mule lane leading to the fields—his own passage to a kindly friend. Sol had walked it without a lantern on many moonless nights, trusting his feet to find their way, much as the horses followed the groove they'd made in the barnyard leading to the stable and back.

But this particular night, having heard his bishop's heart-rending lament, the old dirt path seemed darker and longer to Sol than ever before.

CHAPTER 22

$\mathcal{N}$ick kept coming to mind as Rose prepared to go to Philadelphia Thursday morning. She felt almost giddy at the thought of traveling to such a big city, taking the gift of comforters and quilts to struggling folk so close to Christmas. But more than that, she secretly hoped to find out something about Nick. Had he fallen prey to the same addiction as his alcoholic mother? If so, how very sad.

When the van pulled into the lane, Rose saw Leah Miller sitting in the second seat, and Rose soon found herself settled in next to Leah, while the Esh sisters and their mother sat behind them in the third seat. Up front, the gentleman driver sat alone, as was typical when it was only womenfolk traveling with a hired driver.

Once they passed through rural Bart and were heading east on Route 30—"leading to the metropolis," as Leah cheerfully referred to Philadelphia—Rose was astonished at how fast they were going. She had never, ever felt like she was flying before. It was one thing to ride with Hen in her car to the Quarryville library and around the back roads, but this . . . this was nearly frightening. She heard the tires whirring against the highway and could just imagine how fast they were spinning.

She watched out the window, amazed at the number of cars speeding past. Mandy and her sister Linda, in the seat behind her, also remarked about the hustle and bustle all around them. "Busier than usual," said Mandy.

"Well, Christmas is near," Rose remarked, and Mandy agreed.

In spite of the rapid pace, the trip seemed to drag on for Rose. Was she simply anxious to see the city where Nick had lived before coming to Salem Road? Many of the neighborhood streets seemed nearly as narrow as Cherry Hill Road, and the redbrick houses were all strung out in a line, exactly the way Nick had once described the row houses. Cars were parked nearly bumper to bumper along the curb, and red-bowed wreaths decorated several of the front doors. An occasional Santa statue sat on the small landings at the top of the stoops.

There were street signs, too many to count, and corner stores advertising beer and cigarettes, men loitering out front.

So this is "the edge" Nick loved. . . .

She recalled something he'd said, years ago—how he was so sure English kids must have exciting lives compared to theirs. *"On the farm, everything's the same boring thing, each and every day,"* he'd said with a faraway look in his eyes.

She'd studied him with great concern; he must've seen the worry registered in her eyes.

"Don't brain me," he'd laughingly said.

But she hadn't found it funny that day, just as she didn't feel settled right now, riding so far past the edge of the imaginary line between Amish farmland and the modern city. Deep into the heart of the place named for "Brotherly Love."

To soothe herself, Rose thought of home—she was glad her father had assented to her leaving for a few hours. Hen and Mammi Sylvia were looking after Mamm, and Dat would be working hard to repair the deacon's old market wagon about now, grateful for the sunshine on a cold day. Bone-chilling as it was, though, Rose knew for certain that she much preferred riding in a horse and buggy to going so awful fast.

You can have your big city, Nick, she thought with a grimace as the van turned into the small parking lot behind the homeless shelter.

～

Never before had Rose seen such grateful recipients. Mrs. Schaeffer, the middle-aged brunette woman in charge of the shelter, smiled warmly and thanked them repeatedly as she exclaimed over the fine handiwork and the bright colors. "There's nothing quite like a handmade Amish quilt," she said. "Is there?"

Leah smiled so broadly, she covered her mouth for a moment, peering at Rose as they stood in the hallway.

"We'll prob'ly come again the end of January or so," Laura Esh told the woman. She explained how the quilters got together every Thursday.

"Really, now? You might be interested to know there's a quilting club just up the street." Mrs. Schaeffer pointed in the direction. "Over there at the old Methodist church. They call themselves the Dorcas Circle." Then she asked if they'd like a tour of the shelter, and Laura shook her head apologetically.

"Unfortunately, we can't stay long. We need to get back home to chores."

"Well, I'd be happy to show you around on another visit, perhaps."

Mandy smiled and nodded, and asked if there was a drinking fountain somewhere, which surprised Rose, knowing how shy Mandy usually was. All the while, Rose kept her eyes open, wondering for the life of her where Laura Esh had seen Nick the last time she was here.

Mrs. Schaeffer directed them to an area where there was not only a water fountain but a soda pop and candy machine, too. "Help yourself to anything—it's our treat," Mrs. Schaeffer said, unlocking the machines to let them choose.

After they'd enjoyed a soda, Rose slipped away to the restroom, down the maze of a hallway. Later, as she was heading back toward the snack room, she realized she was quite lost. Somehow, she'd made a wrong turn.

Trying now to get her bearings, she noticed the back of a tall, slender young man dressed in blue jeans and a faded gray long-sleeve shirt, walking away from her down the long hallway. His stride and the tilt of his dark head made her think of Nick . . . except for the missing ponytail.

But that quick, she remembered his long black hair had been cut off the day of Christian's accident. She assumed that if this was indeed Nick, he was living here because he had nowhere else to go. Considering the circumstances, Rose wasn't sure she ought to even try to get his attention.

Best to leave him be. . . .

Even so, her heart raced as memories of happier days together came rushing back. And because she was so curious, afraid she'd never know for sure, Rose mustered up her nerve. "Nick . . . Nick Franco?" she called.

The young man stopped walking and turned, frowning. But in a second his familiar face broke into a slow smile and his haunting dark eyes brightened. "Rosie? Is that you?"

She stood there in disbelief as he moved quickly toward her, the light from the window shining across his dear face. *Oh, Nick.* "I didn't think I'd ever see you again," Rose said, tears in her voice. Happy as the sight of him made her, she felt downright peculiar, unable to forget the cryptic confession in Nick's burned-up note.

And now, because of me, Christian is dead. . . .

Nick's eyes remained fixed on hers. "What're ya doin' here—so far from home?" he asked.

"We brought Christmas gifts to the shelter, quilts and comforters." Rose couldn't keep her smile in check. "Goodness, ya still sound Amish to me."

He shook his head. "Not sure how that could be."

She looked into his face—this young man who'd caused so much trouble for the bishop and the People as a community.

Nick unexpectedly reached for both her hands and pulled her into a small room. Closing the door, he grinned down at her. "I can't believe you're here, Rosie. I've missed ya so!"

Softly, nearly in a whisper, she replied, "I miss you, too." *More than I dare say.* "I found your note to me in the old tin box, Nick." She raised her eyes to him.

"I had a feeling ya might."

He'd written that very thing in his note. And as badly as she wished to know more about the scuffle between Nick and Christian that fateful day, she would not mention it. Not when this moment was so precious!

Truth was, her heart went out to Nick as they stood together alone in the vacant room. What must it be like to have no place to call home—gone from the safety of the bishop's house and farm. She fought back the lump in her throat.

"I think about you all the time," he said, studying her face.

She was half scared to look at him, so near he was. It wouldn't be right for her to reply the same, but it was true even so.

"I hope you haven't forgotten what I said in the ravine." His eyes searched hers.

She shook her head.

"My Rosie," he said and slipped his arms around her as fervently as he had the night they'd gone riding double on Pepper.

Rose was torn right down the middle of her heart, thinking

of her pledge to Silas Good. Yet why did she feel this happy, even content, in Nick's arms?

They quickly stepped apart and she looked up at him, no longer afraid. She was still overcome with amazement. Finally, she found her voice again. "Nick, are ya stayin' here now?"

He nodded.

"Ach, I'm so sorry."

"No, no, don't be." He explained that he had a room there in exchange for helping with the homeless. "I also have a night job—savin' up money, like I've been for some time. But I spend a lot of time here nearly every day."

She first felt surprise, then a sense of relief as she soaked up this news.

"My way of showing some gratitude," he said.

Not understanding, she shook her head. "What do ya mean?"

"My mother lived here for a while. Mrs. Schaeffer took care of her, till she . . ." He nodded awkwardly. "Helpin' out now is the least I can do."

"Oh, Nick."

He stuffed his hands into his jeans pockets. "I'm awful glad to see you again." He leaned toward her again, so very close.

She was about to say more when she heard Mandy Esh calling to her out in the hall. "Rose Ann, can ya hear me? We best be goin' now."

"I'll be right there," she called back quickly.

Rose looked at Nick, worried now what Mandy might think of her being alone with him. Then, pulling the picture of his parents out of her pocket, she gave it to him. "I found this caught under your mattress when Barbara and I were clearin' out your room. I brought it along today, just in case I saw you." She paused, watching him look at it fondly. "I thought you'd want it."

"Denki." He opened his wallet and placed it inside without explaining.

She wanted to ask why he'd left it behind but dared not press the issue.

"How's my Amish Mamma?" he said. "I miss her sometimes. . . ." His fragile words trailed off.

Rose scarcely knew what to say. Truth was, Barbara cared deeply for Nick, just as Rose did. And she would be heartened, too, to know Nick had asked about her. "Barbara struggles," Rose said warily. "I know she misses you, too."

"Wish I could get word to her somehow." Nick blinked hard and glanced away. "Tell her I'm doin' all right. Will you do that for me?"

Rose nodded. "I'd be happy to." Then she heard Mandy calling louder. "I better go." She reached for the door.

Suddenly Nick clasped her hand. "You won't forget me, will ya, Rosie?"

The vision of Silas Good appeared before her. Oh, he'd be so hurt by all this endearing talk meant for someone other than himself.

Knowing she could not answer Nick without feeling guilty later, Rose turned the doorknob and left the room.

Moving into the hallway, she saw Mandy at the far end with her mother and sister and Leah Miller, their eyes accusing, or so it seemed. It was then Rose realized Nick had brazenly followed her out of the room. They were clearly upset at seeing him.

They must be thinking, what's Rose doing alone with Christian's wicked brother?

Perturbed yet sad, Rose glanced back to say a quick good-bye to Nick, but he was already gone. She guessed he was equally embarrassed, as well as wanting to spare her more distress. Still, her heart pounded in her ears.

"Not a single day goes by that I don't think of you," Nick had said in the ravine the day he'd revealed his love.

She shrugged off the memory, both pleasant and painful. Oh,

the many things she'd wanted to tell him just now! But what she should've said was that he could help the bishop in a wonderful-good way, if he'd just return home and confess to the brethren before the New Year. If only he'd do that to help the dear man who'd raised him!

Feeling panicked now, Rose wished she'd had time to give him that important message. Nick alone had the power to alter the course of their beloved bishop's future ministry. And his life.

Rose felt dejected and more alone than ever as she walked toward Mandy and the others.

CHAPTER 23

*D*uring the ride back, Rose was terribly distracted. She wasn't good company for Leah Miller, who tried repeatedly to strike up a conversation. Rose didn't mean to snub Leah, but she couldn't stop thinking how miserable Nick had looked when she'd first spotted him. As if he carried all the weight of his past, present, and his future—what was left of it—on his shoulders. *Just as he looked that first day at the bishop's so long ago . . .*

But his face *had* changed when he'd turned to see her—lit up nearly like a full moon. Her heart had not ceased to sing for joy at the remembrance, despite the fact that Mandy and her family hadn't made a single comment about his being there—or Rose's impromptu encounter with him. Quiet as they were, she was fairly sure they were miffed that she'd had the gall to talk to someone so looked down upon by the People, yet supposedly forgiven. It was beyond her how confusing all of that was.

To think he's helping at the homeless shelter, Rose thought, still surprised. She wondered if Mamm might not see this as a sign that Nick wasn't a bad seed after all. *If she knew . . .*

An hour or so later, when the van pulled into her lane, Rose was surprised at Leah's request to "stay and visit awhile." Still feeling awkward about seeing Nick—and being caught doing so—Rose reluctantly agreed.

She turned in her seat and asked the Eshes if they, too, would like to come in for something hot to drink. "It would cheer up Mamm." But Laura piped up that they needed to get home to make dinner right quick. Rose assumed they were disgusted with her, and she'd never hear the end of it. *Oh, the grapevine will swing fast now!*

When at last the van pulled away, Leah announced that she wanted to go to Christian's grave but didn't want to go alone. And because the cemetery wasn't far from her father's house, Rose understood why Leah had asked to be dropped off there. It made perfect sense.

"I'll go with ya, sure . . . but I'd like to see Mamm first, if ya don't mind." Rose invited her inside to have some hot cocoa, and as soon as she opened the back door, the delicious aroma of simmering corn chowder and baking biscuits welcomed them. Mammi Sylvia greeted her and Leah, then pushed more wood into the belly of the cookstove.

Rose wanted to make up for being so detached during the ride home from Philly, so she invited Leah to sit at the table and offered her warm carrot cookies to nibble on. Then she scurried off to look in on Mamm. Seeing Hen there and that Mamm was resting, Rose soon returned to the kitchen, where she made hot cocoa for herself and Leah.

Mammi Sylvia seemed happy to see Rose visiting with a friend, and invited Leah to stay for dinner, "perty soon now."

Leah accepted right away but whispered to Rose that she still wanted to go to the cemetery before leaving for home. Rose suggested they go as soon as they'd warmed up a bit, and Leah agreed, her soft brown eyes suddenly sad at the prospect of visiting her deceased beau's grave.

～

The occasional gusts were chilling as Rose and Leah walked down the road toward the old Amish cemetery. Black crows flew low overhead, and from the distance came the howl of a dog. A long strand of Leah's brown hair had come loose on one side, flapping against her black outer bonnet. Rose wondered how her own hair looked now . . . and when Nick had seen her. Had she looked as disheveled as the times they'd gone riding together? The thought gave her a hankering to go and get Pepper from the bishop's stable and take him out riding, maybe tonight. A gallop in the brisk air might help set her straight—brush the cobwebs of Nick Franco out of her head.

Rose breathed deeply, glad she'd worn layers beneath her woolen shawl, just as Leah had, having borrowed an extra sweater from the wooden kitchen pegs.

As they went, Leah began to talk about Christian, recalling him so fondly Rose tried not to cry. "Was it hard for you, seein' Nick today?" Rose asked somewhat tentatively as they skirted the shoulder of the road.

"Oh, something awful." Leah's breath hung in the frigid air. She looked askance at Rose. "Let me be plainspoken with you: Nick just isn't for you, Rose—but surely ya know that."

Rose was astonished. So was this why Leah had asked her to go to the cemetery—to speak her mind?

"The People are concerned, after what happened to Christian and all. 'Tween me and you, surely you won't be takin' up with him again. 'Specially now that he's looking so awful fancy."

Rose spouted before thinking, "Philly's a long way from here, ain't so?"

"But I'm worried, Rose." Leah looked at her skeptically and

shook her head as the black strings on her candlesnuffer bonnet blew over her shoulders. "I saw how happy Nick was to see ya. And you looked mighty pleased, too."

Rose couldn't deny that. But for Leah to try to lessen the memory of that for her made Rose feel even more defensive.

"There's more," said Leah. "I don't mean to alarm you or worry you, though."

Rose clenched her toes in her shoes. "May as well tell me everything," she said, resigned to whatever might come.

"Christian knew something about Nick that would keep him from ever joining church," Leah said.

Rose's interest was sparked, given that Christian had been so anxious to talk to her that one afternoon . . . and then died before she had the chance to hear what was on his mind. Had he shared *that* with Leah?

"It was the reason they went riding that terrible day . . . so Christian could try 'n' get Nick to give up his plan."

Rose cringed. "What plan?"

"Nick was getting his GED on the sly."

Rose was stunned. "Was Christian sure?"

"Oh, absolutely. He thought you should know, since higher education would seal Nick's fate—as being outside the Amish community, I mean."

Rose felt sad and didn't know what to say.

"Would you have continued your friendship with him if you'd known?"

"What're you askin'?"

Leah looked chagrined. "I mean, would you have been so happy to see him today, for instance?"

"If I'd known he was working toward something considered worldly?"

Leah nodded. "Precisely."

Rose couldn't answer that. She'd never held high hopes for Nick's becoming a baptized church member, come to think of it. Secretly, though, she'd wished he might . . . but that was long ago.

Leah continued as they turned into the path leading to the cemetery. "Christian really wanted you to know. I guess he thought Nick was sweet on ya."

Rose felt strange knowing the pair had talked about her. She told Leah she'd encountered Christian on the road, "a day before he died." She paused a moment. "It was peculiar, really. He was running alongside my horse and buggy. But I was so busy to get home, I disregarded his request to stop and talk. I've been kickin' myself ever since."

"That was prob'ly it, then. Christian said it weighed heavy on his mind . . . that it just wasn't right for you not to know."

Rose sighed. "Well, did Christian ever tell you flat-out what he thought about Nick's and my friendship?"

"Only that he thought you must be the dearest girl."

Rose didn't understand.

"To put up with the likes of Nick," added Leah.

Rose wouldn't say what she was thinking. The fact was, if folk had given Nick a chance—given him the time of day—they would've known how gentle he really was. Had she and Barbara been the only ones to see that?

Nick had good traits—so once had Christian. She walked with Leah solemnly through the rows of small white tombstones, all alike. Leah's forthright remarks made it seem as though Christian had somehow spoken a warning from the grave.

She stood next to Leah as they stared down at the still-fresh plot where the bishop's son's hand-built coffin had been lowered and buried weeks ago. Christian may have fought for pecking-order rights with Nick those many years, but he'd always been kind to Rose.

He cared enough to try to tell me of Nick's worldly ambitions.

Rose felt awful about ignoring Christian's plea to talk to her that day. She also considered what she knew now of Nick. Drawing a deep breath, she felt as though something precious was dying in her . . . and she was helpless to revive it.

～

After supper that evening, Dat remained seated at the head of the table while Rose washed and dried the dishes. It was a rare occasion when her father stayed put following a meal. Usually he headed right back out to the barn or his woodshop for a couple hours before time for devotions. "Is something on your mind?" She glanced over her shoulder and stacked the clean plates into the cupboard.

"I have a confession to make." He shifted in his chair and turned to look at her. His cheeks were flushed from the warmth of the cookstove. "I'm very concerned that you make a wise choice in marriage."

Rose couldn't help but wonder if Hen's marital troubles were plaguing his mind. How could they not be?

She stopped drying the handful of utensils, unsure what to expect.

"I hardly know how to tell ya, Rosie. But I feel you should know."

"Know what, Dat?"

She recalled his stern warning about staying away from the likes of the bishop's foster son. Had he heard of her encounter with Nick? But how could that be? It was just this morning.

"Reuben Good told me some time ago he'd move heaven and earth to have Silas stay in the area to find a wife." Dat drew a long breath.

"He told ya that?" Rose let out a sigh. Nick was *not* the topic. Yet what was this talk of Silas? It was hard to believe, but because Dat and Reuben were good friends, this shouldn't come as too big a surprise.

Dat seemed reluctant to go on. "He told me he was beginning to worry . . . downright discouraged at the thought of Silas thinkin' about an out-of-state girl."

Silas's father knew about his interest in Rebekah? Rose was flabbergasted.

"So once your grandfather recovered from his stroke, Reuben and I talked about how Silas and you would make a fine match." He paused. "Not that we were forcing the issue . . . seein' as how a young man's choice in a bride is a personal thing." He smiled briefly. "Still, I encouraged Reuben to have Silas seek you out once again. Evidently he knew his son had been seeing you some earlier in the year."

So does Silas care for two of us? Rose was bewildered.

"Reuben decided to turn the farm over to Silas sooner than planned if he married a local girl."

This revelation shocked her—she wished Dat hadn't told her. But then, contemplating it further, she realized she'd much rather know. Wouldn't she?

Rose couldn't utter a word. *Silas didn't have the courage to tell me everything. But then again, why would he fess up to this?*

She shook her head. Since when did a man steer his son in the direction of a wife—even dangle the carrot of a lucrative dairy farm to influence his choice?

Dat continued. "I'm sure Silas cares for ya. He wouldn't be courting you if he didn't."

Rose was beginning to understand how her sister could say she doubted she'd ever feel all right again. At last, Rose knew the whole truth about why she, and not Rebekah, was Silas's intended.

Her hands trembled as she finished drying the rest of the utensils and, lastly, the pots and pans. Her mind was in a whirl at her father's startling words. *Does his father's farm mean everything to Silas? Or does he truly care for me?*

CHAPTER 24

For old time's sake, Rose waited till after nightfall before she slipped over to the bishop's stable. She quietly freed Pepper, offering him a sugar cube, then led him down the lane and out to Salem Road, recalling the summer wind in her hair and the sound of the horse's hooves on the pavement.

They trotted past the little Amish schoolhouse and the cemetery before heading over to the next road, cautiously staying on the far right shoulder, in case cars should come their way.

Rose Ann rode for all the past memories of Nick, still much too raw . . . yet dear. Glad as she was to know he was helping at the shelter, in light of the news Leah had told of his hankering for a GED, Rose was beginning to think she'd been rather mistaken about Nick. It seemed he'd always planned to leave the People—with or without her.

And, too, she struggled with a rising concern about Silas and the genuineness of his affections. She urged Pepper even faster, galloping the horse. Had her beau honestly needed a nudge from his father to court her? It felt as if Reuben had bribed his son to keep him from pursuing Rebekah.

Would I be engaged to Silas now if it weren't for Reuben Good?

"What part did love play in any of this?" she muttered aloud. She talked out her sadness and fears to the wind . . . and to Pepper. It was impossible to think she hadn't known Nick as well as she thought. Nor did she seem to know her own fiancé very well.

To think Silas could be manipulated in such a way!

Sorrowfully, Rose called out to the black night sky, wishing for all the world Nick's knowing eyes weren't still before her, probing her face . . . her broken heart. Had he looked into her soul today, sensing her desire to linger and talk? Did he suspect how much she'd resented Mandy Esh's calling her away?

All that aside, I'm engaged to Silas.

With the day's encounter burning in her mind, Rose took Nick's horse deep into the night, riding him as fast as Nick ever had, pondering and praying as she went.

∾

Hen felt forlorn on Friday and considered canceling her free consultation with the Lancaster attorney. She'd picked the name at random from the Yellow Pages based on the headline: *Divorce and Family Law—know your rights, protect your children.*

There was only one reason she would emerge from her comfort zone and drive to town, despite her father's furrowed brow— assuming he guessed where she was going- -to talk to a stranger about her failing marriage. It was all for Mattie Sue, to preserve her innocence and Hen's desperate hope of continuing Mattie's Plain upbringing. For no other reason would she cause Brandon further strife. Nor herself . . .

Hadn't he himself suggested she get a lawyer? Anymore, though, she had no idea what he truly thought. Or felt. His coming to take

Mattie Sue away last Saturday was completely out of character—he must be fraught with stress. In spite of her annoyance, her heart went out to him. After all, wouldn't she do the same in his place?

Hen felt terribly conflicted as she parked in front of the law offices of Clark and Whitney and Associates. With a prayerful plea for wisdom, she got out of the car and trudged up the steps.

I must not lose heart!

~

Sol was troubled as his daughter revealed having seen Nick Franco in Philly, even talked to him. "You don't mean it. Why'd he go there?" he asked.

Rose frowned, her eyes serious as she stood near the sawhorse in his shop. "I didn't mean to upset ya. I thought you might tell the bishop so he'll know where to search for Nick."

"Search?"

She nodded earnestly. "So Bishop Aaron can defend his ordination."

Sol shouldn't have been surprised at what he saw clearly on Rose's innocent face. *She still cares for Nick more than she ought. . . .*

"It was Providence that led me to Nick yesterday—to save the bishop's ministry here." She went on to add that just maybe Nick's heart was softening toward God. "He's helping others, Dat . . . he really is."

She looked so sincere, he believed she meant precisely that. But beneath it all was a tenderness he sensed as Rose spoke of the man deemed responsible for Christian's death. Perhaps she thought Nick could be talked into returning and making his lifelong vow to the church. Was that what Rose mistakenly hoped for?

"Well, this is something to think about," he said, running his fingers through his beard.

"Will ya tell the bishop where Nick is, then?"

"I'll do ya one better: I'll offer to go with him to Philly."

Rose's face beamed. "You'd do that?" She reached for him, her face wet with tears.

"Rosie . . . dear girl, are ya weeping for the bishop . . . or for Nick?"

She stepped back and wiped her eyes with a hankie. "Ach, I don't know what got into me, Dat. I really don't." With that, Rose turned and slipped through the woodshop door, leaving Sol to wonder many things.

~

The lobby of the attorney's office was spectacular, more posh than any entrance Hen had ever seen. An area rug in a taupe and maroon design lay beneath an enormous coffee table—a shellacked piece of wood sliced right down the middle, its knots and lines plainly visible. The ecru-colored leather couch was so comfortable, she felt nearly embraced while waiting for her appointment, still wearing her woolen shawl and outer bonnet.

I can't believe I'm here. . . .

A young woman about her age sat across the lovely space with a man who looked old enough to be her father. Hen could hear them discussing the woman's pending divorce and the worries she had about dividing custody of her two young children between two households. "Little Kimmie's going to be so confused by this," the woman was saying, her lower lip trembling, "if that's what it comes to."

Hen tried not to eavesdrop, but she couldn't help hearing the woman go on now about a beloved dog, Hamlet, worrying aloud that her husband might try to take the pet away, as well as her children. Hen felt so sorry for the woman. And for herself, too, the more she sat there and thought about what she was about to do.

"Marriage isn't to be entered into lightly . . . or in haste," her sister-in-law Suzy had warned before Hen ran off with Brandon years ago.

How true that is, she thought, removing her bonnet and shawl.

After paging through a magazine for the longest time, Hen was called to meet the attorney. "I'm Ms. Whitney," the lawyer introduced herself with a professional smile as Hen entered her office. Hen was struck by the many silver-framed certificates nearly covering one whole wall. *She's well educated.*

Hen wondered where *she* would be today if she'd taken more than a handful of classes at the local community college. *Who would she be? Only a mother?* But the thought triggered something in her, and she knew she loved the role of full-time motherhood. For her, it was the highest calling, and the very motive behind her coming here today.

"How can I help you, Mrs. Orringer?" the attorney asked while shaking her hand warmly.

"Please, call me Hen." She glanced down self-consciously at her Plain dress and black apron. "As you can see, I'm Amish." She quickly explained how she'd abruptly left home to marry a man who was "anything but Plain." She paused a moment to collect herself, terribly uncomfortable. "Brandon and I have a child together—a beautiful little girl. Mattie Sue is only four . . . and has no idea which end's up."

For a moment, Hen could not speak, she so feared losing control of her emotions.

"And you and your husband are separated, is that correct?"

Hen had mentioned this when she'd called for the appointment from the phone shanty on Monday. "That's right. And he wants to move ahead with a divorce, as well as seek full custody of our daughter." She sighed. "He wants to take Mattie Sue from me . . . as far away as he can get her from the Amish."

"Has he filed divorce papers, do you know?"

"I don't think so. But he's threatened to if I don't return home immediately." Hen looked away, toward the window. Never in her life did she think she'd be divulging such personal things to an outsider. "He urged me to get a lawyer."

"Well, Hen, first let me tell you that, in this state, sole physical custody—or primary custody—is hardly ever awarded. What is more common here in Pennsylvania is something called partial or shared physical custody, or in some cases court-ordered visitation."

"What are my chances of getting primary custody of Mattie Sue?" Her breath gave out on her and she could scarcely utter the last words.

"Are you in touch with your husband at all?"

"Somewhat." Yet she hardly thought that was the right description of their current relationship. "He's opposed to me raising Mattie Sue Amish."

"But that's what you intend."

Hen nodded.

The attorney went on to explain that it wasn't up to Brandon to decide those things. "Remember, the two of you are Mattie Sue's parents. Neither of you can arbitrarily choose her custodial arrangements. You must come to a joint agreement."

Hen felt deeply anxious. "But that's just it—we don't agree on how she should be raised, where she should live, or who should raise her. Not at all."

"Have you seen a counselor? Someone to run interference, perhaps?" Ms. Whitney smiled briefly. "You understand what I mean."

"We can't even agree on which counselor to go to. Brandon refuses to go with me to the bishop for counsel."

"And you? Would you go to a counselor of *his* choosing?"

She felt mortified. "I believe I'd go to a Christian counselor."

They talked further, and the attorney gave her printed information about her rights as a parent, what legally ending a marriage entailed, and the drawbacks of representing herself in a *pro se* divorce. Hen learned that self-representation could drag out a case for months, even up to a year, causing tremendous aggravation and difficulty to everyone involved—Mattie Sue in particular. Ms. Whitney also cautioned that the court would not permit Hen to skip over any procedure prior to the court hearing.

"Having independent counsel—in short, a professional legal advisor, such as myself—is the very best way to navigate a divorce. It is highly recommended, especially when there are child custody issues."

Hen felt overwhelmed, unable to process all that she was taking in.

"Would you like me to represent you, Hen?" the attorney asked, her brown eyes seemingly intent on closing the deal.

Hen's heart pounded as she glanced at the papers on her lap. "I'm an Amishwoman, Ms. Whitney. All of this goes against the grain . . . in every way imaginable."

"I understand there are differences between you and your husband in many respects. Religion being paramount."

Why isn't it this hard to get married? Hen recalled how simple it had been to get a marriage license and run off to a justice of the peace. The process had been so swift, the memory of it made her dizzy.

"I need time to decide what to do, Ms. Whitney."

The attorney rose from behind her desk and came to shake hands as Hen got up from her chair. "I'm happy to give you the legal help you will need, and I'll do my best to see to it that Mattie Sue's best interests are taken into consideration by the court."

"Can you win primary custody for me?"

"I'd see to it."

Hen thanked her and said she'd call to make another appointment if she decided to retain her.

"I wish you all the best, Hen."

She nodded her awkward thanks and made her way to the hallway, noticing the young woman who'd come with the older man wiping her eyes with a tissue as she leaned on the man's arm. *I have no one to encourage me in this,* thought Hen as she opened the main door and made her way alone to the car.

She worried that if she lost custody of Mattie Sue to Brandon, it would be deserved . . . God allowing Hen to be punished for marrying outside the faith. She'd been taught that good things came to those who made wise choices—to those who followed God's ways. And did His bidding.

On the drive back through Quarryville, Hen felt perplexed and torn. Why had she disregarded Dad's wishes and gone to see the attorney? And what about the bishop—would he also be displeased when he found out? Surely he'd know soon enough . . . the grapevine had a way of uncovering everything.

Ms. Whitney's legal instruction buzzed in her brain till Hen felt nearly ill. And once she'd pulled into the secluded parking place behind the barn and released the key from the ignition, she leaned her head on the steering wheel. She'd known what to do and rejected it. *Therefore to him that knoweth to do good, and doeth it not, to him it is sin,* Scripture warned.

Opening the car door, she breathed in the bitter cold and pulled her dark shawl close around her. She saw Mattie Sue playing with one of the barn kitties on the back stoop, all bundled up in mittens, an outer bonnet, and one of Hen's old black coats.

She pasted on a smile and waved to her daughter as she walked toward the Dawdi Haus, more confused than ever before.

What if I just took Mattie Sue and left?

CHAPTER 25

With the end of the year fast closing in, Sol wouldn't dawdle about proposing to hire a driver to take him and the bishop to Philly. There was no time to waste now that he knew where to catch up with Nick Franco.

Sol still pondered Rose's running into Nick while dropping off the quilts the women had made. He'd been all too aware of the real spark of interest in Rose's eyes as she talked about having seen Nick at the homeless shelter.

He'd also seen Hen drive off in her car earlier this morning and suspected she was going to town to consult a lawyer. Both of his daughters so ferhoodled! Only the dear Lord knew the end from the beginning.

He feared the next few days would be difficult, but he had learned years ago not to anticipate trouble. *Live like the ordinary sparrows, dependent upon the heavenly Father's care. How much more does He care for me?* Solomon thought. *And my dear family . . .*

∼

The next day was Saturday, a day Solomon typically worked extra hard, knowing the Lord's Day was to be kept holy, a quieter yet cheerful day. Today, however, found Sol and the bishop, who remained reluctant to confront Nick, up early and leaving for Philadelphia. Though still dejected, Emma seemed a bit stronger again physically, and Sylvia had offered to look after her, so Sol felt comfortable going for only a few hours.

The day was bright with sun but bitter cold, and Bishop Aaron remarked how there hadn't been a speck of snow yet this month. The bare maples and oaks were dark silhouettes against the brown pastureland just outside Bart. The horses stood in each other's shadows, and Sol imagined what those same fields had looked like blanketed in snow last winter at this time.

Soon the van was entering the ramp and merging onto the highway leading to Philly. He assumed it was the same route Rose and her women friends had taken recently. The traffic was horrific and made Sol yearn for the quiet of the countryside. *First things first*, he thought, talking in Pennsylvania Dutch to his neighbor and friend, who was quite restless, fidgeting with his hands. Even his feet were going. "We'll just see Nick for a few minutes, and let things unfold from there," Sol advised.

"In case you've forgotten, Nick won't want to be cornered about anything," Bishop replied.

"No, but he might find comfort in knowin' you're eager to see him . . . considering everything." Sol hoped that would be true.

At last, they located the shelter and found the director, Mrs. Schaeffer, who greeted them warmly. "It's a delight to have you here today. Some lovely Amishwomen from your area recently brought the prettiest quilts I've ever seen." Sol mentioned his daughter had been with them, careful not to sound boastful, considering the way Mrs. Schaeffer was so effusive about the wonderful handiwork.

After she offered them some soda pop, Sol inquired after Nick Franco.

The woman's eyes brightened. "Oh, Nick . . . he's no longer here, but he's been one of my best volunteers, more than ready to help wherever he could. And all for the sake of people who've lost everything, wandering the streets without knowing where their next meal might come from," Mrs. Schaeffer explained. "Our Nick has a real heart for the needy."

Our Nick . . .

Though Rose had mentioned a little of this to him, Sol was astonished at this picture of a young man so unlike the one they'd known. But when Mrs. Schaeffer went on to say that Nick had talked of possibly enrolling in a community college somewhere, the bishop's face immediately fell.

They thanked the woman kindly and made their way outside to hail the driver and to head home. On the ride back, the two men talked quietly, lest the driver overhear their concerns.

Sol tried to soften the blow of a college-bound Nick by pointing out that perhaps some of the important things Aaron had taught Nick had, in fact, stuck. "Though as far as helpin' at the shelter goes, who knows what Nick was really thinking," Sol said as an afterthought. "It might've seemed like penance for whatever went on with Christian, ya know."

Slowly, the bishop nodded. "I wondered that, too."

"Emma's said in the past that Barbara thought Nick had a soft spot for children and older folk. Maybe he also had a caring side toward those less fortunate."

"Could be," said Aaron, clearly deep in thought.

The closer they got to Salem Road, the more Sol presumed the chances of getting Nick to return home and join the church were slim to nothing—not if he was bent on enrolling in college, as Mrs. Schaeffer had said. No, once an Amishman got a taste of higher education, it was pretty much over as far as ever again getting his attention for God and the church.

～

Hen felt compelled to get the afternoon mail before Rose did. Intending to take Mamm's circle letters to her, as those usually arrived on Saturday, Hen was shocked to see a letter with Brandon's return address on the envelope.

Not waiting until she was inside, she opened it quickly.

Dear Hannah,

I've finished up the paperwork to get our divorce and the custody complaint under way. Unless you've acquired your own lawyer, you will be expected to come to my brother Lawrence's office to fill out financial information and meet with the psychologist next Friday, December 20. Dr. Greta Schmidt has been assigned to evaluate both of us, beginning with you. She will also assess Mattie Sue to determine the best custodial arrangement for our daughter, since this has become an obvious and irresolvable conflict.

Sincerely,
Brandon

Dismayed, Hen stumbled back to the Dawdi Haus, putting off delivering the two circle letters for Mamm until she could pull herself together.

So Brandon had meant what he said, moving ahead just as he'd threatened and asking his brother Lawrence to handle the legal matters. And even though she had guessed at what he would do, the reality didn't hurt any less.

Indoors, she kissed Mattie Sue's sweet head, and commented on the pretty coloring page of butterflies she was filling in at the kitchen table. Her daughter's toy puppy, Foofie, sat next to the box of crayons. "I can't wait to see your picture when you're all done, honey."

"Do ya like it, Mommy?"

"Very much."

Mattie Sue looked up at her. "I'll color another page for Daddy, too. Okay?"

"That's very nice of you." Her tongue felt frozen, but she managed to say she was going upstairs for a little while.

Lost in her art, Mattie Sue nodded and continued coloring.

In her room, Hen tried to read the letter again, struggling to see the words for her tears.

Custody complaint?

The words pointed fingers, accusing her of being an unfit mother. Perhaps that was precisely what Brandon was hoping to prove. But how? He knew that she was anything but unloving or unfit. Just because she embraced a simple lifestyle, did that make her incapable in his eyes? Did he really think he could rip Mattie Sue away from her because she wanted to live a Plain and peaceful life, one pleasing to God?

"Will the powers that be rule in Brandon's favor?" Hen carried the letter to her dresser and slipped it into the drawer as fear took hold of her. "Next Friday . . . just five days before Christmas," she whispered. "What would happen if I just didn't show up?"

～

Before Rose served the supper of pork chops and scalloped potatoes that evening, Dat came in to wash his hands at the sink, looking repeatedly at her. *Something's on his mind*, she thought. Moving away from the table, where she had been setting out the utensils, she went to the kitchen counter. Was it about Nick?

She had seen Dat and the bishop get into a van together early this morning. They had been away for several hours, so she couldn't help but wonder if they'd gone to Philly.

Dat turned his attention back to lathering his hands, and when he said nothing at all, Rose awkwardly resumed her work preparing for supper. Leah's words spun round in her head, but she dismissed them, knowing she dared not ask Dat about that.

All through the meal, it seemed peculiar how her father occasionally looked her way but said nothing. Apparently he was thinking about something important.

Did the bishop talk Nick into returning? Rose wondered, worried and hopeful both.

∼

That night, in the wee hours, Rose was awakened by the sound of sniffling. When she opened her eyes, she saw Beth kneeling beside the bed, praying. Rose groggily got up and went around the bed to Beth, whose short hair fell forward in the darkness of the room, hiding her face. "Beth, honey . . . what is it?" Rose knelt next to her. "Are you thinking 'bout your grandpa?"

Beth shook her head, then sighed softly. "I had another dream," she said between breaths. "Oh, Rosie, it was so real . . . like I was right there. I could see everything so clearly."

"Do you want to tell me about it?"

"Not just yet."

"Did you dream about someone we both know?"

Beth nodded. "Your mother." She paused. "But I want to write down everything I remember in my notebook."

"Tomorrow?"

Beth agreed. "You can read it if you want."

Concerned as she felt, Rose did not press further, uncertain how Beth might react. Still, she couldn't help but recall what Beth had once told her—that sometimes her dreams about people dying came true.

Rose put her arm around Beth as they prayed silently together. She comforted the young woman and wished for someone to comfort *her* in that moment. Beth's slender shoulders moved with her quiet whimpers, and it touched Rose deeply that she cared so much for Mamm. She'd never witnessed such a close connection in someone who wasn't kin.

After a time, she helped Beth back to bed. When Beth was settled again, Rose crept downstairs and stood at the back door, gazing out at the sky, alight with stars. There, she whispered the question that now weighed so heavily on her heart: "O Lord, are you preparing us for Mamm's heavenly Homegoing . . . at Christmas?"

CHAPTER 26

The first snowfall of the season came like fine white dust that Lord's Day morning, drifting drowsily from a gray sky. There was not the slightest hint of wind, and Rose felt almost as if she were floating upward from her vantage point at the bedroom window. The strange sensation lasted but a moment, just until she looked away to regain her equilibrium.

Rose had awakened to muffled crying as it seeped through the wall from the attached Dawdi Haus. At first, the sound startled her, because she'd thought she was dreaming, but sadly, she was not. Hen had been sobbing her heart out, and Rose could only assume what might be causing her dear sister such heartache. *Must be Brandon. What else could it be?*

As it turned out, Hen didn't come over for breakfast before Preaching service, nor did she stop in to see Mamm after Hen and the family returned, following the common meal. Rose spent the entire afternoon reading aloud from the New Testament while her mother flitted back and forth between sleep and wakefulness.

Dat had spent an hour away from Mamm, over at the bishop's

house talking with Deacon Esh and the two preachers from their church district. Rose had seen the men arrive, their driving horses familiar to her. Because of the sudden meeting, she prayed that whatever was happening there might above all benefit their wonderful-good bishop.

Before it was time to prepare a light supper, Mammi Sylvia and Dawdi Jeremiah came over to sit with Mamm. Mattie Sue wandered over from next door, too, asking for Beth, who was still upstairs resting.

"Is she sick?" her niece asked.

"No, honey . . . just napping." Rose didn't explain that Beth had been awake for a while in the night due to a vivid dream.

"Can I see if she's up yet?" Mattie Sue persisted.

"She'll be down soon, I'm sure."

Mattie Sue turned and went into the kitchen, and Rose followed her. She wanted to make some paper chains, so Rose found some construction paper Mamm always kept on hand in a cupboard for the grandchildren's visits.

"I think Mommy's sick," Mattie Sue said quietly, not looking at Rose. "She cries a lot."

"Aw, honey . . ." Rose went and sat on the long bench beside her at the table.

"She misses Daddy. I know she does." Mattie leaned her head against Rose's arm. "And I do, too."

"Of course ya do." Rose patted Mattie's head and hugged her. Then she went to the drawer where Mamm kept some blunt-edged scissors. "Do you want to cut the paper strips for your chain?"

Mattie nodded and began to cut as Rose set out the makings for a simple cold supper. From time to time, her niece looked up to watch the snow coming down, faster now, in much heavier flakes, nearly weighty enough to make a sound when they landed on the roof. "Can bein' sad make you feel sick, Aendi Rosie?" asked Mattie Sue, dispelling the silence.

Rose pondered that as she put down a plate of cheese slices and a bowl of a sandwich spread consisting of minced green tomatoes, peppers, celery, and onions, mixed with mayonnaise and a little mustard. Dat especially liked this quick way to make a sandwich or two, especially on Sunday evenings. "I s'pose if a person cried a lot, they could get a tummy ache. Is that what ya mean, Mattie?"

"No. Mommy's so awful sad she can't sleep at night."

Rose worried that Hen's sobbing had perhaps awakened Mattie.

"I pray for her . . . don't you?"

Rose said she did. "Every morning and night, and plenty of times in between."

"Do you pray for Daddy, too?"

Rose couldn't say that she had lately. "Your mommy prays for him, though, doesn't she?"

"Sometimes." Mattie's eyes were serious. "I hear her after she tucks me in bed. She doesn't know it, but I pray for Daddy then, too . . . in my bed, while I hold Foofie."

Rose smiled. "God hears you when you pray, sweetie. I know that for sure."

Later, when Beth came downstairs, her eyes looked bright, compared to how droopy she'd looked in church. Rose had noticed Beth dozing off during the sermons, her head bobbing repeatedly. She didn't dare ask if she'd written about her dream yet, because she didn't want to bring it up in front of Mattie Sue. Her poor niece didn't need anything more on her mind.

Rose hadn't stopped thinking about it, though. She hoped to look at Beth's notebook later tonight, after returning from the Singing—and her buggy ride with Silas. The thought of *that* did not bring the usual joy.

What if I just stayed home tonight? Would Silas even notice?

∾

It was Dat who insisted on taking Rose to Singing and dropping her off. On the short ride over to the barn gathering, Dat mentioned that Nick Franco no longer lived at the homeless shelter, where she'd seen him.

She couldn't help but frown.

Dat sat tall at the reins. But he didn't offer an explanation, which surprised her.

She also wondered what it meant that Nick had left the shelter. "Do ya think he'll come home, maybe?"

"That's unlikely now."

She had to agree, what with Nick's past behavior. He was like a crow feather fluttering in the wind. Here . . . then gone. "I'm sorry ya went all that way for nothin'."

"Ain't your fault, Rosie. How could you know?"

"He must've gotten jumpy about seein' all of us there, maybe."

"No, I don't think that had anything to do with it." Dat ran his fingers over his lips. "He's headin' for higher education, Rose Ann. I hate to tell ya."

"What?" Hearing this made her feel off-kilter . . . and unsettled in the stomach. Mattie Sue's remark rang in her head: *"Can bein' sad make you feel sick?"* And yet Rose wondered at this news. Hadn't Leah said he was pursuing his GED even before leaving for Philly? Maybe this had been a part of his plan. *All along.*

Rose stared at the golden spots of distant light coming from the large bank barn where the Singing was to take place. Once, years before, she had felt flickers of excitement as she arrived, wondering just who might invite her to ride home after the gathering. And more recently—since September—an even stronger quiver after Silas Good's letter had come inviting her to go with *him.*

Tonight, however, she almost dreaded going. She thanked Dat for bringing her and even had a momentary urge to lean over and kiss his cheek—something she rarely did—because he seemed so downtrodden. And she somehow felt his sullenness was *her* doing, since she'd told of seeing Nick.

If only I hadn't breathed a word.

"Have yourself a nice time, Rose."

"Denki," she replied as she got down from the carriage. Beth's recent dream came unexpectedly to mind then, but she hadn't had the heart to bring it up to Dat during the ride here, or before now. Even so, the dear Lord surely had her mother, and all of them—including poor, sad Hen and missing Nick—in the palm of His loving hand. Nothing was going to happen to any of them that was a surprise to their heavenly Father.

~

Rose was hardly in the mood to sing the "fast" songs typical of their barn gatherings, but she sang anyway. Her heart wasn't in mingling with the other courting-age young folk between songs, either, but she put on a pleasant face and mingled anyway.

Usually, Silas didn't sit across from her at the long table, nor did he tonight. Instead, she ended up across from Cousin Melvin Kauffman's younger brother Noah, who'd just turned sixteen and seemed exceptionally pleased to be present for his first ever Singing. Rose waved casually at Leah Miller, who'd just started coming again, no matter that she must still struggle with mourning Christian.

Yet even though Silas sat down the table from her a ways, Rose was very much aware of him. They traded furtive glances, Silas's expression questioning, as if he'd noticed her somber mood. Thankfully Rebekah was nowhere to be seen, and Rose started to feel more relaxed. With the twins to care for, most likely Rebekah would not be coming to the youth gatherings for many weeks, if not months.

Later, when the fast songs were finished, the fellows started to blend with the girls. Silas caught Rose's eye and gave her a warm smile. She nodded and even smiled back, hoping the night might end up better than she'd anticipated. Who was to say that Silas didn't love her?

Just then, the big barn door slid open and in walked Rebekah Bontrager. She appeared shy at first, glancing about as if she wasn't sure of herself. Then, spotting Rose with several of her girl cousins, Rebekah waved. One of the cousins invited her over warmly, and Rebekah greeted them all, looking somewhat relieved.

The merry buzz of fellows talking with their prospective dates filled the bank barn, punctuated by the occasional bellow of a cow in the lower level. Some of the young men had briefly opened the outside door in the haymow, as well as the main door, bringing in some nice, cold fresh air.

Rose was aware of Silas's gaze in her direction as she and her Kauffman cousins talked with Rebekah. Returning his smile, Rose waved discreetly back to him. Then, just as Silas seemed about to make his move toward her, the cousins disbanded, leaving Rose alone with Rebekah.

Reaching for Rose's hands, Rebekah said, "Silas says the two of you are planning to tie the knot next year." She kept her voice low.

"That's right." Rose looked around for Silas, but he must've stepped outside. "You'll keep it to yourself, jah?"

"I promised I would." Rebekah regarded her, then smiled ever so broadly. "There's no one quite like Silas Good, I should say. You surely are fortunate."

Rose suddenly felt uncomfortable. It was almost as if Rebekah was hinting at her own affection for him. *She must've dated lots of young men. But how odd to compare them to Silas to my face . . . if that's what she's doing.*

Quickly, Rose changed the subject. "How're Annie's baby twins?"

Rebekah ran her hand across her forehead. "They're precious. I can hardly wait to have children of my own someday."

Rose fully understood the yearning for young ones. "Who's helpin' Annie tonight?" It may have sounded tactless, but she was very curious to know how Rebekah had managed to come to the Singing.

"Oh, it was her idea to shoo me out the door. I would've gladly stayed with the babies. After all, that's why I'm here in Lancaster."

Is it, now? Rose thought sarcastically. Almost immediately, she chided herself, feeling bad that she'd thought less of Rebekah, if only for a second. "What did they end up naming the twins?"

"Mary and Anna. That way, when they're called in from play, it'll sound like one name: Maryanna."

"Oh, I like that."

"Me too." All of a sudden, Rebekah's face lit up. And just that quickly, she blushed pink.

Rose couldn't help but notice Silas looking their way again. Was he the one having such an effect on Rebekah?

"Well, I'd best be talkin' with some of the others," Rebekah said, nearly out of breath.

Rose didn't dare look back over her shoulder again; she would let Silas seek her out as he always did. Feeling out of sorts over Rebekah's comments and behavior, she went to find her woolen shawl and stepped outside into the cold night, glad she'd worn her sturdy black leather shoes.

The air was crisp and smelled like more snow soon to come. Dat had always said there was something sweet about the atmosphere prior to a big snowstorm. Thus far this evening, they'd gotten only a skiff of the white stuff.

She noticed Cousins Melvin and Noah walking with two girls, but she couldn't make out who they were. It was nice to see two brothers double-date in the older one's courting buggy, especially on a wintry night. She smiled fleetingly, then felt sad, thinking of Nick and Christian.

*Never close enough to double-date . . . and always so opposed to
each other.*

After a few minutes, she headed back inside the barn to get
warm. In just the short time Rose was gone, Rebekah had managed to find Silas, or the other way around. The two of them were
talking and laughing in a circle over in the corner with three
young men.

Rose stood there quietly observing, feeling quite left out . . .
puzzled. Silas was caught up in conversation with Rebekah nearly
to the exclusion of the others, and the more Rose watched him,
the more she realized he must be oblivious to Rebekah's apparent
interest in him, or he would be more guarded.

Rose moved about the barn, hoping she might somehow attract
his attention. But to no avail.

Eventually, she became frustrated—and hurt—at her inability
to catch her own fiancé's eye. A thought struck her: Was this the
way Silas had felt about her friendship with Nick? Oh, she hoped
not! Perplexed, she turned quietly and headed for the barn door
again. This time, though, she took off walking toward home without
waiting for Silas to finish talking with Rebekah, who'd said quite
distinctly that she knew why she'd come back to Lancaster.

The wintry scent that hung in the air earlier answered its promise with a cloudburst of white. The snow fell fast around Rose as she
hurried home, thick flakes multiplying as she pressed on, thankful
for no wind. Rose came upon the Amish cemetery, its rows of white
markers rectangular mounds of snow against the night.

It was then she heard the gut-wrenching sound of a man weeping—heard it before she saw the dark figure hunched over a single
gravestone. Concerned, she stepped near to peer over the white
picket fence lining the perimeter. Much to her surprise, she saw
Bishop Aaron kneeling on the ground, his hatless head leaning
against his strong arms as he clung to the small tombstone.

"My son . . . my precious son" came his cries, lingering in the air as wet flakes swiftly covered the ground.

Her heart went out to him, and she wished with everything in her that somehow time could be reversed, that Christian could still be alive.

The bishop's keening rang into the snow-dotted sky as Rose whispered a prayer. "Our bishop is a desperate man, O Lord. Please send someone to help him this night, this week. And may his heart be open to receive that help, whatever it may be . . . and whenever it comes. Amen."

CHAPTER 27

With Christmas fast approaching, extra attention would need to be given to cleaning the house from top to bottom, similar to a thorough cleaning in the spring or in preparation for the Preaching service. There would also be baking frolics and cookie exchanges, as well as time spent carefully washing decorative plates and cups and saucers.

Today, though, Hen was going to Arie Zook's to enjoy some midmorning coffee and sweets. She was glad when Rose offered to babysit Mattie Sue for an hour or so that Tuesday morning. Beth had seemed anxious to take her turn reading the Bible to Mom when it was time for Hen to leave the room. Hen kissed her mother and said she'd be back before the noon meal. Mom smiled and nodded drowsily and closed her eyes, seemingly more at peace today than usual.

She's in and out of herself, like Dad says.

Hen bundled up before going out to hitch up the horse and carriage. As she worked, she realized how accustomed she'd become to traveling by horse and buggy and dreaded the thought of ever driving her car again—even to go into town Friday to meet Brandon's attorney and begin the required evaluation. After a solemn talk with Dad yesterday, Hen had promised her father she wouldn't take things into her own hands further. She had made her stand to Brandon about what she felt mattered, and that's all Dad felt was necessary. He was quite outspoken about it, too.

Yet as much as she desired to please her father and the bishop, Hen still felt ill at ease about what this meant for her and Mattie Sue's future. Despite that, Dad had urged her to trust in God for the outcome.

" 'The Lord will give strength unto his people; the Lord will bless his people with peace.' " Hen quoted the psalm as she lifted the reins and headed up Salem Road to make her way to her dearest friend's house. Arie had seemed so excited after Preaching service when Hen agreed to visit her, going on about the delicious goodies she planned to bake. *"Another time I'll have you and Mattie Sue over, so your daughter and mine can play together,"* Arie had said with joyful anticipation.

And because of the way Arie had stated it, Hen felt sure this morning's get-together was sure to be a friendly heart-to-heart. Oh, she could scarcely wait to spend this special time with her cherished friend.

As Sol watched his older daughter take the family carriage out onto the road, he hoped she wouldn't be gone long. She'd asked for George, one of the driving horses, as well as the family buggy, but hadn't said when she would return.

Sol had errands to run, one involving the pending end-of-year ruling of the oldest bishop in the county. Seventy-seven-year-old Ezekiel was the most respected and most unyielding of all the ministerial brethren in the area, including the other bishops.

It had been Bishop Aaron who'd said that if things weren't resolved between himself and the local ministers that Ezekiel would step in and decide what must be done. Since Nick wasn't Aaron's flesh-and-blood son, the heated debate continued to brew. Yet Nick's decided lack of interest in joining church in a timely fashion pointed to what some of the brethren said was a shoddy upbringing, one that reflected poorly on Bishop Aaron.

Nick just ain't one of us, mused Sol. *That's all there is to it.*

The People expected each of the bishop's offspring to be a church member in good standing—something frequently considered before a man was nominated for the divine lot in the first place. But Aaron's children hadn't all been grown at the time of his appointment, and Nick had come along as a foster lad, so Aaron had argued with the local preachers that this should *not* be an issue. That Nick hadn't bowed his knee to God and the church wasn't Aaron's fault.

Sol went back to finishing his work, nearly ready to take the garden cart over to Jonathan Esh's place—the deacon's brother. Jonathan was pinching pennies, so Sol had decided to sell him the commissioned cart for just half of what he'd normally get.

Just then, Sol heard the sound of tires creeping along the snowy gravel. He looked out the window to see the mail truck coming and Rose running out to meet it. Checking his pocket watch, Sol wondered again when to expect Hen back with the buggy, feeling mighty restless now. He wished to goodness the brethren weren't breathing down Aaron's neck like this! He stepped back to admire his craftsmanship and thanked the Lord for the ability to work with his hands. It kept his mind from worry . . . most days. "Jonathan will find this cart mighty useful," he muttered to himself.

He pulled on his heavy work coat and made his way through several inches of snow to the house. Inside, he heard Rose calling happily to Beth, saying she had a letter from her aunt Judith in Illinois.

Beth appeared at the doorway to the sitting room where Emma liked to rest and peeked her head out, eyes shining. "Goody, Aunt

Judith must've gotten my letter," she said, going to sit at the kitchen table, envelope in hand.

Meanwhile, Rose was opening a letter of her own, but her expression was quite the opposite, a trace of exasperation in her eyes as she read.

Sol went into the sitting room and closed the door. He stood beside the daybed and looked at his wife sleeping so peacefully and wished there was something the Lord—or even a doctor—could do to allow her to look as relaxed when she was awake as when she slept.

Slowly, reverently, he moved to her side and leaned down to touch her face. "Emma, my dear . . ."

Her eyes fluttered open, and when she looked up at him, Sol leaned down to kiss her.

~

Hen couldn't recall ever feeling so completely at ease with another person. Arie animatedly recounted the year she and her husband had planted too many hills of watermelon. They'd gone up and down the neighborhood, leaving melons on back porches at dusk as "gifts."

"Same thing happened to us one year with zucchinis and tomatoes," Hen said, remembering the greens and reds of the squash and tomatoes. "They took over the kitchen—nearly every square inch, and then some."

"I know what ya mean. It's like you'd turn your back and they'd multiply, ain't so?"

Hen laughed heartily. "My brothers helped us out a little, though. They had tomato fights, of all things."

Arie burst out laughing.

"It's good they didn't smash the tomatoes in the backyard, though. Dad would've had their hides."

Arie poured some more coffee and offered sugar to Hen. She

paused and bowed her head slightly, looking at Hen with her expressive light brown eyes. "Mind if I ask ya something?"

"Not at all."

"I'm just curious . . . since you've come back home, you tend to call your parents Dad and Mom. Why's that?"

Hen wasn't surprised she should ask. "Guess I just got in the habit of referring to them that way when I lived on the outside."

Arie looked out the window, sad suddenly. "We won't go our separate ways ever again, will we, Hen?"

"No, never." *No matter what happens,* Hen thought. A tremor of concern rushed through her as she exchanged glances with Arie.

Then, quite simultaneously, each of them reached for another slice of cherry strudel.

~

Rose looked over at Beth, who was obviously pleased with her letter. "Aunt Judith is coming to visit me," Beth said. "Next month sometime."

"That's so nice," Rose said, wondering why Donna Becker hadn't dropped by again with further word from Gilbert. She hoped his widowed mother was doing all right but wouldn't worry, since Gilbert had been so conscientious about keeping Donna informed thus far.

Beth glanced at Mattie Sue, who was laying out a checkers game on the kitchen floor. "Did you get a nice letter, too?" she asked Rose, leaning forward on her elbows.

"Nice enough." Truth was, Silas had written rather pointedly to Rose, concerned that she'd left the Singing so suddenly.

Why didn't you wait for me, Rose Ann? he'd written. She guessed he might as well have asked, *What got into you?* But he was more tactful than that. Still, she could read between the lines. He was upset with her, and rightly so.

Now that she thought of it, she'd made him look bad, though not intentionally.

He'd written to ask her to meet him this coming Saturday night, after dusk. *We should talk*, he'd written before signing off, *With love, Silas*.

She didn't know how she felt about seeing him, because if they did talk about the things that bothered her, she wasn't sure how to make him understand. At first, she'd wanted to befriend Rebekah, make her feel included in the group . . . since she'd been Rose's friend years ago. But the more Rose had gotten reacquainted with Rebekah, the more she felt concerned about her obvious regard for Silas—and his friendship with her. Rose had witnessed an undeniable spark between them.

Beth interrupted her thoughts, asking if they could go upstairs for a while. Rose agreed, glad to have the chance to dismiss Silas's letter. She wondered what was on Beth's mind.

When they were upstairs, Beth closed the door to Rose's room. "I want you to read something real nice . . . since you look so sad." Beth went to the drawer where Rose had cleared a place for her things. Beth brought her notebook to Rose and held it open to the page titled "Healing Love." Then Beth went to stand near the frost-covered window, her face alight.

"This is what I wrote about my dream," she said. "You've been so busy, I couldn't show it to you before now."

Rose sat on the bed and began to read the surprising account of a woman who could not walk because of a mysterious buggy accident. She suffered horrible pain and went to see a special kind of doctor—*a surgeon in York, not far from here*. A doctor who was able to quiet her pain.

What does it mean? Rose wasn't sure how to react, or what to say to Beth. So she closed the journal and thanked Beth for showing her. "Your writing is beautiful."

"I believe God gave me the dream to help your Mamma," Beth said as she took the journal.

"Beth, I don't want to disappoint you, but my mother absolutely will not go to a specialist," said Rose. "She doesn't really trust doctors."

"Well . . ." Beth's eyes shone. "Sometimes God lets people have very real dreams to give them hope."

Rose agreed. "Jah, and there are accounts of dreams in the Bible like that." She sighed, not wanting to hurt Beth's feelings. "But . . . not all dreams come true," she added softly.

"I know." Beth held the journal close to her heart. "I've been praying, and I really think God gave me this dream as an answer to my prayers. I really do, Rosie. Will you talk to your father about taking her just one more time?"

"Against her will?" Rose was perplexed.

Beth's face was bright with joy. "What if she could live without pain? Just imagine that!"

Imagine it? Oh, there had been literally hundreds of hopeful days—years filled with them—when Rose had clung to that expectation just as Beth did now. But reality had set in long ago, and Rose had resigned herself to Mamm's never being free of pain.

"Please don't give up, Rosie. We mustn't."

Looking into Beth's sweet face, Rose wondered what would happen if Mamm was told about the dream from Beth's own lips. Would it change her mind? "I have an idea," Rose said, getting up and going to her bedroom door.

Beth's eyes lit up. "What?"

"Let's go back downstairs."

"All right," said Beth, following close behind.

Dear God, if this is your will for Mamm, let her be openhearted to Beth's strange, yet remarkable dream.

CHAPTER 28

Once Hen returned from Arie's, Solomon took the team over to Deacon Esh's farm. The two local preachers had already arrived, their buggies parked on the side yard, the horses tied to the hitching posts. Bishop Aaron was turning into the lane, as well.

The gathering had been planned to include several long-standing church members, including Solomon. When Sol had first heard of it, he'd immediately decided to go in support of his friend and bishop. And even though he wasn't an ordained minister—and never would be nominated due to Hen's marriage to an outsider—Sol wanted to give his opinion on behalf of his closest neighbor and friend.

Over the period of an hour, a handful of church members gave their say-so, one way or the other. While much of the talk surrounded Nick, a couple men present also reluctantly faulted the bishop for giving sermons that were too long—something they said smacked of pride.

Sol could scarcely believe anyone would accuse humble Aaron of anything near pride, but he held his tongue until he was called upon to sum up his own thinking. He then restated what those present already knew. "From the first day onward, our bishop has been a faithful, diligent, patient, and compassionate father to Nick . . . never wavering even in the face of the boy's belligerence. An exemplary minister, to be sure."

The men listened intently as Sol continued in that vein, emphasizing Bishop Aaron's repeated efforts where Nick was concerned. When he'd concluded, the ministerial brethren dismissed Sol and the other church members from the deacon's wife's kitchen. As Sol turned to leave, Aaron caught his eye, and in that instant, he realized anew how gracious and benevolent a man their bishop had always been.

How could anyone force such a man out of leadership? Sol trudged across the driveway to his horse and carriage. He reached for the buggy's ice-cold frame to pull himself inside, wishing he'd worn gloves. He pondered the real possibility of Aaron's being forced to step down as bishop. *Silenced, they call it. And for what reason? A rebellious son not even of his own flesh?*

It was beyond Sol how the actions of Aaron's foster son could shed a speck of light on the nature of *his* spiritual influence in their church district. Surely the Lord God, who'd chosen Aaron in the first place, would not allow such a sad end to come of his ministerial calling.

How can mere men make such a judgment?

Sol blew his warm breath on his hands and rubbed them together briskly before picking up the reins. For all the many years he'd lived neighbors to Aaron Petersheim, Sol had known his friend to be a man who wholly followed the Lord, always openhearted to what was right and good.

"O Lord, make your will known in this," Sol pleaded as he drove.

~

Sol lay next to Emma, who was sleeping so serenely he dared not doze off. His wife had passed a new threshold of lethargy, and he could hardly stand to see her this way. Yet which was worse—the uncommonly cruel pain, or this near stupor? Emma did seem less afflicted, which was a blessing after all these years.

Perhaps it was partly because of an endearing—and surprising—conversation he'd overheard between Beth and Emma earlier today. And as he lay there, resisting sleep, the scene played over in his head. Beth had apparently had a rather vivid dream, and she'd explained to Emma that God cared for her so much that Beth believed He had shown her a doctor who could help her. *"I have peace that God will answer my prayers, and you will be healed from your pain,"* Beth had said, eyes ever so hopeful.

But what had surprised Sol even more was Beth's ability to impart the optimism she herself clung to. For a fleeting moment, Emma had seemed to catch a glimpse of it, too, before going away, back into herself.

He didn't know if this was a sign he should pursue a new doctor, or even take another look at the list of specialists Emma's original doctor had strongly recommended.

Was this God's answer to Sol's own fervent prayers for his wife? To be sure, there had been something too special for words that passed between Beth Browning and his dear wife. Even his Rose had witnessed it.

What now? Sol didn't honestly know but would take it to prayer this very night. And reaching over to touch Emma's frail hand, he began to beseech the Almighty.

Later, in the absence of any inclination to rest, Sol rose from the bed and went over to the antique bureau. He pulled out an old tan folder containing the names and addresses of Pennsylvania specialists and surgeons.

Going to the kitchen, Sol lit the gas lamp and scanned the page, moving his finger down the row, stopping at the only orthopedic surgeon in York, about forty miles away.

Might this one help my Emma, most gracious Lord?

∽

Hen sat all curled up in bed the night before her required meeting with Brandon's lawyer. Mattie Sue was already asleep in the next room as Hen plumped her own pillow and paged through the small wedding album she'd brought from home.

Our home.

She studied her husband's face, his expressions. In several photographs he looked humorously like the cat that caught the mouse. She'd never noticed it before. Then, in yet another picture, she was very sure she saw love in his alluring blue eyes, just as her own face reflected the same, standing next to her handsome groom.

Surely, we loved each other. . . .

Her mind had been in turmoil all week, contemplating tomorrow's grilling at the lawyer's office—questions no doubt focused on her parenting abilities and intentions. She broke out in a cold sweat at the uncomfortable nature of what was ahead.

Even so, she would follow through with her promise to Dad to honor the way Brandon wanted things done. *I'll simply bite my tongue.* She imagined the awkwardness of the psychological assessment. The whole process seemed so unnecessary. *Why must I be the first to be questioned? Has Brandon told them I'm unstable?*

She could just imagine her brother-in-law Lawrence having set things up in favor of Brandon. But would he also prejudice the judge against her, when all was said and done?

There were times when her grief and anguish moved easily toward anger. But because she desired to demonstrate a meek and gentle spirit from here on out, Hen slipped out of bed and knelt to pray. *May your will be done on earth as it is in heaven, O Father, at tomorrow's meeting. This frightens me terribly, dear Lord. You know all things, and you see deep into my quivering heart.*

She paused and breathed deeply, attempting to surrender her will to God's. Why was it so hard to trust her Maker?

Hen realized that, as much as she desired to follow God in returning to the ways of her past, she had been doing so without regard for her husband. Had she driven a deeper wedge between him and the heavenly Father through her actions?

O Lord, I've been so blind. . . .

Yet at the same time, Hen wasn't ready to admit that this way of life wasn't the best for her and her daughter—for all of them, really. Her heart heavy, Hen began to pray once more. *I know you are working in Brandon's and my life, to will and to do of your good pleasure. But, Lord, it is so hard to see a good path through this. Please save our marriage . . . our family. Guide us for Jesus' sake. Amen.*

Feeling quite weary, she rose to stand at the frosty window. "*Keep showerin' dei Mann with love,*" the bishop's wife had told Hen when she first returned home. Somehow, Hen must find a way to do that even in the difficult circumstances of tomorrow.

Lantern light flickered from the upstairs windows across the long meadow, and she wondered if the man of God might still be up as she was, pacing and pleading for divine guidance, as well.

∼

Hen wasn't the only one for whom Brandon's tardiness brought uneasiness on Friday. As Lawrence Orringer, attorney-at-law, briefed her on the various forms she was required to fill out, he glanced repeatedly at the open office door.

She had interacted with Brandon's brother on a number of occasions, namely New Year's and Easter. Brandon had always referred to Lawrence as his closest brother of three. The other two lived on the West Coast near LA and were too busy climbing corporate ladders to keep in touch with their small-town brother—or so Brandon had often quipped.

Sitting now in the comfortable office chair, across the gleaming desk from Lawrence, Hen wished Brandon would arrive. Her neck and shoulders tensed as each minute passed and still there was no sign of him. Was he testing her, guessing she would not show up? She pushed away the ridiculous notion and willed herself to have a kinder attitude. This was what Brandon wanted, right?

Yet secretly, she hoped he might've gotten cold feet. If only that were so!

Lawrence apologized several times for his client-brother's delay, although Hen could see by his impatient expression that he, too, was weary of waiting.

At last, there were hurried footsteps in the hallway, coming this way. Both she and Lawrence turned to see a woman dressed in a burnt orange tweed suit knock on the slightly open door and then breeze in. The young woman, no older than her late thirties, gave Hen a rather professional once-over, then introduced herself as Dr. Greta Schmidt. "I'll be handling the parental evaluation."

"My client has obviously been detained," Lawrence stated, glancing now at Hen. "This is Mrs. Orringer—Hannah."

"Please call me Hen," she said, accepting the woman's firm handshake.

Before Dr. Schmidt could continue, Lawrence pulled at the sleeve of his navy blue sports coat and looked at his watch. "Uh, excuse me, but perhaps it would be best not to move ahead just yet."

"How necessary is it for Mr. Orringer to be present?" Dr. Schmidt asked before admitting to an exceptionally tight schedule. The psychologist glanced at Hen again, appearing to take in her long dress, her gaze coming to rest on the Kapp.

Lawrence rose from behind his desk and moved toward the door, motioning for Dr. Schmidt to follow. Hen could hear them talking in muffled tones as Lawrence pleaded with her to wait around a few more minutes.

Oh, what stress! Hen thought, a knot in her stomach.

Hearing their footsteps moving farther away, Hen leaned back and attempted to relax. She recalled the first time she'd met Brandon's brothers, following her and Brandon's elopement. It was after Christmas, a few days before New Year's Eve, when Brandon's brothers and families had gathered at their parents' sprawling home in New York's Finger Lakes region. She'd sat in an upholstered leather wing-back chair similar to the one she sat in presently, but in Brandon's father's aristocratic home office, with its duo of cherrywood desks and matching credenza. Custom-made Italian drapes had swept down from the high ceiling and fell in puddles against the polished hardwood floor. Hen had waited to fully take in the magnificence of the room until Brandon stepped outside with his father, who smoked a cigar. The pungent scent had seeped through the French doors as she sat there, marveling at her choice in a mate—and his family.

Why did I marry Brandon—and he me? she'd mused that day. Although she'd known very little firsthand of love, she'd quickly concluded she was eager and ready to love him for all the days of her life. What else could she call her feelings for the man with whom she'd fallen head over heels? There was no other relationship to compare her strong feelings to, but even then, Hen had suspected their affection was a fragile thing. Neither had really known how to nurture that love to maturity.

She thought back to their wedding, so simple compared to the opulence in which Brandon had been raised. The justice of the peace had been a tall woman who had recited the required legal words with little or no feeling. At the time, Hen had felt cheated somehow, remembering how zealous Bishop Aaron and their two preachers were in their instruction of young couples during Amish weddings.

But now all of that—the words spoken that day in the judge's drab chambers, including her and Brandon's vows—had vanished in the sea of paperwork there in front of her, waiting to be filled in for yet another judge.

The thought entered Hen's mind that she'd never told a soul—not even her own dear sister, who'd known something was up—about her plan to marry Brandon that day. With no guests other than the photographer they'd hired, everything had been very basic, mostly because of their haste to marry. Neither she nor her groom had remembered to buy flowers for the other. *No music or boutonniere . . . no engraved invitations or bridesmaids. Like an Amish wedding in its simplicity,* Hen realized with a start.

Much to Solomon's surprise, Emma admitted that morning to being heartened beyond her ability to explain because of Beth's faith-filled dream and her handwritten prayers. "I saw the great hope in her eyes . . . and I believed the dream must be from God," she said, tears in her eyes. "I want you to call the York orthopedic specialist you talked about."

Sol's spirits soared at this decided change of heart. *Thank you, Lord!* Later, in the phone shanty, while Sol dialed the York office, it struck him that the phone number of the orthopedic surgeon had remained the same, after all these years. Surely it pointed to divine providence.

The receptionist offered a post-Christmas opening that had just come up for a week from today, Friday, December twenty-seventh. Otherwise, the doctor was booked solid well into January. Gratefully, Sol said they'd take it.

As he walked back toward the house through the ankle-deep snow, a siren rang out in the distance, then another. He cringed inwardly, just as he had the day the ambulance wailed down Salem Road, coming for the bishop's son. *Too late.*

"Lord, help whoever is in need," he whispered, his breath crys-tallizing before his eyes.

Once inside, Sol jotted down the appointment day and time. Feeling invigorated by the hope burning within him for Emma, he prayed she would not back out prior to the trip to York next week.

He went to the sitting room to see Emma and found Rose Ann there reading aloud to her. Smiling a greeting to his wife and daughter, Sol made his way out to the woodshop, still conscious of the intensity of the sirens' cries.

CHAPTER 29

Hen started when Lawrence's desk phone jangled loudly. She leaned forward to look into the hallway as the phone continued to ring. At one point, she nearly felt compelled to answer it herself.

Finally the phone ceased its ringing. Within a minute or so, Lawrence returned to the office, alone. "Hen . . . I don't know how to say this." He looked like a man sleepwalking. "I've just received very bad news . . . about Brandon."

"Bad news?" The words caught in her throat.

"There was an accident." Lawrence stared at her in a daze. "Head-on collision. Brandon's in the ER, where the doctors are assessing his injuries."

Brandon hurt?

Lawrence went on talking, something about the critical condition of the other driver. But Hen froze in the chair, unable to hear or comprehend his words, lost in the air as they were. Her mind and heart entangled in a great knot of concern, distress, and fear.

In a daze, she rose without speaking. From a concealed closet in the wood panel behind his desk, Lawrence snatched his overcoat off a hanger. "I'll drive us to the hospital," he said.

Hen mutely nodded her thanks and placed the financial papers back on the desk. Then, pulling on her woolen shawl, she made her way out to his car, parked in a reserved spot behind the law building. She shivered not so much from the cold as from nerves. It was impossible to think of her strong, energetic husband lying injured—or worse—in a hospital.

When they arrived at the emergency room, the receptionist was surprisingly strict about permitting only one family member to visit at a time. She also stared, as if unmistakably curious about Hen's Plain attire. "Are you a close relative of Brandon Orringer?" she asked.

"His wife," Hen said, scarcely able to speak. *For now . . .*

The woman said Brandon was in the critical area of the ER. "Room number eight—headed soon for surgery on his fractured arm."

"Which arm?" Hen thought aloud.

"His right."

Brandon's right-handed.

The woman eyed Hen yet again. "Please adhere to the five-minute rule."

Lawrence seemed reluctant to let Hen go in first, and he followed her to the locked double doorway and stood to the right of it, his hand in his trouser pocket, jingling coins. He wore a frown as he stared through the round windows.

Feeling out of place, Hen waited until the woman gave the signal and the doors opened outward. Hen tiptoed inside, looking for the correct room number posted on the wall panels. She held her breath as she at last stepped into the curtained-off area, moving quickly to the side of the bed.

Brandon looked worse than she'd feared: His head and neck were attached to a long board, and the bed railings were up on both sides. His face was badly bruised and his forehead was bandaged.

Her knees felt weak at the sight of him, and Hen suddenly realized just how terrible it would be to lose this man—the husband she loved. *How could I forget what he means to me?* She folded her hands and peered down sadly at him. *Is he asleep or unconscious?*

The sounds of several machines filled the room. A clear tube for oxygen had been inserted into his nose, and another tube with a needle on the end was going into the vein in his left arm. His heart was also being monitored, and the steady beeping was a comfort to her as Hen's own heartbeat pulsed loudly in her ears. Her husband looked so pitiful, so pale and lifeless.

Glancing about her, she noticed a clipboard at the foot of his bed. She peeked at it and saw the letters TBI. A moment or so later, a nurse came in to check his blood pressure and oxygen levels. The nurse told her Brandon had suffered several broken ribs, as well as a badly fractured arm.

"What is TBI?" Hen asked.

"Traumatic brain injury. We'll be watching your husband closely over the next forty-eight hours to determine the extent of the damage." The nurse explained that because Brandon had been unconscious for more than fifteen minutes following the impact, they were treating him with medication to keep brain swelling to a minimum.

Brain swelling? Her breath caught and tears sprang to her eyes. No, she must not cry. Brandon needed her now . . . needed her to be strong.

"The doctor will be in soon to give you further updates," the nurse said, offering her a sympathetic smile.

Hen did not want her precious minutes to slip away too quickly. Praying silently, she gently touched Brandon's exposed left wrist. No response came and she was struck by how very warm his skin was to the touch.

Tears blurred her ability to see clearly the man she'd married so eagerly . . . so happily. The English man who did not understand

Hen's renewed fondness for Plain living, nor her concerns regarding Mattie Sue's upbringing.

The man who wants to leave me . . .

She looked at his broken body—his right arm in a temporary blue sling. It was impossible not to wonder how badly Brandon's brain was injured. Yet she refused to give in to fear.

O Lord, please help my husband. She closed her eyes, unable to bear the thought of his being so terribly hurt.

The curtains moved and the ER doctor appeared and introduced himself as Dr. Baker. He shook her hand kindly. "I understand you are Mrs. Orringer," he said.

"I am." She waited a moment before asking, "How badly hurt is he?"

"Considering the force of the collision, I have to say your husband's a lucky man."

His words were hardly reassuring.

"The initial scan indicates Mr. Orringer has suffered a moderate to serious concussion."

"What does that mean for him?"

"A head injury of any kind is a grave matter, and according to the report, your husband was unconscious for a considerable amount of time." He picked up Brandon's chart and made notes as he checked the various monitors. He leaned over the bed and raised Brandon's eyelids, one after the other, shining a small penlight. "The first few hours are not as critical as the next twenty-four and beyond. We will be watching for any brain swelling or bleeding."

It crossed her mind to ask how long he'd be in the hospital, but her legs felt so weak it was all Hen could do to simply cling to the bed railing. She felt as if she was walking in a stupor. All of this had happened so fast.

Dr. Baker went on to say that Brandon's right arm was severely fractured and that surgery was essential to reset it. Several ribs were broken, as well, but there had been no puncture to either lung, according to the X-rays.

Thank the dear Lord! she thought.

Although five minutes had already passed, it was difficult to think of leaving Brandon there among strangers.

Hen memorized the form of her husband's long and once robust frame beneath the white sheet. *Please let Brandon recover,* she fervently prayed again. "My husband's brother is waiting to come in next," Hen told the doctor as she stepped back from the bed, her eyes lingering on her injured husband. "I'll return tomorrow."

After his brief visit, Hen's brother-in-law offered to drive her back to her car at the parking lot behind the law offices. And although the trip wasn't long, the mood between them in the car was tinged with tension, despite Lawrence's efforts to make small talk. They were both filled with apprehension.

Lawrence mentioned he would contact his brothers in California and his sister, Terry, in Maryland. Hen was quite relieved. She did not wish to go to the empty house to look up the pertinent phone numbers. "I'll notify my parents, too, of course," he added.

She heard the catch in his deep voice. The man was worried sick, just as she was. And thankfully, nothing more was said about filing divorce papers.

They pulled into Lawrence's parking spot and Hen thanked him as she reached for the door handle. "I plan to visit Brandon again tomorrow," he told her.

"Thank you," she said. "I'll be there, too."

As Hen got out and walked toward her car, it occurred to her that she should have stayed at the hospital while Brandon underwent surgery. But she needed to get word to her family, who would be expecting her back by now. She sighed, well aware that mentally she would be standing next to Brandon's bed the rest of the day, her hand holding his.

Once home, she entered the main house, where she quietly relayed the news of the accident to her father and sister. Both were shocked and concerned, as well as ready to assist in any way possible. Neither Dad nor Hen was in a hurry to tell her mother, at least until tomorrow, when they knew more.

But Hen could not put off telling Mattie Sue. Gently, she sat down with her daughter. "Daddy's been in an accident. He'll be staying in the hospital for a while."

Mattie's eyes grew solemn, but surprisingly she seemed less frightened than Hen thought possible. Hen took her daughter into her arms and held her near, making a great effort to be calm as they prayed together for the man they both loved.

CHAPTER 30

The next morning, Hen sat across the breakfast table from Mattie Sue and told her she was going to visit Daddy again at the hospital. When Mattie pleaded to go along, Hen explained that children under the age of twelve were not permitted to visit.

Much to Hen's relief, this seemed to suffice as she kissed her good-bye. "Mind your Aendi Rose and Mammi Sylvia, won't you, honey?"

Mattie Sue smiled and nodded her little head. "Tell Daddy I miss him."

"I certainly will." Her heart was made tender by her dear girl's remark, and she hugged her close.

As she walked around the barn to her car, she was once again glad she hadn't sold it just yet. She would need a car to visit Brandon each day, until he was released.

When Hen arrived at the hospital, she made her way to the information desk amidst discreet stares to ask what room Brandon had been assigned to, following yesterday's surgery. She was directed to his floor and room and, after noting that Brandon was sleeping, she sat in the chair near the window and settled into doing a bit of needlepoint. Every few moments, she looked over at him, recalling happier days. Truth was, she was waiting on pins and needles for Brandon to wake up and talk to her, or for someone to come in and give her an update.

For the first half hour, Brandon remained at rest, eyes closed. When the nurse assigned to him arrived to check his vitals, she indicated it wasn't unusual for a head injury patient to require lots of rest. In fact, it was strongly encouraged.

Hen felt sure her husband must sense she was near, even though she had been reticent about speaking, not wanting to disturb him. And although her hands were occupied by embroidery, her thoughts were of his having survived the accident. *What if he had died yesterday? What then?*

As time passed, everyone who entered Brandon's room, including one of the paramedics who'd come to see him briefly, mentioned how remarkable it was that he was alive. "Your husband must be living right," the paramedic told her with a broad smile. Evidently the other driver had a fractured vertebra and faced a second surgery today to stabilize his left leg, although he was expected to make a full recovery.

Hen was thankful to hear this and wondered how long Brandon's own recovery might take. It was hard for Hen not to worry that, along with his inability to use his right arm for weeks, Brandon could very well suffer great pain, like her mother. She prayed that would not be her husband's plight.

Hen's concern deepened when Brandon's doctor stepped into the room and asked to have a word with her. "Your husband has been more alert this morning—an excellent sign. Unfortunately, we've discovered that his head injury has affected his vision—a condition known as cortical blindness, and a situation we expect will be only temporary."

Hen felt unable to absorb this news. "Blindness?" she repeated. "He can't see *anything?*" Her lower lip trembled at the thought.

"Yes, I'm afraid that's the case." The doctor nodded. "I know the news is disconcerting, Mrs. Orringer, but his prognosis is good, and I wanted to alert you to the situation before Brandon wakes up again. He's naturally very concerned right now."

Hen thanked him for telling her, but her own worries were multiplying by the moment. How would an independent man like Brandon handle the loss of his sight for even a short time?

"The longer the loss of sight continues, the more cause for concern." The doctor paused. "But again, we have every reason to believe it will return soon."

He handed Hen a booklet describing various kinds of head injuries. "This will help you understand your husband's concussion-related symptoms. In addition to the cortical blindness, he has a nasty headache, as well as some nausea, both of which are very typical. Additional indicators of the initial trauma can show up over time . . . even during the next weeks."

Weeks? Brandon will never stand for that!

The doctor said he would return in a few hours, then wished her well. Hen sat musing on what she'd just learned, too dismayed to return to her embroidery as the oxygen whistled through the tube.

Later, Brandon's nurse came back to take his blood pressure. Even though he appeared to be asleep, she talked quietly to him, describing what she was doing. Brandon's eyes fluttered a bit, and Hen's heart beat faster when she saw that he'd opened his eyes, blinking them repeatedly. He mumbled something Hen could not make out from where she sat.

The nurse glanced at Hen and motioned for her to come to his bedside. "Yes, your wife is right here," she said, looking at Hen.

Brandon continued to blink, his face turned in the direction of the nurse. "Hen—thanks for coming," he said weakly. "You didn't . . ."

She patted his hand.

"Has the doctor been in yet?" he murmured.

"He was just here," the nurse said.

"What day is this?" he asked.

"It's Saturday," Hen told him.

"Are you sure?" He seemed terribly agitated.

The nurse intervened. "It's Saturday all day today," she joked, winking at Hen. "You're just a little confused—very common after your type of injury." Hen knew she'd said it for both their benefits. "That should clear up soon."

"But my eyes—why can't I see?" he asked, moaning.

Hen's heart went out to him. "It's best to rest," she said softly.

He turned his head toward her, staring blankly. "Is Mattie Sue with you?"

"She asked to come, but it's against hospital policy. She misses you . . . and is praying for you. My whole family is."

Brandon shifted in the bed, as if uncomfortable. "Last night the doctor said I could go home soon, if there's no more swelling in my head." His voice sounded vacant, and Hen sensed he was discouraged. "I have an important business deal to close on Monday. I can't afford to miss out." He paused, frowning. "Or is it on Tuesday?" He groaned, frustrated. "Why am I so mixed up?"

The nurse touched his arm. "You have a bad concussion, Mr. Orringer. Give yourself time to recover."

"Time? I need to go home."

The nurse assured him he would be discharged the minute the doctor thought he was ready.

Hen thanked the nurse for her good care. And later, when the nurse left the room, Hen slid the chair closer to Brandon's bed and sat near him, wanting to be a comfort. Silently she prayed, hoping Brandon's sight might return quickly.

What will he do otherwise?

Yet by two o'clock that afternoon, Brandon still could not see.

~

After supper that evening, Barbara Petersheim came over to Hen's for a visit, bringing freshly baked brownies and a Jell-O salad with homemade whipped cream and crushed pineapple over sliced bananas. While enjoying the treat, they talked about Brandon, as well as the quilt Hen was making.

The cheery visit touched Hen deeply, and when Barbara rose to leave, she embraced Hen caringly. "The People are prayin' for your husband, dear girl. You can rest assured of that."

Hen thanked her for coming; she felt exhausted as twilight fell. Mattie Sue had spent much of the day with Beth and Rose Ann at the main house. Just now she could see Mattie Sue running across the yard, calling "Mommy."

Hen went to the door and watched Barbara wave kindly to Mattie Sue. The bishop's wife had been the ideal person to drop by this night. Of all women, Barbara understood about grief and fear, having watched her own son struggle to live that short time following the accident. Dear Barbara's light brown hair had begun to gray suddenly in the last two months. Deep grief could do that, Hen had read somewhere.

Mattie Sue came rushing into the house. "How's Daddy today?"

Hen sat down with her darling girl and explained that her father needed their prayers more than ever. "Daddy's arm and ribs are getting better, but his head hurts really bad, honey . . . and right now he can't see. The doctor says he might by tomorrow, though."

A deep frown appeared, but Mattie Sue did not cry. She nodded her head and offered to say a prayer for Daddy right then. "Dawdi Sol says God hears our prayers, ain't?"

Hen smiled. "That's right, honey."

"He says sometimes God says yes, or no, or maybe—or wait for a while longer."

Hen kissed her daughter's cheek. "And sometimes the prayers we pray help change *us* most of all," she said, following Mattie Sue upstairs for bed.

"Dawdi Sol told Aendi Rosie the same thing at the noon meal today."

Hen wondered what she'd missed—had Rose asked about prayers for healing? For Mom, perhaps? *Or for Brandon.* Hen knew that she would continue to pray for both her mother and for her husband.

Dear Lord, may your will be done for Brandon . . . and for our marriage.

⁓

Courting couples met after nightfall on the Saturday evenings before the no-Preaching Sundays. Some rode about the countryside for hours in the young man's open buggy, while others went to relatives' to play Dutch Blitz and other table games, or Ping-Pong.

Because the night was bitter cold, Rose assumed this date would be spent riding and talking for only a brief while before Silas took her home. When Silas arrived, she was grateful to note he had several warm lap robes and heated bricks in the courting buggy. He was well prepared, and she wondered if what he wanted to discuss might take some extra time.

She still felt uneasy about the note he'd sent her this past week. To ward off discussing that, Rose instead brought up Hen's husband's accident. "My brother-in-law is in the hospital with a concussion," she told him, "and a seriously fractured arm . . . and broken ribs."

"Oh, awful sorry."

Brandon's accident had weighed heavily on her mind since yesterday afternoon, when she and Dat had heard about it from Hen.

To think it happened on his way to the law office!

Rose still had a hard time grasping the fact that her sister's young marriage was ending. And now this? What did it mean? She believed the Lord allowed things to happen, whether good or bad, for the "trying of our faith." Out of the bad, good could also come in due time. No matter what, Rose understood it was important to trust in God's will, regardless of how things might appear, or what others might think or say about the situation.

"Hen says Brandon's sight is also affected, but the doctor anticipates it will come back soon," she told Silas.

"I sure hope he's right." He said no more.

Rose felt odd about carrying the conversation like this. She decided not to say another word, except to respond to Silas—if he finally loosened his tongue again.

The perfect half-moon was a lovely sight as the horse pulled them slowly along the road, heading east. Rose missed hearing the chorus of crickets in the underbrush—summer was long gone. The steady snows of the last few days had covered the fields and meadows, as well as the lanes leading into farmhouses and other homes in the area. Winter draped the road, where horses' hooves had packed the snow into ice, and buggy wheels had carved furrows into the treacherous roadway.

She huddled beneath the woolen lap robes, trying to keep warm. She breathed in the icy air through her nose, lest she freeze her lungs as the steady sounds of the horse's hooves clomped against the hardened snow. Mammi Sylvia had warned her and Hen to do this when helping bundle them up for school in the deep of winter, years ago.

When Silas finally did speak, Rose was nestled down in the heavy lap robe, her nose and upper face the only parts showing. "Rose, it's beyond me why you left so quickly last Sunday night," he said. "Why would ya do such a thing?"

"I didn't do it to embarrass you, if that's what you think."

"Well, I kept wonderin' where on earth you'd disappeared to."

She listened, then replied, "It didn't look right . . . you standin' over there talking to Rebekah like that. It was like you'd forgotten I was even there."

He was quiet again.

"I wouldn't have left the Singing if you'd noticed me. But once Rebekah showed up, well . . ." *And you couldn't seem to stay away from her,* Rose added mentally.

"That's beside the point."

"I'm sorry to disagree with you, Silas, but how can ya say that? We're engaged . . . and betrothed couples stay together."

He turned to face her. "Why are you so upset 'bout this?"

"Like I said . . . it just didn't look right." Taking a slow, deep breath, she withdrew from his side. Evidently, Silas did not understand how she felt, which made her even more frustrated.

"So now you're goin' to pout?" He sounded bewildered.

They rode without speaking for a long and awkward interval.

"Silas?" she said at last. "Could it be you still care for Rebekah?" Rose held her breath, waiting for his answer.

"I care for *you.*"

She pondered that. "Then why did ya seek her out like that?"

"She sought *me* out at the Singing."

For certain, it seemed as though Silas was bent on defending his behavior. Why? The things he had said didn't make her feel a stitch better.

"Look, Rose, I don't want you to think you're not important to me. You are." He turned to look at her. "I've always thought highly of you. So has my family. Why, my father even prompted me to court you again last spring. He's a good judge of character—and a man of high integrity. It seemed like a confirmation when I realized he and I were both thinking the same way."

Rose was surprised he was telling her this, though he did not mention the land. Would he answer her honestly if she asked? Her concern over that—and his evident lack of understanding of her own feelings regarding last Sunday—stole away any desire Rose had to talk further. Yet she could not help but wonder if his father's farm had played a role in settling Silas's choice on her.

Has he suppressed his true feelings for Rebekah? The thought went round in her head like the continuous spinning of a windmill.

After another long stretch of silence, Silas said, "I think we should call it a night, jah?"

Surprised, she glanced at him.

"Seems we're getting nowhere," he stated flatly. He hurried the horse, and when they came to a side road, he directed the animal to turn and then back up. Once they'd straightened again, he clicked his tongue and they sped back toward Salem Road.

As they approached her father's house, Rose said softly, "I don't know, Silas . . . if I'm not speakin' out of turn, maybe we shouldn't see each other for a while."

Silas didn't reply—didn't even reassure her with his wonderful smile. And, considering everything, she didn't feel crushed by his silence as she climbed down, out of his courting buggy. In fact, his lack of a response right now seemed to point to the truth.

CHAPTER 31

Hen fingered the end of a loose strand of Mattie Sue's blond hair that evening. "Looks to me like you need a good brushing." She smiled down at her daughter.

"Oh, Mommy . . . do ya think I'm a pony now?" Mattie Sue giggled, prancing around her bedroom. "Giddyup, Pepper."

"Pepper? Have you been riding the bishop's horse?"

Mattie nodded. "Dawdi Sol took Beth and me riding on him this morning."

Dad did this? Hen was surprised. "But Pepper's a driving horse."

"Well, Dawdi says he's the best horse for us to ride double on, since he's nice and slow with the bishop's littlest grandchildren, too."

"Does Dawdi Sol lead Pepper along when you ride?"

"Jah, he wants us safe. And that way, Pepper won't start trotting." She giggled. "But Beth said she'd like it if he did."

Hen reached for the brush on the dresser and sat on Mattie's bed. She began to undo the bobby pins and let out the little bun at her neck. Down tumbled a cascade of thick locks. "Goodness, just look how long your hair's getting."

"Show me where."

Hen patted Mattie Sue's midback. "Halfway between your neck and your waist."

"If ya brush it a lot, will it grow faster?"

Smiling, Hen said her own mother had always thought so. "When I was a little girl, I asked the same thing."

"Did ya want your hair to grow real long . . . down to your knees?"

"No, not that long."

"How long, Mommy?"

"Well, to my waist, like my grandma's," Hen replied.

"*Grossmammi* Sylvia?"

"No, Dawdi Solomon's mother had the longest hair I've ever seen. It took nearly a full day for it to dry."

Mattie sighed. "I don't remember her."

"I was just ten when she passed away . . . long before you were born, honey."

Mattie fell silent, and Hen picked up the length of her daughter's hair with her left hand and began brushing gently with her right. "Daddy's not going to die, is he?" Mattie Sue asked softly.

A similar worry had plagued Hen when she'd first stepped into the emergency room critical care center. But now she believed differently. "Daddy has a wonderful-good doctor and nurses taking care of him. You mustn't worry."

"Why can't he see?"

In terms Mattie Sue could understand, Hen explained that a blow to the head could hurt the brain and so affect other parts of the body. "Like Daddy's eyes. But the doctor thinks Daddy's sight will return soon."

Mattie Sue turned and put her arms around Hen's neck. "I really miss him."

"It's possible Daddy might be able to go home tomorrow. We'll just have to wait and see." She hoped that what the doctor had indicated today was correct—that Brandon was responding well to the neurological tests so far and might indeed be discharged. "He'll have to rest quite a lot once he does go home," she said.

Might be weeks before he can return to work, though.

"Will Daddy live at his own house again?" Mattie got resituated so Hen could finish brushing her hair.

"I'm sure he will," she said, but suddenly she wondered how Brandon would manage.

Mattie's questions ceased suddenly, and she remained very quiet until Hen tucked her into bed. "Beth wrote a prayer for Daddy in her notebook," she said.

"How nice!"

"She read it to me," Mattie Sue said, reaching up to kiss Hen good night. "I'll miss her when she leaves."

Hen hadn't heard that Gilbert Browning was returning. "Did Beth say her father was coming for her?"

"Their neighbor came to see Aendi Rosie this afternoon."

"Donna Becker did?"

Mattie nodded her head and rubbed her eyes sleepily.

"Well, I'm sure you'll still see Beth plenty, sweetie," she assured her, then kissed her cheek and blew out the lantern.

Downstairs, Hen sat on the settee with her Bible, reading in 1 Peter. She must have dozed off, because the next thing she knew, her father was calling to her from the back door. "Come in, Dad."

He joined her in the small front room and surprised her by saying that Mom had agreed to go to an orthopedic surgeon in York.

"Amazing! When will you go?"

"Next Friday morning." He looked toward the window. "Honestly, I haven't seen your mother like this since before the accident."

"What do you mean?"

"She's surprisingly hopeful." His chest rose and fell. "It's so unlike her."

"Many prayers have been offered for her through the years, Dad."

"That's the truth." He then asked how Brandon was doing today.

"Well, his surgery was successful, so things are better than yesterday. Apparently, though, he's lost his sight due to the blow he took to the head, but the doctor said it should be only temporary."

Her father looked grave. "Temporary?"

She nodded. "That's the expectation. Either way, the doctor said it really shouldn't be much longer and he'll be going home—maybe even tomorrow."

"The Lord's Day," he said softly. "Will you visit him again?"

"Yes."

He gave her a knowing smile. "You know, you've seen your husband more in the last two days than in the last two months."

She realized suddenly he was right. "Between you and me, I wonder what'll happen now to Brandon's plans for divorce."

"Honestly, I wondered the same thing."

A soft thump came overhead, and Hen guessed one of Mattie Sue's beloved toys had fallen to the floor. "Mattie misses him so much, Dad. Should I take her with me to see him once he's released?"

"Well, that depends on how you think she'd handle the loss of his sight. She'll certainly need you right there when she first sees him."

"Surely by tomorrow he'll see." *Surely.* Hen couldn't let herself think otherwise.

Later, after her father left for home, she made some warm peppermint tea and sipped it, thinking that if tomorrow weren't the Lord's Day, she would have invited her dad to ride with her to the hospital. His presence would provide a buffer, especially if Brandon was more alert and broached the dreaded topic of divorce.

O Lord, please let something good come from this accident.

CHAPTER 32

*R*ose helped clear away the plates and utensils from the table on Sunday noon. Her own words came back to plague her: the bold suggestion that she and Silas not see each other for a while. Why hadn't he spoken a word in reply? Was Silas irritated at her for being so brazen as to broach it?

She went upstairs to her room and looked at the library books piled on her dresser. All of them were historical novels, just waiting to be read. Right now fiction was one of the best ways for her to deal with the turmoil swirling around the family. Hen's pending divorce, and now Brandon's accident and recovery—*and this awkward thing between Silas and me.*

The book she was enjoying most took her far away from her worries, if only for a short time. Oh, the joys of living near an adventure-filled land as did Elnora Comstock—the lonely girl lived in the Indiana Limberlost and spent her leisure hours collecting and selling beautiful moths. *Nearly as forlorn as I am.*

But Rose did not reach for the cherished book. Instead, she opened her dresser drawer and removed a small writing tablet and pen. Going to her chair and the side table near the window, she sat in her quiet room with the door securely shut. She stared out the window at the bishop's house in the distance, through the windbreak of black trees.

Rose sighed deeply and stared at the lines on the tablet. In the past, when she'd been feeling this addled, she'd always poured out her heart to Nick—*he* had always understood her. Maybe she would be able to think through everything more clearly if she simply wrote down her thoughts to her best friend. It was worth a try.

Sadly, she began to write, knowing that at least the Lord would see this letter. All of a sudden, she hesitated—Rose hoped He would not frown upon her for these words. Truth be told, she was searching her heart, just as she'd told Silas to search his.

Dear Nick,

I might burst if I don't write my thoughts here, though you'll never see them. So much is bottled up inside me since I saw you unexpectedly in Philly. I wish I could talk to you like I always did when you were here. Oh, Nick, I miss those days!

When I saw you at the homeless shelter, I wanted to tell you that your bishop-father is in dire trouble with the neighboring bishops over his ordination—especially Old Ezekiel. I know nothing can be done now, and that his fate is in the hands of God. But still, it breaks my heart—Dat's, too.

I told you in Philly that I found your note in the tin box. You wrote that you feel responsible for Christian's death. And surely everyone here believes that you are. But I refuse to think, my dear friend, that no matter how angry you may have been that day, you would have taken the life of another. I simply do not believe it, Nick!

No matter what you say, God is surely watching over you. He cares for you . . . and so do I. I really wanted to tell you this before you left home. Maybe you knew it all along.

And even though it makes no sense at all, I realize more and more that I'm engaged to marry a man I might never love as I ought, and I love a man I can never marry.

I miss you, Nick.

~ Rosie

Rose stared at the shameless words, nearly shocked that she'd had the courage to commit them to paper. Carefully, she tore the page out of the tablet. Then, getting up, she placed the tablet and pen back in the drawer. She folded the letter in half twice and pushed it deep into her dress pocket. Finding her warm navy blue sweater, she slipped it on and buttoned it all the way down, then hurried downstairs to retrieve her heaviest wool coat and black outer bonnet from their hooks at the far end of the kitchen.

Rose did not tell a soul where she was going, but it wouldn't have mattered anyway. No one could keep her from hiding this. Truth was, she knew the very best spot for the letter. Somehow, it felt like the right thing to do.

The best place, after all.

Rose went out to the haymow and found her old riding britches for under her dress and long apron. Then she went to the stable and got her favorite horse, George, taking him far out of her way just so she could approach the desolate ravine at one of the points where the road lay lower and closer to the creek bed. The horse picked its way over the snow-covered area near the frozen creek, and she eventually found the boulder where Mamm's tin box was still pushed deep into the crevice behind the rock, concealed beneath the decaying leaves. She removed all of the money her mother had taken along eleven years ago to make change at market. Then, wadding up the bills, she stuffed them into her pocket and removed her letter to Nick from the other. Her fingers shook despite the warm gloves she wore.

A strange feeling came over her as she placed the letter where she'd found Nick's unexpected note a month before. She firmly pressed down the lid and put the tin box back into its nest. Then she turned and mounted the horse to head back down the creek, amidst huge rocks and ragged trees, mere silhouettes now that their branches were barren.

The letter would be safe there, where no one would think to look for it. No one knew that Nick had found the abandoned tin box, the sole remembrance of Mamm's horrid accident, or that he'd taken Rose there to show it to her . . . and to speak tender words of love. How astonished Rose had been!

Even so, Rose was fearful. She wondered suddenly what would happen if the note was unearthed years from now, perhaps long after she was Silas's wife . . . and mother to his children. What then?

"What if all the People come to know how I feel at this moment?" she said into the frosty air, her breath billowing up to the sky. But she'd done what she had set out to do and was not going down there to retrieve it. The box had been untouched for more than a decade. Surely there was no reason to expect anyone would discover it now.

Once she was back up on Bridle Path Lane, Rose passed Jeb Ulrich's little house. The poor man was said to be mentally unstable, and most of the time slept his days and nights away. There was no movement or even a single light coming from inside as the horse trotted past the tumbledown dwelling. Rose felt strangely comforted by the knowledge that not even Jeb had the slightest notion of her trek through the deep ravine that Lord's Day afternoon.

∾

When Rose returned home, the kitchen was empty, a rare thing. She quietly placed the money from the old tin box in the empty cookie jar on the counter that her parents had always used for the purpose of storing pin money. The additional thirty dollars would easily mingle with the jam and jelly money and the earnings Rose had made recently on sales of her faceless dolls.

No one will ever question it. My visit to the ravine is safe.

CHAPTER 33

Brandon gingerly sat on the edge of his hospital bed Sunday afternoon, fully dressed, his middle wrapped securely and his right arm in a cast. Hen had pulled up a chair as she attempted to encourage her husband, whose sight still had not returned. It was obvious he was depressed.

In the midst of Hen's inability to reassure him, the on-call doctor came into the room. He glanced at Brandon with a smile. "Someone's rarin' to go home." He directed his gaze to Hen, then continued. "We've studied the MRI test results, and I'm happy to say they're normal. As soon as the paperwork is finished, you're free to go."

"That's all great, but I still can't see," Brandon stated. "How am I supposed to function like this? I need to get back to work."

Again, the doctor reiterated that the blindness was temporary. "Most probably."

"Can't you give me more to go on than that?" Brandon rubbed his eyes and grimaced. "I can't even see light!"

The doctor assured him that given enough rest, his brain and his eyesight should fully recover.

Brandon needs my help, Hen thought, reaching to touch his shoulder. This was more than he could manage on his own. "How about I take you home?" she offered. "We'll get through this together."

He turned toward her, surprise registered on his features. "You'd do that, Hen?"

Just then, she realized he might be confused, thinking she meant their house in town. "I'll take you home with *me*."

"Amishville?" he muttered, scowling. "I hope you're not serious."

The doctor waved at Hen. "I'll leave you two alone," he said, moving quickly to the door.

"Thank you for everything," she called to the doctor.

He nodded and smiled. "Remember, rest is key." Then he was gone.

Brandon sat there silently.

"I can best take care of you at the farm, Brandon," she said more quietly. "It will also be more peaceful for you—fewer distractions while you heal."

He hung his head. "I'm not going there."

"All right, then. But don't you need someone to help you get your bearings?" She wondered if his sister might return to stay with him. But when she asked, Brandon said Terry had used up all of her vacation time.

"Where's the phone? I'll see if I can stay with Lawrence . . . just until this nightmare's over."

Hen cringed inwardly but handed the receiver to Brandon to dial the number. Standing up, he shuffled about, looking so pitiful that Hen guided him back to the bed, where he sat while fingering the keypad on the phone. He talked himself through it, mumbling the whole time, as if picturing the keypad in his mind. It took more than a minute for him to locate the numbers to call his brother. Hen patiently stood by but did not assist him.

When Lawrence answered, Brandon greeted him warmly. Hen heard him ask if he might stay there for a while, but soon it was quite evident that Lawrence could not—or would not—accommodate Brandon's request. He was too busy.

"What about your parents? Couldn't they come stay with you?" Hen suggested when he'd hung up.

Brandon shook his head. "They have all kinds of holiday social commitments." He blew air out of his mouth. "Besides, I don't want to put them out."

She waited, wondering what other options he might have.

Then, almost reluctantly, he said, "Why don't you just take me to the house in town. I'll figure out what to do when I get there. Who knows, maybe I'll be able to see later this afternoon."

"Sure, I'll drive you there . . . if that's what you want."

"I need to check on Wiggles, too." He mentioned the neighbor who looked in on the new puppy when Brandon was at work. "I had Lawrence call her to let her know I might be in the hospital for a few days."

She glanced around the room. "Did your briefcase come along with you after the accident?"

"I assume the nurse put my belongings somewhere nearby."

Hen spotted what looked like a narrow closet near the door. "How'd you get dressed earlier?"

"Lawrence dropped off fresh clothes yesterday." He shrugged. "And I had some help today." A look of recognition crossed his determined face, and he stopped talking for a moment. He drew in a long, contemplative breath. "Okay, I see your point. I'm entirely dependent on someone."

"Well, not really. It's all how you think about things. For instance, there are only so many strides from the door of the Dawdi Haus to the kitchen table. And a certain number of steps to the stairway . . . you get the idea." She paused. "And Mattie Sue will be thrilled to help out, of course."

He shook his head slowly. "I don't want my daughter to see me like this."

"Okay. It's your decision." She opened the small closet and found his briefcase, car keys, and wallet. She placed his wallet and keys in his hand. "I'll carry your briefcase, unless you want to."

"I can do it." He stuffed his wallet and keys in his pants pocket. He held out his good arm and took the briefcase from her, then winced as he remembered his broken ribs. "On second thought, maybe you'd better keep it."

The nurse arrived with a wheelchair for Brandon, and when he was seated Hen placed the briefcase on his lap.

In the elevator on the way down to the main entrance, Brandon asked about the other driver. "Any idea how he's doing?"

She hadn't heard an update since yesterday but knew he was expected to remain in the hospital longer than Brandon due to a fractured vertebra and badly broken leg. "He may be worse off than you are . . . but I don't know for sure."

"I feel bad for the poor kid." He shuddered just then.

His melancholy demeanor was typical after a head trauma, or so the booklet the doctor had given her had indicated. She'd also read that Brandon might experience confusion and disorientation, abrupt mood swings, and even weakness on one side of the body. He was no longer experiencing nausea, but his headache and broken bones were enough to warrant a prescription for pain medication.

Once downstairs, she headed to the parking spot and brought the car around to the entrance. A nurse wheeled Brandon out to the curb and helped him into the front passenger's seat.

Hen thanked the nurse, then inched the car forward and out of the drive. Brandon mentioned something about maybe not staying at home after all.

"Your doctor did say yesterday it's important for family to observe head injury patients for several weeks, even months," she reminded him.

They rode for a ways before he relented. "Well, don't expect me to wear that ridiculous black felt hat or those suspenders your father wears."

She smiled to herself. "Deal. Let's stop first to pick up some more of your clothes from the house. And Wiggles, too?"

Brandon turned toward her. "What day did you say it is?"

"The Lord's Day."

He ignored the religious reference. "I really need to contact Bruce Kramer, my business partner."

"You can use the phone at the house while I find your clothes." She smiled again. "I doubt I'll have time to sew up a batch of britches for you."

"Hen, please . . ."

"If you rest like the doctor said, you should be able to resume your work and return to the house in town in a couple of weeks."

"Two weeks? Is that what he said?"

"Two weeks to two months," she replied.

He groaned loudly, looking quite pathetic there in the passenger seat. "I hope you're driving carefully," he said. "I'm a little gun-shy about getting into a car. I'd prefer not to get creamed again."

"Sounds like you might actually prefer some slower travel in a horse and buggy."

He blanched. "No, Hen. I refuse to rot away in Amishville."

"Why not think on the bright side? You might actually enjoy yourself and soak up the peace of the place. Besides, it's almost Christmas, and Mattie Sue will be thrilled to spend it with you."

The three of us.

Hen sighed, her heart in her throat. "And if you still want to divorce me when you're well again, that'll be up to you."

∾

Rose held her breath and watched Hen lead Brandon carefully across the driveway after helping him out of the car. Wiggles was nestled in Hen's free arm as Brandon stepped gingerly across the driveway. Rose's heart sang, seeing her sister and husband make their way toward the backyard together. "Mattie Sue, come welcome your daddy home!" she quickly called up the stairs.

Mattie's footsteps were on the stairs in an instant, and Rose went to look in on her mother. "Hen's brought Brandon home from the hospital," she said softly. "Isn't that wonderful-*gut?*"

Mamm's eyes were suddenly alert. "You don't mean it!"

"Jah, it's just amazing."

Mamm looked at the ceiling, exhibiting her gratitude to God.

Rose excused herself to put on an old coat. Then she hurried to the back porch to welcome her brother-in-law. Mattie Sue was already chattering about the big cast on his arm and his bandaged forehead. Meanwhile, Beth peered out the back door, shaking her head no when Rose asked if she wanted to come meet Mattie Sue's father.

"That's all right," Rose assured her. "I'll be back in a jiffy."

Rose slipped her arm around Hen as Mattie Sue clung to Brandon's uninjured arm. "I'm glad you're both here," said Rose softly. *At last . . .*

Dat opened the door of his woodshop and came across the backyard, calling his greetings, as well. "*Willkumm,* son!"

Rose's breath caught and she had to look away. Her father's warmhearted greeting touched her so deeply. With all of her heart, she hoped Brandon understood just how truly it was meant.

∾

Later in the afternoon, when Beth had finished eating an ice cream cone, Rose wiped off the table. Dat came into the kitchen from the sitting room where he'd been attending Mamm and glanced at the money jar. "Rosie, do ya know anything 'bout the extra money in there?" he asked. "A *gut* thirty dollars has just appeared—on the Lord's Day, yet. More than I counted the other day."

Caught, she bowed her head. She'd been naïve to think no one would notice. "Jah, Dat . . . I know about it."

He tilted his head, eyeing her. "What's to be ashamed of? Did ya sell some more of your little dolls?"

"Not lately."

"Well, what then?"

"You might not remember, but Mamm took thirty dollars' worth of bills and change to market . . . the day of her accident."

His face turned white.

"Oh, Dat . . . I found the tin box with the money in it, behind a boulder near the crick . . . in the ravine."

"*You* did?"

She paused. "Well, not exactly me." Dare she reveal the full truth?

"Nick happened upon the box first. He took me there later to see it."

His eyes locked on hers. "You . . . and Nick?"

She nodded.

He chuckled a little, his face still pale. "Well, I'll be a horse's knee."

She'd never heard him talk so, and she bit her tongue, bracing herself for further questions.

Just at that moment, Beth came out of the bedroom. "Can you carry Mrs. Kauffman to the bathroom?" she asked shyly.

Immediately Dat turned without saying more, leaving Rose alone, her heart beating ever so hard. *Might've been better to leave the money where Nick first found it.* She wondered if Dat would also ask why she hadn't brought the tin box home, as well. But he was occupied now, and Rose dismissed her concern. Actually, she rather liked the notion of a secret hiding place . . . especially because Nick had thought to leave his letter to her there.

And now mine's there, too. . . .

CHAPTER 34

*H*en's heart was gladdened at her father and sister's welcome of Brandon, but seeing Mattie Sue's response earlier had been best of all.

Mattie was far less concerned that her daddy could not see than Hen expected. Without prompting her, Hen noticed Mattie was eager to help Brandon as he tentatively walked about the house.

Presently, her husband and daughter were seated side by side at the table. Mattie talked happily as she "showed" him the coloring book page she'd made for him, describing the picture of butterflies in pinks, reds, and yellows. Brandon sat stiff and straight due to his bandaged ribs, his cast resting on the table.

So far, so good. Hen filled Wiggles's doggie dishes with kibble and water, reveling in the fact that her husband was actually here with them. *Here, on Salem Road!*

She wanted to pinch herself, though she wouldn't be hasty with excitement, given the reason for his stay. Any moment his sight could return, and he'd want to head right back to town.

A few minutes later, when Mattie Sue ran upstairs to get several of her faceless dolls, Brandon mentioned how drafty the house was. "And I sure miss my La-Z-Boy."

"Sit closer to the fire if you're cold," she encouraged him, slipping several more logs into the cookstove. "I can drape the rocking chair with a soft afghan to make it a little more comfortable for you." She offered to help move him to the rocking chair near the stove, but Brandon shook his head. He looked downright pitiful.

"Would you like some hot coffee?" she asked cheerfully. "I'd be happy to make some. Or would you prefer cocoa?"

"Coffee's fine." He got up and inched across the room, waving his left arm in front of him so as not to bump into something.

But seeing he was heading straight for the opposite wall, Hen hurried to clasp his arm and redirect his steps toward the stove. "Do you want to stand here to warm up?" she asked.

Brandon faced her. "Well, I guess what I *want* and what I'm stuck with are two different things."

Wishing she could make him feel more at ease, Hen paused a moment. Then, realizing she was staring at her wounded husband, she headed back to the kitchen. *Happiness isn't wanting what you can get, but wanting what you have,* she thought, hoping Brandon wouldn't continue to let his frustration spill out when Mattie Sue returned.

But he was already so sunk into despair that even Mattie's attempts to "show" him a few Amish dolls fell on deaf ears.

He can't see with his eyes . . . or with his heart, Hen thought sadly.

As the supper hour neared, she made chicken salad sandwiches and warmed up some homemade tomato soup. When she set the plate before him she told him, "The sandwich is at nine o'clock, near your left hand." He didn't wait for the table blessing. He reached for it and began eating.

Hen and Mattie Sue raised their heads from the silent

prayer—Brandon was struggling to eat his soup. Quickly, Hen realized she'd made a mistake in offering it, seeing Brandon fumble to spoon it up using his left hand, the hot soup dripping down his shirt. He huffed and shook his head.

"Oh, Brandon, I'm awful sorry," she apologized. "Obviously I didn't think this meal through very well."

"I can help you, Daddy," Mattie Sue offered, going around the table to stand beside him.

"I don't need your help!" he protested.

"But, Daddy—"

"Go back and sit down."

Mattie Sue began to cry. Hen opened her arms and held her for a moment, then led her into the sitting area, away from the kitchen.

"Why's Daddy mad at me?"

"No, no, darling . . . he's not mad at you. He's in pain, and it's hard to do things when you can't see."

As if struck by an inspiration, Mattie Sue closed her eyes and tried to find her way back to the table. She stumbled and ended up peeking, but finally sat back down at the table. "I'm sorry, Daddy," she said. "It's just like the faceless dolls."

"No, Mattie, it's not the same." Brandon pushed aside his soup bowl. "Not even close."

Hen cringed and held her breath, hoping Mattie Sue would pipe down. She realized she should have encouraged Brandon to lie down for a while after arriving. He seemed so taxed now.

Once supper was done, she and Brandon and Mattie Sue sat together on the settee, covered up with an old afghan as Hen read from the Psalms. Despite his glum expression, Brandon did not protest the Bible reading. And she was relieved that none of her family had stopped by this evening, perhaps recognizing Brandon's need for time to rest and acclimate.

The irony of his being here lingered in Hen's mind and heart as she lay awake in her empty bed while her husband slept in the spare room down the hall.

Who would've thought Brandon would consent to stay here? Hen hoped she had not made an error in judgment. The harmony of the little house had already been altered with his presence.

∼

After breakfast Monday morning, Rose stood at the kitchen window with Beth, watching the snow fall and waiting for Gilbert Browning to arrive. She thanked Beth for being so caring toward Mamm, and for all she'd shared with them. Smiling sweetly, Beth's eyes remained fixed on the road, eager for her father's return.

When Mr. Browning came, he brought a thank-you gift for Rose, a large fruit basket with a big red bow on top. He opened his wallet, offering to remunerate them for taking care of Beth. Rose refused politely, adamant that having Beth there had been a gift. "Especially for my mother," she added, smiling at Beth.

Mr. Browning's face was drawn with grief. Rose had never seen him look well rested, and he certainly didn't look so today, either, as he reached down for Beth's suitcase and carried it out to the trunk.

When he'd gotten Beth settled inside the car, he hesitantly asked Rose, "I really hate to ask—you've already done so much—but would you mind coming over to clean tomorrow morning . . . and do a little cooking, too? I realize it's Christmas Eve."

"Not at all, if I can finish up before the noon meal." She thought of the Christmas program planned at the one-room schoolhouse. "We always go to the school play over yonder." She pointed in the direction. "You should come, too . . . and bring Beth along. We ride over in the big two-horse sleigh with the neighbors, our bishop and his wife."

Mr. Browning smiled wearily and glanced at Beth.

"Oh, could we, Daddy?" she pleaded.

"We might just do that. Thanks for the invitation, Rose." He looked toward the woodshop. "Would you also extend my thanks to your father and mother, as well?"

Rose said she would. "I'll see you bright and early tomorrow, then." She waved and watched them go, glad to have helped Beth's father during his time of need, especially so near Christmas.

~

After Rose finished her work at the Brownings' the next morning, she urged the horse quickly back home, wondering if maybe today she'd receive something in the mail from Silas Good. Perhaps a Christmas card? She'd taken time to make a lovely one for him but had ended up simply signing it *Yours, Rose Ann.*

The sky had opened in the last hour and was dropping enormous white flakes, some as large as a half-dollar. *If this keeps up, we'll go tobogganing on Christmas Day!*

She hoped all of her seven brothers and their families might attend the school program later this afternoon, and she wondered if even Hen would brave the weather with Mattie Sue. Feeling as though it was a good idea to keep her distance and let Brandon settle in, Rose hadn't ventured over to their Dawdi Haus at all. And since her father's arrival and Beth's departure, Mattie Sue had spent her hours with her parents. Surely the three of them needed this precious time to catch up, given all the weeks apart.

Back home, Rose checked the mail for a card from Silas but found nothing at all. Concerned, she unhitched Alfalfa from the buggy and Dat came over, offering to give her a hand. He leaned down and waved her off into the house. "Go on in and get warmed up. Your Mammi's made a big pot of hot apple cider."

"Denki, Dat."

He nodded. "You don't think Brandon's goin' to make it out to the Christmas play, do ya?"

"My guess is he'll stay put."

"Prob'ly best," Dat said.

Rose could tell by the way his face drooped that her father wished Brandon could see—and be touched by—the wonderful presentation the children put on each year.

∾

"You mean it? Amish don't put up Christmas trees?" Brandon said to Hen after awakening from a long nap. "Are you kidding me?"

"Well, some Plain folk decorate their front doors with holly and greenery," she replied. "Or string up cards over a doorway."

"That's it?"

"Sometimes there are candles in the windows on Christmas Eve . . . to welcome the Christ Child."

"That's silly," he mumbled.

"We celebrate in ways other than decorating. We make all kinds of cookies and cherry pies, and keep a pot of cinnamon-spiced hot cider simmering all day long," Hen said, helping to layer Mattie Sue in enough outer clothing for the chilly sleigh ride.

"And Aendi Rose says there are carolers, too," Mattie Sue chimed in.

Hen explained that children and youth particularly liked to go from door to door singing "Joy to the World" and other old carols.

"So if there's no tree, then Santa doesn't come for good little Amish children, does he?"

"Brandon, please," Hen whispered. "Are you really sure you'll be all right here alone?"

"I'm fine," he replied.

"I wish you could come to the program, Daddy. It's my first time going," said Mattie Sue.

Brandon shook his head.

"Well, we need to leave the house pretty soon," Hen said, trying to overlook Brandon's grumpy mood. "It looks like Dawdi Sol has the horses hitched up to the sleigh."

Mattie Sue was awfully cute in her black bonnet and warm coat and boots, all marked inside with her name for the occasion. "Who's stayin' with Mammi Emma?" she asked.

"Dawdi Jeremiah and Mammi Sylvia offered to." Hen shooed her daughter out the door, saying she'd catch up. She went over to Brandon on the sofa and gave him another afghan. "I'm sure you know . . . but Christmas here is really about the Lord Jesus," she said, hoping he might understand. "The reason for the celebration."

He thanked her for the extra afghan. "Are you saying Mattie Sue's really okay with not getting tons of presents under a Christmas tree?"

"You'll know soon enough," Hen said, pleased with how readily Mattie had taken to the Old Ways. "We'll be back in about two hours."

He nodded, head down.

"Is there anything else you need?"

"No . . . thanks."

She felt sorry to leave him alone. "I'm only going for Mattie's sake," she admitted.

"Go on . . . have a good time."

"My grandparents are right next door and can check on you, if you'd like."

"Please, Hen. That's not necessary."

He doesn't want anyone's help.

"Well, all right, then." As Hen stepped out the door, she spotted Gilbert Browning arriving. He and Beth climbed into the sleigh, and Mattie Sue jumped up and moved to sit smack-dab between Beth and Rose. Poor Rose looked unusually solemn, but she brightened when Hen caught her eye.

What's going on with Rosie?

CHAPTER 35

*D*ozens of coats and bonnets were piled up outside on the schoolhouse porch. And because each item of clothing looked similar, Rose was glad they'd taken care to sew colorful name tags inside with special embroidery that glowed in the dark. The sun would be down by the time the Christmas Eve program was over.

Inside the schoolroom, paper snowflakes decorated each window. So many folk were in attendance, they had to double up at each student's desk, and the benches set up across the back and side walls were filling quickly.

When Rose had attended as a girl, she'd volunteered her fourth-grade year to do a chalk drawing of a wintry scene on the blackboard. And now, recalling that particular Christmas, she realized it had been Rebekah Bontrager who'd helped her draw the row of snowmen in the picture.

Rose dared not look to see if Rebekah had come to the popular program. Could Annie Mast get along without Rebekah more often than once every other Sunday night for Singings?

Still, Rose felt uncomfortable, knowing the Reuben Goods were present. She'd seen Sarah and Anna Mae and their mother coming up the road in their family buggy. Rose hadn't been able to see if Silas was indeed scrunched in the back, but she was certain he'd come along, too. Who'd want to miss this?

A large curtain hung across the front of the open room, allowing the students to line up without being seen. Rose saw no sign of the teacher, who'd planned this occasion for quite some time, hoping her pupils would do well and remember their memorized poems and skits, just as they'd rehearsed.

All the happy memories of special school days came rushing back as Rose scooted over to share a desk with her newlywed cousin, now Esther Glick. They dared not speak or even whisper, since the place would be in chaos if everyone did so. Accordingly, they merely exchanged smiles.

When it was time to begin, a tiny first grader came out from behind the curtain and stepped onto the small square box of a platform. Rose could see Mattie Sue clasp Hen's hand and lean forward where the two of them sat on a bench on the side, over near Silas's mother and sisters. Rose held her breath, hoping the young pupil would remember every line of his Christmas poem, which he was reciting in English. She let out a relieved breath when he did, and there were many encouraging smiles and even a few little chuckles, perhaps from the boy's parents or older siblings. But, as was their way, no applause.

There were eleven poetry recitations, five short skits, and two readings in all, and everything culminated in the students singing "O Come, All Ye Faithful" as a rousing end to a wonderful-good afternoon. After that, there was a half hour of audience singing—one of Rose's favorite parts. She joined her voice in unison with the others as they heartily sang the familiar carols, beginning with "It Came Upon a Midnight Clear."

By the time the play was finished, the children were eager to give their presents to the teacher—apples and oranges, links of sausage, jams and jellies, embroidered hankies, quilted potholders, and even a couple of hams. Each of the children in turn received wrapped candies and two new pencils and a pen from the teacher.

The members of the audience were remembered, as well, with candy canes. Rose noticed Mattie Sue removing the wrapping from hers, all smiles. *Dear little girl,* Rose thought, hoping her Christmas might be truly happy in every way. She wondered how things were going for her sister and brother-in-law, since Brandon was clearly reliant upon Hen to get around.

When will his sight return? And what then?

Sometime later, during the merry mingling which followed the conclusion of the program, Rose noticed Silas present for the first time. Just as she presumed, he'd come, though he wasn't standing with his family, but rather was wedged into the far corner.

At first, Rose thought he was alone, but the young woman standing near him turned slightly—Rebekah. The two of them appeared deep in conversation, though Silas was definitely doing most of the talking. He was laughing now, and Rebekah beamed in evident delight as she shifted, allowing Rose a better view. Rebekah was a very attentive listener, her eyes focused on Silas as he leaned forward, face alight as they talked. Had he ever looked at Rose with such tender affection?

Then, as if Rose's steady stare had sent out a signal to him, Silas turned and caught her eye, his face reddening. Suddenly, Rose's face felt too warm as an uncomfortable moment passed between them . . . and lingered. Yet, in that awkward moment, the truth was laid bare: Silas's heart plainly yearned for Rebekah.

All during the sleigh ride home, Rose considered the undeniable affection she'd witnessed between them. She recalled the other times she'd inadvertently observed their fondness for each other. The shared looks, the furtive smiles—it was as if they were magnets, unable to stay too far apart. Even Rebekah's returning to Lancaster County confirmed that.

The sky was windswept and blustery, and Rose shivered in the straw as the muted *clip-clops* of horses' hooves padded against the snow. She slipped her arm around Mattie Sue, who was sandwiched cozily between Rose and Hen. Mattie's hands were burrowed deep into her fluffy white muff, and she kept her head down against the cold.

Manes flying, the horses pulled the sleigh around the bend and into the driveway. Rose filled her lungs with the frosty air and sent a silent prayer for wisdom heavenward.

And then, amidst the sparkling snow and crisp air, she knew just what to do.

After all, it's Christmas, she thought.

∼

Christmas morning, Mattie Sue woke up early and crawled into Hen's bed to snuggle. She whispered that she'd made a present for Daddy. "But don't tell, okay?"

Hen sleepily agreed.

"He doesn't think Santa Claus comes here . . . but that's all right."

Hen gave Mattie a peck on the forehead.

"It's more fun to give presents, anyway," Mattie Sue announced. "I like watchin' people when they open them."

"That's so true, honey. It's better to give than to receive." Hen kissed Mattie's forehead and hoped Brandon's eyes might somehow be opened to the wonder of Christmas this year.

Her husband was still sleeping when Hen made her way down the steps to start cooking breakfast. She made a few notes on her small tablet near the sink as she thought ahead to the big turkey dinner scheduled for just before noon. Three of her married brothers—Josh, Enos, and Mose—were coming with their families. Her four remaining brothers had plans to have Christmas dinner with their in-laws. Often such holiday celebrations extended well into February, given the many siblings and combinations of in-laws and other relatives eager to see them and share a feast.

Hen looked forward to Brandon's finally meeting all her brothers, yet she knew she ought to go easy with him on any social expectations. The pain in his ribs and broken arm, as well as his continuing headaches, made him uncomfortable and touchy, even with pain medication. He'd come here, after all, to rest and be cared for. Hen had seen to it last evening after she and Mattie had returned from the school to have a quiet supper alone as a family. Brandon had seemed somewhat subdued, though he had appeared to make an effort to be pleasant. Even so, she sensed he was already weary of his predicament.

She tried to put herself in his shoes, hampered by sudden blindness and, as time passed, wondering if today would be the day his sight might return . . . or if seeing again was even possible.

When Brandon came slowly down the stairs in his bathrobe and slippers, he ran his hand along the wall to find his way into the kitchen, then reached out to locate the counter, where he came to stand near her. "Merry Christmas, Hen," he said. "I didn't have time to get you or Mattie Sue anything." He blinked and rubbed his stubbled chin. If her husband went much longer without shaving, his face would soon blend in with Hen's father's and brothers' . . . and their beloved bishop's.

"Oh, don't worry," she said, guiding him. "After all, the best gift is being together." When Hen smiled up at him, she wished with all of her heart that Brandon could see the smile meant just for him.

∾

Sol was thankful Hen, Rose Ann, and their brothers had swiftly prepared the large kitchen to accommodate the extra family members now seated around the extended table. Red and green Christmas decorations, brought along by their school-age grandchildren as surprises for Sol and Emma, adorned the windows. Sol was especially pleased his wife had made an effort to be present, as well, sitting in her wheelchair to his right at the head of the table.

While the womenfolk scurried about to get all the hot dishes on the table, he looked down the row on the right side and noticed Hen's husband perched stiffly there on the long wooden bench, his cast situated between his chest and the table's edge. Mattie Sue leaned her head against Brandon's good arm, stroking his hand, and Sol struggled to keep his emotions in check.

Once the stuffed turkey and gravy, mashed potatoes, corn, homemade noodles, lima beans, and chowchow were set before them, Sol waited till everyone was seated with folded hands. Then he said a warm "willkumm" to Hen's husband. His elder daughter's face shone with both joy and perspiration from working over the hot cookstove. "Most of all this Christmas, we are grateful to God for sparing Brandon's life," he said.

Everyone at the table nodded and said "jah" in agreement, and Brandon offered a somewhat self-conscious nod in return.

Then, bowing his head, Sol prayed the silent *Sege*—blessing— for these gracious provisions from the Father's own hand. He made the customary sound in his throat and raised his head, reaching for his water glass. He looked toward dear Emma and asked her what she'd like to eat. When she indicated she wasn't very hungry, he coaxed her to at least have a small slice of turkey and some potatoes, which she accepted.

The tinkle of Emma's fine glassware and best china was soon accompanied by the pleasant hum of family chatter. Josh and Enos, the more talkative of his sons present, tried to strike up a conversation with Brandon as they sat across from him. Even Hen attempted to draw out her husband, but the man was silent, clearly wounded inside and out.

Solomon ate his fill, ever mindful of his family and precious wife. Halfway through the meal, he leaned toward her. "Just say when you're ready to lie down again, dear. I'll help ya back into bed."

After all the serving dishes had been passed, Mattie Sue slipped out of her spot on the bench and came over to ask Emma if she wanted any food from the far end of the table. Sol's heart was warmed by Hen's little girl. He thanked the Lord for each grandchild there at the table today, as well as those celebrating Christ's birth with other family members nearby.

Keep them ever in your loving care, O Father.

~

Hen and Brandon excused themselves to return next door, and Mattie Sue asked politely if she might stay and play with her close-in-age cousins. Hen agreed, pleased to see her daughter so anxious to be well mannered. *She's come such a long way.*

At the little Dawdi Haus, Hen stayed with her husband to help him up the stairs to rest. He said his head was throbbing and had been all during the dessert offerings of fruit pies, carrot cake, and chocolate chip cookies. "I thought dessert would never end," he concluded.

"My family does love sweets," she agreed, letting him lean on her arm as he moved toward his bed.

Hen fetched Brandon an extra quilt in case he was chilled. She suspected Dad was assisting Mom to a nap about now, as well. Brandon sat on the bed in the spare room, looking forlorn. A single tear rolled down his cheek and he brushed it away, turning toward the wall.

"Brandon, hon . . . it's all right. You've been through the wringer. Of course you're feeling lousy."

"I don't want sympathy." His voice was soft, not accusing.

She stepped back, away from the bed. "Okay, then, I'll leave you be."

Brandon leaned back slowly, cautious of his fractured ribs and arm. "If only I could see, I think I could manage the rest of this nightmare." He groaned as he lowered his head onto the pillow. "I really need to return to work in a couple of days."

In due time, Hen thought, trusting God for Brandon's healing. Oh, she truly wished she could do something more to ease his pain, but she'd already given him the prescribed dose of pain medication for now. The doctor had warned him not to take more so as to prevent his becoming addicted to the very thing that could bring him momentary comfort.

～

Hen returned to the main house to help with clearing the table and doing up the mountains of dishes, thankful for some time with her sisters-in-law and Rose Ann. They talked together in the front room as the children played games, and then joined in singing a few carols.

Later, Hen slipped in to see her mother, who was lying on her daybed, looking at the ceiling. Hen went over and kissed her on the cheek. "A blessed Christmas to you, Mom," she whispered. "Not long now until you see the specialist."

Mom's eyes sparkled. "I'm holdin' on as best I can."

"Is there anything I can do for you before I return to Brandon?"

"No, dear girl." Mom shook her head slowly. "You just take care of that husband of yours. First things first, jah?"

Hen patted her hand. "I'll see you this evening at supper-time." Then Hen had an idea. "There are oodles of leftovers from dinner. Would you like to invite the Brownings over for supper tonight?"

"Oh, could we?" Mom's eyebrows rose. "That'd be awful nice."

Hen realized once more how much Beth's compassionate attention had endeared her to Mom. "I'll see what Rose or I can do."

With that, Hen pulled up the soft crocheted afghan to cover her. "Try to rest now."

Nodding, Mom closed her eyes, a contented look on her sweet face.

I'll ask Mose to stop by Brownings', she thought. Mose didn't like to sit in one place for very long and was probably already itching to be outside again. Hen went to find him, feeling excited about trying to make the heartfelt wish come true for her mother on this most joyful of days.

CHAPTER 36

After Brandon's rest, Hen and Mattie Sue brought out all the beautiful squares for the bed quilt Hen was in the process of making for Mattie. They sat together in the little front room, describing the design, as well as the colors for the Double Nine Patch quilt design. With his fingers, Brandon examined the difference between the interior and outline stitches.

When the squares were neatly put away again, Mattie Sue had the idea to let her daddy smell the various berry jams Hen had canned. "Can ya guess what flavor this is?" Mattie Sue said as she sat on his lap, holding one small spoonful after another up to his nose.

Hen thought Brandon's expression seemed softer . . . but then, it was Christmas Day. She hoped he wasn't merely tolerating Mattie's and her attempts to entertain him and make him feel like a part of their lives.

Soon Mattie gave him the paper chain she'd made, placing it in his left hand. He seemed pleased as he felt each one of the loops. He kissed Mattie's cheek and thanked her, promising to buy a belated Christmas present for her after he felt better, then donned the chain around his neck as a sort of paper scarf. Mattie Sue giggled and offered to take him outside to help feed the baby goats.

Brandon shook his head. "I've had enough for one day," he said somewhat brusquely, more to Hen than to Mattie Sue. "Don't feel bad, Mattie Sue, all right?" His tone was kind again as he spoke to her. "I just need to sit here and rest."

"Okay, Daddy. Maybe tomorrow, then?" Mattie Sue went to the stool beneath the wooden pegs and got down her coat, scarf, and black outer bonnet.

After Mattie had gone outdoors to tag along with Dawdi in the barn, Hen told Brandon she was scheduled to work at the fabric shop tomorrow. "But I'll be glad to take the day off to stay with you," she offered.

"Tomorrow?" He looked helpless suddenly . . . even disappointed.

"I can call in first thing in the morning from the phone shanty to let Rachel know I'm not coming. She'd understand."

"Would you, Hen?" he asked, relief flooding his voice.

"I certainly will." Rather taken aback, Hen realized again how dependent Brandon was on her while he waited for his sight to be restored. Her husband had put his life on hold, and at least temporarily, he could not look farther ahead than a single day. The thought that Brandon needed her gave her hope.

∾

Rose was thoroughly delighted when Beth and her father arrived at suppertime. All smiles, Beth sat beside Mamm during the meal consisting mostly of leftovers, though Beth and her father had brought along some fudge prettily wrapped in green cellophane to share. Beth made a point of saying that her father had helped her make it as a Christmas surprise for their neighbors and friends. "Especially for you, Mrs. Kauffman," Beth said, turning toward her.

While they ate, Rose wondered whether the Brownings might soon pull up stakes to move to South Carolina to be near Mr. Browning's widowed mother, as Beth had feared. But Mr. Browning spoke very little, though he seemed to enjoy their company—perhaps he'd chosen not to speak of it on such a happy day.

Meanwhile, Beth told Mamm she was counting the hours until her aunt Judith arrived, "sometime in January." Mamm reached over and stroked the back of Beth's head, smiling and nodding and treating her like one of her own daughters.

The evening ended on a blissful note when a group of Amish couples knocked on the back door and sang "Silent Night," which moved Mamm to tears as she sat in her wheelchair near the woodstove.

As the voices rang out into the cold, moonlit night, Rose thought how much fun it would've been to carol around the neighborhood with this group . . . and her betrothed.

If Rebekah hadn't come to town and spoiled everything, she thought. Nonetheless, Rose knew the truth was more complicated than that. She and Silas had grown apart because each of their hearts was drawn to another.

∼

After dark, Rose was very surprised when she saw Silas's courting buggy pull partway into the driveway. She had been redding up the kitchen after yet another round of desserts with her parents, who had already retired to their room.

Not knowing what to think, she wrapped up in her warmest shawl and went outside to meet him. "Hullo, Silas."

"Merry Christmas," he said with a quick nod. In his hands was a large green box with a silver bow, which he offered to her. "I didn't want you to think I'd forgotten to get you something, Rose Ann," he said almost shyly.

"Oh, Silas . . . it's nice of you." She realized how cold it was and invited him inside. "You can warm up by the kitchen stove," she said. "No one's up just now."

He agreed and followed her inside as she carried his gift, wondering what it could be. Then she remembered what she'd planned to do. Waiting till they'd pulled chairs up next to the cookstove, she turned to him. "I appreciate your present, Silas, but there's something I'd like to say."

A frown passed over his brow.

"I've been thinkin' quite a lot lately," she began. "About us— our engagement, I mean."

He reached for her hand. "Rose Ann . . . what're ya saying? Is it about what you said last time—about us maybe spending some time apart?"

"Jah, 'tis." She paused, gathering strength. "I've seen how you look at Rebekah, Silas. And honestly, I believe you care more for her than you prob'ly realize."

In the flickering light from the belly of the cookstove, he looked down at their entwined hands. A second or two passed before he spoke. "Rebekah's coming was unexpected." He looked at her, his gaze steady. "Truth is, I didn't realize till lately that I still care for her." He shifted a little in his seat. "But I don't want to hurt you, Rose Ann. I'd never want to do that."

She nodded; she'd anticipated that he'd be the dutiful beau. "That's awful nice of you, Silas. But . . . really, it's not reasonable for you to be engaged to me when Rebekah is the girl you truly love."

He squeezed her hand, then released it. "You needn't be so kind about this, Rose." His voice was thick with emotion.

"Kindness has nothin' to do with it." Her heart hammered

in her ears—never had she imagined speaking so freely to Silas about such things.

"Rose . . . I've asked you to marry me, and I am fully prepared to do so. Perhaps our affection will grow even more with time."

Rose made no answer. She looked down at the beautifully wrapped box, and he urged her to open it. "There are two more boxes in the buggy yet," he added.

She removed the bow and tore open the wrapping. Inside, she found delicate glassware with etched floral designs. Stemware for water or iced tea, just like Mamm had received from Dat years ago.

"Oh, Silas . . . these are just beautiful." She lifted one of the glasses out gently to look at it more closely. She guessed by boxes he meant there were many more of the same outside in his court-ing carriage.

"It's a set of twenty-four," he told her, smiling. "For big family gatherings, ya know."

She paused, looking at him. "And I have a gift for you, also."

"No . . . no," Silas protested. "Ain't necessary."

"It's not what you think," she said. "But it's a gift all the same."

His eyes registered bewilderment. "What do ya mean?"

"I'm releasing you from our engagement, Silas. I believe you and Rebekah are meant to be together." She paused and offered him a small smile. "After all, a good marriage needs lots of love to help make it strong. I want that for you and Rebekah, just as I do for myself . . . someday." Her voice trembled.

Silas looked surprised, but his relief was equally evident. "If you're sure," he said slowly, then offered to take her for a ride. "It's Christmas, ain't so?"

Her first thought was to decline, but then, seeing the gracious smile on his face, she accepted his invitation. As Silas helped her into the buggy, Rose thanked him and settled into his open carriage for the very last time.

A light snow began to fall, dusting them with soft white flakes. She felt sure it was a sign, if not Providence. "Joyous Christmas, Silas," she said.

"And to you, too, Rose Ann."

They rode quietly side by side, and Rose did not feel the slightest speck of sadness or regret. If anything, there was a tangible peace between them as they rode up Salem Road in the silvery moonlight.

CHAPTER 37

As sometimes happened on the heels of Christmas, the weather began to turn warmer, akin to an Indian summer. The drastic change was a blessing to Sol, considering their long trek ahead to York that Friday morning. He was thankful for sunshine, especially since Emma hadn't been outdoors in quite a while.

They were traveling on clear roads, the sun pouring down on them. It was truly a brilliant day in every way—or so he hoped. The closer they came to the city across the Susquehanna River, the more he trusted this was a wise move for Emma. He did not, however, want to be tricked into doing something risky or unreasonable. Nor would he allow his wife to be treated like a guinea pig!

When they arrived, he and the driver got Emma safely situated in the wheelchair. Together, they pushed her up the ramp leading to the doctor's office. Once inside, Sol and Emma waited for her name to be called after Sol signed in with the helpful receptionist.

Going to sit with Emma, Sol didn't see how a single visit to a doctor could change the course of their lives, but because of his and Emma's firm belief in prayer, he was optimistic. He still wasn't sure what to make of Beth's dream, but it had made Emma want to move forward with this, and he was forever thankful for that.

Emma, for her part, was adamant that God had planted the dream in the innocent young woman's heart for this very purpose. Truly, Beth Browning was a godsend.

"No matter what happens," Sol said quietly as he and Emma waited, "we'll always trust in God's will."

No matter what.

Dr. Robertson surprised Sol with his attention to detail during Emma's initial exam. Sol asked if the surgeon thought he could help alleviate Emma's pain.

"I'll need to do further testing before we can decide on a course of action, but yes, I believe I can help your wife." The doctor said it with such confidence, Sol was taken by surprise, and tears shone in Emma's eyes.

"I'd like to do some X-rays today, while you're here." Dr. Robertson explained that several advancements had taken place in the decade since Emma's accident. "There is good reason, Mrs. Kauffman, to assume surgery would enable you to live without much pain."

Sol held his breath for a moment, astonished.

"I'm confident I may be able to help you in many ways." Dr. Robertson went to the wall switch and lowered the lights. He touched another switch, and a large screen descended behind his desk, displaying an enormous diagram of the spine. He pointed out the area that required further testing. "If the vertebral column is turned or fused in either of these areas, then surgery might eventually return some feeling to your legs, though I cannot promise that you will be able to walk again."

Emma gasped and reached for Sol's hand.

"We'll know more when the X-rays come back. After that, we'll want to follow up with an MRI and possibly a CAT scan."

While sitting in the waiting room during Emma's X-rays, Sol spotted a handmade wall hanging and rose to look at it more closely. In cross-stitch was a Scripture verse he'd learned as a boy . . . one he and Emma had often recited together during their courting years. *Cause me to hear thy lovingkindness in the morning; for in thee do I trust: cause me to know the way wherein I should walk; for I lift up my soul unto thee.*

Seeing this particular verse displayed here on a simple wall hanging took Sol aback. Was it a sign to them—a sort of divine confirmation?

When Emma was finished, Sol wheeled her over to look at the cross-stitch. She was quiet for a time. Then she folded her hands in her lap and looked up at him. "I daresay it's the handprint of God on this day . . . on our coming here," she said in a hushed voice.

Later, as they rode back to Lancaster County, Sol questioned why he hadn't taken Emma to this surgeon years ago. *She doggedly resisted, that's why,* he reminded himself.

And in that moment, he knew precisely where his beloved daughters had come by their stubborn streaks.

～

Preaching Sunday arrived, and Sol climbed into the buggy with Jeremiah and Sylvia, leaving Emma at home in Rose Ann's care. Word had gotten out amongst the district that a decision regarding their longtime bishop was being announced today after the second sermon.

All through both sermons, Sol fidgeted, which was unlike him.

With his whole heart, he held out hope that Bishop Ezekiel would rule in favor of Aaron's remaining the bishop over the local district. Sol didn't see how the older and wiser man of God could do otherwise, given the vague nature of the issue at hand. To think one could be expected to dictate the actions of an offspring, blood kin or not. And the talk of Aaron's sermons being any longer than those given by the other ministers—it was downright ridiculous! For sure and for certain, Sol had never noticed any such prideful tendency.

Soon enough, the time came for Bishop Aaron to stand for the reading of the Weltende, or the end-of-the-world scriptures from Matthew's gospel. The place was hushed.

" 'But of that day and hour knoweth no man, no, not the angels of heaven, but my Father only. But as the days of Noah were, so shall also the coming of the Son of man be. For as in the days that were before the flood they were eating and drinking, marrying and giving in marriage, until the day that Noah entered into the ark, and knew not until the flood came, and took them all away; so shall also the coming of the Son of man be. Then shall two be in the field; the one shall be taken, and the other left. Two women shall be grinding at the mill; the one shall be taken, and the other left. Watch therefore: for ye know not what hour your Lord doth come.' "

Still holding the open Bible in his hands, Bishop Aaron looked out at the congregation. A long pause ensued and his eyes held Sol's gaze. *Does he already know the outcome?* Sol worried what it would do to their already grief-stricken bishop, and poor Barbara, if Old Ezekiel had ruled against Aaron.

Taking his seat, Aaron looked nearly despondent. Sol's ire rose even as the People bowed in contrition, turning to kneel at their seats. He was ever mindful of his own failings and shortcomings. Having taken the scriptural warning to heart, he silently asked now for God's mercy and forgiveness, just as he did each and every day.

By the time the final hymn was sung, Sol had chewed his fingernails down to the quick. Old Ezekiel was not in attendance this day. For that reason alone, Sol clung to the last shred of hope.

After the nonmembers and children were dismissed, one of the neighboring bishops rose stoically to speak. A look at the minister's grave expression and Sol felt certain what was coming.

Even so, the dreaded pronouncement to silence their long-standing bishop came like a punch in the gut. *Such a sad, sad day for the People!* Sol felt sickened. No longer would Aaron oversee the two local church districts, nor would he preach at area weddings or funerals. He had no further ministerial influence over the community that loved and respected him—he was relegated to the status of church member only.

Surely God doesn't remove a ministerial calling from a man who has wholly followed Him, thought Sol. *How can this be?*

Returning home, he was torn between the grave judgment put on his friend and, on the other hand, the brighter possibilities before his Emma. Dr. Robertson had been encouraged enough by the X-rays to schedule Emma for yet another round of tests, including blood work, coming up in a few days.

"*A fine way to begin the new year,*" the doctor had told Sol and Emma, who were both convinced it was God's will they follow the advice of this man.

As for today, Sol secretly doubted the will of God had been performed before the People. The decision appeared utterly unsound.

~

Distraught over Dat's news of their bishop's silencing today, Rose Ann left the house and headed up Salem Road for a walk.

She lifted her face to the heavens and soaked up the warmth of the sunshine. It felt so good to see the blue of the sky after the heavy storms during Christmas week, and the brown fields were already emerging from their snowy blankets. The road, too, was beginning to clear.

Not caring where she walked, she wandered all the way over toward Bridle Path Lane. The day was entirely jumbled up in her mind as she considered the decision made against Aaron Petersheim. It was beyond her to think Nick's actions had the power to set such a terrible thing in motion. Somehow yet another tragedy had been laid at his feet.

Alone with her thoughts, Rose found herself at the bottom of the ravine, sitting on the boulder near where the tin box was hidden. *Nick would surely be sorry at this sad outcome. If only he knew . . .*

Resting there, she realized how very short the daylight hours had become. Winter solstice had occurred just a few days ago, and she felt thirsty for light. Even with every tree stripped of leaves, this area was bereft of much sunshine.

She sighed, feeling colder and knowing she should head home before dusk. Turning, she glanced at the spot where she'd pushed the tin box back into the earth the last time she'd come. She pulled the old box from its hiding place and pried open its lid. Looking inside, she found that it was empty. Her letter to Nick was gone.

Rose gasped. "Where is it?"

Had her father come searching for Mamm's precious box and found her letter? She *had* told him about finding the tin box here . . . and about the market money, too. But would he even do such a thing?

No . . . no. She tried to calm herself. The area was too vast—too dense. How would Dat ever find it? He was much too busy to be traipsing about the wooded, precipitous area in search of such a small item.

Still, she trembled. What if Silas ended up seeing the letter—or hearing about it? Would he think she'd released him from their engagement because she was in love with Nick? "Oh," she groaned. "Why'd I take such a risk?"

She was afraid, too, about what might be said about her, should the letter find its way into the wrong hands. *In any hands, amongst the People, it will destroy my reputation!*

Holding the box, Rose didn't know whether to put it back or take it with her. She turned around to look for footprints in the mud but remembered that more than a few inches of snow had fallen and then melted here since her last visit.

She saw no evidence of her father's large boot prints or anyone else's. Her stomach ached and she didn't know what to think. So, deciding not to stir up further concern at home, she returned the box to its hidden spot and picked her way back up the ravine slope.

When at last she made it to the top, she walked briskly, trying to clear her aching head.

"Hello there," someone called to her.

Looking just ahead, she saw Jeb Ulrich sweeping off his wooden stoop. He was surprisingly spry as he waved at her, but his gaze made her feel terribly uneasy. Had he seen her in the ravine before today?

Her heart pounded. *How could he possibly see clear down there?* Rose shuddered. *And what would he do with the letter, if he somehow managed to find it?*

She opened her mouth to ask, then realized how ridiculous such a thing would sound to the elderly man. Poor thing, he rarely got out of his house, let alone into the steep gorge. No, she wouldn't bother him with her unreasonable thought.

Rose kept walking the narrow dirt road and dismissed her

notion of Jeb's having found the note where she'd unwisely revealed her love for Nick Franco—outcast that he was. And now to think his own foster father—their dear bishop—was nearly considered likewise!

Earlier this morning, while keeping Mamm company when Dat was at Preaching service, Rose had read a verse in 1 Peter, chapter four . . . one she hadn't paid much attention to before. Mamm knew it well, though, and asked Rose to read it more slowly a second time. The verse referred to the kind of love that covered a "multitude of sins," and Mamm had said she hoped the brethren remembered that love when it came time to judge their bishop. But it seemed they'd forgotten.

God expects us to have that kind of devoted love for one another, Rose thought, her eyes on the lights of home as she made her way down Salem Road. Hurrying now, she knew she must face whatever fallout might come from having declared so unashamedly her feelings for a man who was not her fiancé—and never would be.

Serves me right for being so foolish!

Rose turned into the long lane, walking toward the house, past the grapevines she and Nick had often pruned together. Woodsmoke trickled out of the chimneys of the main house and two smaller attached houses—one where her grandparents made their cozy home, the other where Hen was attempting to create a new one out of the ruins of her marriage.

Rose reached for the back door, realizing she could not live bound by fear. If her father, or even Silas, had happened upon the letter, then so be it.

She glanced behind her and looked up at the bright stars appearing one by one. One way or another, she must forge a new path. The thought of the New Year, just days away, gave her a measure of assurance. *An uncluttered slate before me.*

After all these years, the truth concealed in her heart was out in the open—in the light—at last. And whether or not anyone would ever read the letter wasn't a concern.

Perhaps Providence had permitted this to happen. Rose smiled at the thought, trusting in that. She must move ahead to do what she knew was right. The Lord would see to the rest.

EPILOGUE

If you're ever lost, always look for the brightest spot along the horizon," my father used to tell my brothers. *"You'll find a river there, which will lead you to people . . . to inhabitants."* And Dat had explained that the light of the sky reflected in the river below.

There are times when I ponder such things in view of all that's happened in these past months, though I'm surely not lost in a strange land. But I *am* on a journey, and sometimes it seems ever so long. Still, little by little, I'll find my way with the help of my heavenly Father. I can never go wrong by clinging to His hand, Mamm always says.

And she ought to know! Dr. Robertson has nearly completed his tests, but the prospect of surgery next month seems quite certain. When Mamm thinks about the possible wonderful-good outcome, her upcoming operation causes her great anticipation . . . and great apprehension, too. Yet who can blame her for being so torn? Surely it's an enormous leap forward for one so reclusive and resigned to living a life of suffering. With all of my heart, I hope and pray the surgeon can lessen her pain. That is my dearest wish of all.

As for my daily work, when I'm not sitting with Mamm, I help occupy Mattie Sue's time for Hen. And what an energetic little girl she continues to be! Hen certainly has her hands full caring for Brandon, who has transitioned better than expected to our life here, though he's anxious to get back to what he calls "normal living." When that might be, the doctors aren't sure, as Brandon's sight has yet to return beyond an occasional flicker of light. Each passing day is a real worry, but Hen is unwavering in her belief that her husband will see again. Amazingly, there's no indication of anxiety on her part—she's become a truly prayerful wife and mother. I just hope Brandon won't break her heart when all's said and done.

To give my sister and her husband some time alone, I take Mattie Sue with me on Thursdays when I work to make quilts and comforters for the Philadelphia homeless shelter with the women-folk. Mattie Sue enjoys playing with the other children, often right near our feet under the frame. The talk is a strange blend of hearsay and solid information. And occasionally I feel a sense of sadness as I am continually reminded why the People were so quick to presume Nick's guilt in Christian's death. It seems not a soul ever really had the chance to know the sometimes-thoughtful Nick Franco the bishop's wife knew . . . nor the softhearted, horse-loving *Kummraad*—friend—I came to know.

So then, which is the real Nick?

But my mother taught me that a friend never gives up on a friend. And this is the reason I privately beseech God's mercy for Nick, who seemingly caused all this chaos, just as I ask it for our former bishop. As far as I know, there has been no further word about Nick, which is probably just as well.

Thinking of friends, Silas wasted not a speck of time asking Rebekah out, according to the flourishing grapevine. More than likely they are a courting couple by now. Annie Mast is helping see to that by giving Rebekah more evenings away from her baby duties than were originally planned. Honestly, I wouldn't be surprised if the Bontragers make a trip back here next autumn for a wedding uniting them with the Goods.

I can't say that I'll be distressed on Silas's special day, because even now, I know I'll be right happy for him. And for Rebekah, too. After all, when two hearts beat nearly as one, like theirs seem to, who amongst us should ever stand in the way?

So it is that I look ahead to my future with God's help, joyfully trusting in whatever He has planned for me. And, really, considering the abundant blessings I've received from His loving hand, how can I do otherwise?

AUTHOR'S NOTE

$\mathcal{W}$ hile the idyllic countryside around Salem Road continues to capture my attention, I am equally fascinated by the spiritual landscape of the people I write about, people so like my maternal grandparents, Omar and Ada Buchwalter, both born in Lancaster County, Pennsylvania. Their spiritual heritage has helped to shape my family . . . and my stories. In chapter 8 of this book, Rose Kauffman refers to the old German prayer book *Die Ernsthafte Christenpflicht*. Many readers will undoubtedly be curious about this clothbound treasure, which has long been dear to Anabaptists like my grandparents and other relatives.

That precious connection led me to compile a selection of excerpts from those very prayers in a newly translated edition just for modern readers. It is my hope that this volume, entitled *Amish Prayers*, might bless you in your life as richly as it has Anabaptist Christians, many of whom first said these prayers as persecuted believers in Europe over three hundred years ago.

On another important note, I offer my continual gratitude to my devoted consultants and research assistants who bring authenticity and great joy to my writing life: the Lancaster Mennonite Historical Society, Brad Igou, Erik Wesner, Carolene Robinson, Judith Lovold, and Hank and Ruth Hershberger. I am also thankful for the complete works of Donald B. Kraybill, John A. Hostetler, and Stephen Scott, as well as my good fellowship with numerous Amish friends who read my books and appreciate my desire for accuracy.

My longtime friendship and partnership with my editors—Dave Horton, Rochelle Glöege, and Julie Klassen—continue to enhance my writing life. "Thank you" never seems enough.

I pray each of my readers will embrace the grace and goodness of our Lord, and choose the path to peace and simplicity.

Soli Deo Gloria.

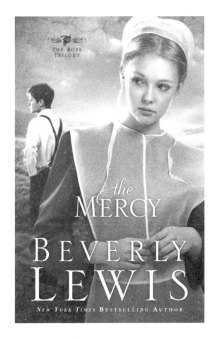

The Mercy

Book Three in THE ROSE TRILOGY

—AVAILABLE SEPTEMBER 2011—

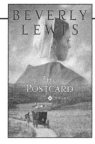